THE MATRIARCH OF RUINS

A Novel of Civilians and the Wounded at Gettysburg

Book II of the Gettysburg Trilogy

EDISON McDANIELS

Northampton House Press

First Northampton House LLC e-edition, 2015. ISBN 978-1-937997-64-9

First Northampton House Press print edition, 2016. ISBN 978-937997-66-3.

Library of Congress Control Number: 2015949197.

10 9 8 7 6 5 4 3 2

THE MATRIARCH OF RUINS

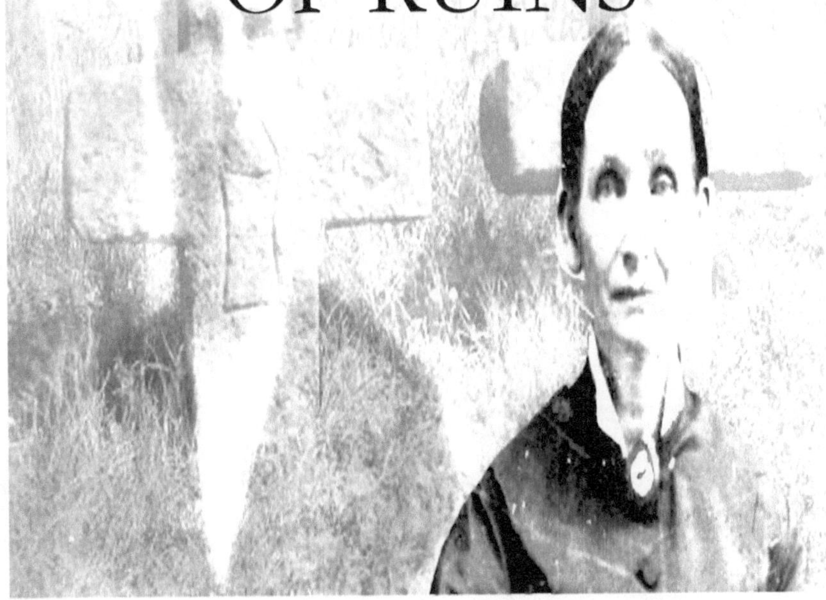

PROLOGUE

The morning twilight washed through the sullied windows, erasing the flickering sepia tones of the candle-lit room and touching the time-worn face of a middle-aged woman. She'd been up most of the night, indeed well into the wee hours, and what little time she'd slept had been fitful, awakened at intervals by the weak, not quite right breathing of her grandbaby, in the arms of his own mother. This younger woman, who had slept but little herself, pulled the boy close against her bosom. His skin was mottled and dusky. He'd spent the greater part of two days skirmishing for breath and mostly losing the battle. Now and then he convulsed, straining for air, heaving his tiny body in the effort. He struggled the way a fish out of water does in its final throes. Baby Noah, who would be four months old if he lived another week, had the gone look of the aged and infirm.

The widow lay on her back, still in the maiden dawn light, chin resting on folded hands in the chiseled nook between jaw and breastbone, her eyes the swollen, shadowed creatures of fatigue. A wispy strand of hair, thin, only recently gone gray, stuck to the sweat of her brow. The only sound was that of the boy's fight for breath, together with a cricket fiddling under the bed. The wind was a whisper in the trees.

The infant gurgled thickly, as if drowning in his own spew. The widow opened her eyes. She swallowed and wiped at a bead of sweat. Each breath of the tiny boy seemed only to bring him a little closer to quitting this world. It was there for all to see, filling the room. The fever that had only singed the rest of them had consumed him like kindling. To look on him was to look on a pile of ashes in his mother's arms, nothing but the dust from which he'd come, and the idea that it wasn't a fair world came to her, not for the first time. Living was an ordeal, a painful condition, like a deep down bellyache you couldn't get at no matter how hard you tried. It gnawed at you like a poorly fit shoe.

Sam's mother hugged him closer, and he gurgled again, followed by a scrimpy cough.

Purdy closed her eyes and tried to bring sleep on, but mostly she found herself just pretending.

Part I:

A Strange and Blighted Land

ONE

Purdy's first thought as she approached the town was for the frozen horses. Nothing in her forty-two years had prepared her for such a sight. How war must use them up, like cordwood in a winter freeze.

Her second thought was for Enoch: *Please God, let him be alive.* She pressed the back of her hand to her mouth, put her wedding ring to her lips, and kissed the gold band he'd given her twenty-odd years before. "I love you," she said in a muted, prayerful tone, and if Enoch had by some miracle been listening, he would have heard the pang of her desire.

"I love you," she said again, and trudged on into the broken town.

What was left of Falmouth wasn't much. She pulled the kerchief wound round her neck up over her lower face. The place stank of sulphur and corruption and the mixture made her eyes burn and her belly queasy. Interspersed among the dead horses, men—or rather the used up skinbags of what had once been men—lay at frequent intervals. The several people walking this corrupted landscape worked with faces half covered, as if the necessary business of taking up the dead made them outcasts, or bandits in their own land. The abundant dead made their efforts appear futile.

At first glance, the inhabitants of the town looked washed-out and pale. Their faces inspired dread, as if every soul suffered from some awful form of insomnia. As if the world entire had taken ill at once. Smiling seemed a lost skill, known only to the before-time. The folks gathered here and there in the yards of ruined homes, or along cobblestone streets. Now a small crowd, now a displaced family, now singly and by twos. Dispossessed of their homes, they fired their furniture and burned their heirlooms to keep warm in the frigid air of a December gone bad.

Enoch wasn't anywhere she looked.

A young girl, perhaps ten, stood beside a scorched tree which looked black and bonelike against the gray sky visible through its branches. The girl wore a dirty dress of some indeterminate color, lighter than the tree. Its tatters blew in the wind. She was stained red across her front, as if she'd pissed herself in blood. Purdy stared hard at the girl, upon whose face was writ the graven image of death. She stood statue-like and Purdy herself finally had to turn away, feeling more the intruder. When she turned back but a heartbeat later, the girl was gone. She might never have been there in the first place. Even if she found Enoch, he mightn't be but a fiction of the mind himself. A person could go crazy here, maybe had no choice in the matter. "Oh God in heaven," she said, "oh God in heaven."

A sort of quasi-life persisted. Quartermasters set up supply houses and ordered a thousand different items in bulk quantities that would take days and weeks to arrive from up north. Hospital clerks counted the wounded, cataloguing their dreadful inventories with studied indifference, as if tallying cattle. Nurses, plain men and plainer women, came and went at all hours of the days and the nights, grudging witnesses to the carnage. Surgeons worked at their anatomical trade, exhausting themselves in their own bloodletting. Orderlies and aides moved amongst this confusion, taking a man here, dropping a soldier there, being generally useful in the thousand terrible ways a broken man needs assistance and support. Seamstresses made diapers, slings, and bandages from all manner of materials: curtains, dresses, fine linens, pillow shams, bedspreads, shirts, tablecloths, napkins, whatever rags or otherwise lay at hand. Cooks boiled meat and baked bread and made hardtack biscuits and turned all of these things out of portable kitchens set up hastily amid the rubble. They cooked grits and turned beans to gruel and boiled ham soup for shattered bodies to slurp through straws. Volunteers fanned out across the ruined countryside to serve up the food and spoon out the soup to those who couldn't spoon it themselves.

And so on.

Purdy Gamble was middle aged, a hard looking woman of stout stature with a narrow face that narrowed still further at the chin. Her eyes were deep set and seemed ever in shadow, as if she had never to get enough sleep. She had survived the smallpox that had killed her sister as a young girl and the scars still marred her. She was not vain. She was in all things a practical woman, who had attained her two score and two through hard work, long days, longer nights, the grace of God, and the love of a man so good she could imagine no other after him. His name was Enoch Gamble, lately of the Army of the Potomac, and she had not seen him in near two years.

She searched the disrupted town end to end and back again.

On her third morning in that awesome and dreadful place she awoke to the grunting and snorting of hogs feeding nearby. She'd hunkered the night in a barn, had slept in her clothes yet again, had not washed in three days. What little warmth had been had come from snuggling with the piled strangers sharing her stall. She disentangled herself and brushed off the straw and took up her few possibles and stepped over the folk and left the barn. It had snowed in the night and with the blood and the dead both covered, the land lay ghostly white and without detail to the eye. The air was raw and smelled of the barn, of manure and gunpowder and dead things.

A rat the size of a loaf of bread ran across her boot.

She spat with the wind and pissed in the slop at the corner of the yard, where was discarded the remains of a fiddle and beside that a doll's head whose china eyes were painted on and so always open. She paid a penny for a biscuit and two for a pot of warm water. She washed her face and hands and that part of her female things she could reach with modesty. She gave the soiled bathwater to a family of three while it was still lukewarm.

She spent the remainder of the day as she had the previous, searching house to house, which is to say from hospital to hospital, since every remaining building housed the injured. Sometimes two or three, sometimes a dozen and more. She went about this business cold and shivering and blue to her carpals. She prayed with every other minute, sometimes that she'd find Enoch and sometimes that she wouldn't. She closed her eyes often and when she opened them not a damn thing had changed.

Scores of dogs roamed the town, so many it seemed they must outnumber the people, and it was no rare sight to see them gnawing on the dead horses. Like rats. She'd heard, and only heard thanks be to God, how some of the bastard dogs had chewed the bodies of the dead soldiers in the first days after the battle. Soulless creatures to be sure, but there was worse out there no doubt.

Near midafternoon she turned into an alley and saw a man well-dressed in a warm-looking overcoat. His pants were around his ankles and he was standing with legs spread. An oldish woman was crouched before him bent-knee'd and he held her head in his hands as it bobbed up and down. On seeing Purdy, the man pulled back and hiked his trousers and walked briskly to the other end of the alley, the woman hollering after him how he'd promised a nickel for the tickle. She turned to Purdy, wiping at her mouth, and spat in the mud. "You owes me a nickel, bitch."

"What? I...I don't know what—"

She came at Purdy, eyes alive with scorn and vinegar. She pressed her up against a wall, stripping her possibles away. The bag fell into the muddy lane. "You dumb bitch."

The woman reeked and Purdy turned her head away from her breath. She pushed back, kicking, clawing at the woman's arms as she in turn fought for the bag. They came apart a moment, then stood an arm's reach each from the other.

"I didn't do nothing 'cept walk down the wrong street," Purdy said.

"That was my dinner you mussed up. Mine and my daughter. We gotta eat." Her breathing hitched and came in quick gasps. She cocked her head, put her arms up, fists at the ready.

Purdy saw the fight in this woman. Her own breathing came hard and fast, and her words ratcheted. "I'm sorry. I know that's a hard thing. Feeding your youngins I mean."

"You owes me."

The woman was younger than she'd first figured, thirty maybe, with a hard, chiseled look about her. One eye was narrowed, just a slit.

She needs it more than I do. "All right." Purdy dropped one hand, kept the other raised before her face. She tried not to look like she was cowering, tried to look bold. "I'm just gonna reach for my purse."

The woman's one wide eye darted up and down Purdy's person, wary and weary both. "Go on. Don't try nothing, cause it ain't just for me. I'll cut ya if'n I need to. I got a knife. You should know that. I got a knife."

But she didn't produce one. Maybe that was just bluster. Purdy slid her hand between the buttons of her blouse, fumbled for the pouch she kept there. She had some coins, mostly pennies, nickels, and dimes, a few quarters. She had paper too, Union scrip, but she didn't want the woman to see that. "Step back a piece."

"If you try to run, I'll cut ya."

"I ain't gonna run. Those're my possibles in the mud." She snapped open the purse under her shirt and felt for the coins, counting them. "All I got is three pennies. That'll do ya good. Your daughter too."

The woman rocked back and forth on the balls of her feet. "You looks like you maybe got more," she said, and her tongue came out and licked back and forth.

"That's for my own. All I got's three pennies for the likes of you." She hesitated, then spat. That was for effect. *I don't wanna fight you, but I will.*

The woman appeared to think on it some. She looked up and down the alley. It was empty, but she maybe couldn't count on that for long. "I got a knife," she repeated.

Purdy took her hand out of her blouse. She held it out in a fist, opened it palm up. "Three pennies. That's all you gonna get."

The woman snatched them up and spat in Purdy's empty hand. "I ain't no whore, no more'n you. You'd do the same, you was me. Me and my girl—she only four—we gonna eat tonight no thanks to you." She turned and ran down the alley in the same direction the man had gone.

On the fourth day Purdy found herself standing before a large brick mansion on the banks of the Rappahannock. A shambled place of shattered windows and pitted masonry. In place of the front doors someone had hung a blanket. The battered walls still stood. The chimneys were tall, barren ruins absent of any smoke. Icicles hung from the broken standpipe above the portal.

A clerk sat inside the front door, on a stool beside a pail where a small fire flickered. It seemed to provide all the warmth the place offered, save for the fevered men beyond, and the clerk was hunched over it like a consumptive. He turned when she entered, her presence made known only by the rush of chill air as she pulled aside the blanket. The warmth inside was thin and a stink of shit and piss wafted out with it.

"This ain't no kinda place ye wanna be," the man said.

"Beg pardon?"

"Ye don't wanna be here," the clerk said, looking up from his warm seat. Like most every other person she'd seen in recent days, he had the look of the damned about him. She wondered what she looked like to him.

"How's that?" Purdy covered a nostril with one finger and blew a string of snot into a cloth and then repeated the process on the other side. "How you know where I wanna be?"

The man had a narrow, bushy nose with hairs bunching about the nostrils. These hairs twitched back and forth as he spoke and the effect was weasel-like. "Like as not ye in the wrong place."

"I'm looking for my husband."

"He ain't likely here."

"You don't even know."

"What I mean is," the weasel was standing now, "ye should hope he ain't in this place, lady. Got nothing but the worst hereabouts. Poor souls evir one of 'em." He blew on his hands.

"I gotta check, you know that much."

"Ye alone? This ain't a place for your sort."

"Soldier" —she had almost said 'weasel'— "this ain't a place for any sort. I been walking this town near a week and I ain't seen nowhere I'd want to be anywhere."

"I got a man back theres," his head bobbed toward the inner doorway, "what got his eyeball on 'is cheek. Just hanging there it is, like a...like a piece a beef on a string. If'n he wanted I suppose he could take it up in his hand and look behind hisself without turning his head a whit. It ain't hardly a thing ye'd expect to see this side a hell. Ye really wanna see that?"

"He got red hair? My Enoch got red hair. Bright red."

"Ain't exactly his hair you notice."

"I guess I'll have me a look then."

"Naw, ye don't wanna come in. Not here. This the divil's place I tell ye. The divil's playground."

"That's damn near blasphemy. And how you think you can tell me where I want to be? What're you, maybe twenty? I'm old enough to be your ma. Ain't your ma taught you no better?"

"My ma, she niver seen hell from the inside. I guess I have."

"How many you got in this place?"

"Maybe fifty. Maybe fifty-five. Depends."

"Depends?"

"On how many come at their end in the night. There's always a few what cross the river. Some nights more 'an a few. I ain't counted since yesterdey."

Purdy said nothing to this.

"I guess there's some here what gots red hair." The clerk finally said, apparently allowing how she wasn't going away.

"Any answer to Enoch Gamble?"

"I dunno. But I sure's hell hope not. It ain't gonna be nothin' good if'n they does."

She pushed around him and went inside.

Here indeed only the worst cases were to be found. Men lay crowded together for warmth, their eyes following her, begging. She wept as she went, fearing to touch them. They didn't look like men at all. Actually, they did and that was the profaning nature of it. Broken in body but stolid in mind one moment, they writhed in agony the next. Being among these afflicted was like being afflicted herself, as if what they had was catching. She was suddenly and completely consumed with a great fear she would find Enoch among these poor souls. A moment later her fear flip-flopped and she thought I won't find him here or anywheres else. He'd died, been buried in some nameless grave alongside a hundred other poor fellows on some godforsaken hillside. Or worse: left to rot on a field somewhere, was even now being chewed on by those bastard dogs….

A curious chittering brought her back to the moment. A heavy and irregular cacophony she had trouble placing at first. It filled the place and was both awesome and claustrophobic at the same time. The noise hurt her ears. It was the sound of many teeth chattering. That such a sound existed on this earth she had not previously known. The knowledge did no good and in fact some little harm, as she became at once hot despite the cold and had trouble catching her breath. She slipped and looked down to see a peculiar red ice caking the floor.

She wanted to run, needed to run. The weasel had been right. *"This ain't a place for your sort."* Another moment in this purgatory and she'd be as condemned. She couldn't go forward and so turned around and there, immediately before her, was the weasel clerk. His pointy nose was a size too small for his face and his front teeth a size too big for his mouth. His nose twitched when he spoke. "You okay? I told ye don't come in here."

She punched his rodent nose. Not hard, but it caught him off guard and spun him back. "Piss off," she said.

"You hit me. Dammit, ye hit me. Jesus lady." He groped at his smeller and blood came away on his hand. "I oughta—"

"Shut up."

He kept wiping the blood and looking at his finger, but he shut up.

Purdy's hand throbbed. She thought of the woman in the alley. *Don't try nothing, cause it ain't just for me. I'll cut ya if'n I need to. I got a knife.* She hadn't had one, of course. Except, in a way, she had. Her daughter, her loved one. Her love was her strength—her knife. The tool that powered her, made her a force.

Maybe Enoch was dead, but she didn't think so. She couldn't. She worked her hand and took a deep breath, then another. The pain felt...good. The air was different now, had somehow turned. Maybe better, maybe not.

She pressed on into the makeshift hospital.

The men reached out, pulling at her with filthy hands, fingers twisted and broken. They wanted for everything: clothes, a drink, a bath, something to piss in, to eat, a smoke, a hand to hold. The air reeked with the stink of their slops. At first she hadn't wanted to touch them, but after a while she found she had to, if only to assure herself of their humanity. She found it an easier way to go too, moving from man to man and wiping their dirty faces with her kerchief, with whatever was at hand.

A few times she thought she saw Enoch, but each time when she drew close he wasn't there. The men asked if she had any tobacco, any paper. A soldier gave her a crumpled letter to post to his folks in Schenectady. His or someone else's dirty fingerprints smudged it. She promised to mail it at the first opportunity and stuffed it in her blouse, alongside the pouch.

Another grabbed her dress and would not let go till she came close. When she did he pled his case; how he missed his girl back home, how he doubted ever seeing her again. The heat coming off him was fierce and his skin the color of burnt walnut. He pleaded, would she kiss him. She touched her lips to his cheek and he said she smelled just like his girl back home and he had known it would be so. His grip slackened and his eyes closed when she pulled away.

She skipped the dead, which she knew by the lack of any visible breath. She teared as she held the hand of a boy who'd been chest-shot. Looking at him, and she couldn't say how she knew this, she knew he was at his end, that he had only another moment or two left in him. His chest yet rose a half dozen times and each time a briefer plume of frosty breath passed from between his lips until at last there was none. His hand remained in hers and she squeezed it but there was no response and she let it go while it was still warm. She stood a long time at his side, staring into his open eyes as if she might learn something of who he'd been. She pressed a thumb and index finger to each eye and drew the lids down.

She cursed the weasel clerk. Not because any of this was his fault, but because she could.

Her first glimpse of Enoch was not much hopeful. At first she thought it was a trick of the light, thought it couldn't be. She'd given up any idea of finding him in this place. Perhaps had hoped not to find him here. But then there he was, chicken-wire thin with threadbare undergarments rusted an ugly gray-brown by skin oils and bits of road dirt. It was only by his flaming hair, grown long and unruly, that she knew him. She'd run her fingers through that hair a thousand times and each of those memories summed to a whole more than their parts now and a sure chill went through her. She'd know that hair anywhere. Would know him anywhere.

He was the best man she'd ever known and the only man she had ever loved.

His face was bushy and overgrown, his beard unkempt, the features underneath uneven, not so much evocative of Enoch but of Enoch as might be reflected in a looking glass, one cracked and tarnished with age so that the glass had gone cloudy. Such a glass dulled the features, but she saw through to the luster underneath.

His right cheek was puffed out and bruised. He had a neat, black hole in the outer corner just below his eye, no bigger than one of the nail heads in her kitchen floor back home. The eye itself was a hideous thing. The lid had fallen open and the globe within was ruptured and sunken and runny. She put a fisted hand to her mouth and bit a knuckle, as if doing so might blind her to the horror before her. She stood in the cold air, her breath a visible, heaving sigh rising over the confused clatter of the sickroom. Somewhere a dish shattered and it echoed hollowly through the mansion's busted walls. Somebody hollering words she heard only faintly. A low moan, then a deeper one. Outside, a man was yelling at a horse, calling it a "dang fool of a animal." Dogs barked in the yard.

She put all these distractions to one side of her mind, away from the here and now, and gasped. Enoch's good eye opened at the sound, searching the piece of room where she stood. The single eye looked too big for his face. He, himself, looked too small for this world.

Not dead. The thought—the realization—hit her like a hard wind and it was all she could do to remain standing.

Purdy felt the gold band on her finger and pulled at her clothes, as if to do so would somehow make her more presentable, as if being presentable mattered in that—what had that weasel called it?—that devil's place. She'd worn the same clothes—a simple gray work dress with a fitted bodice and a straight paneled skirt gauged at the waistband—for four or five days now. Muck crusted the hem of her skirt and the brogans beneath. Specks of blood and pieces of the men she had touched on her way to this moment clung to her clothing. She pulled at a sleeve and picked at the waistband of her dress, even felt the bump of her small purse, before coming back to the notion he was still her husband and she still his wife.

She took another moment to regain herself, which mostly meant she wiped her face on her sleeve and ran her tongue over her lips, and stepped forward. "Enoch," she whispered, afraid to disturb him. Then, afraid not to, she said, "Enoch? Honey?"

He still wore the ring she'd given him all those years ago, and her lips turned up in the bare semblance of a smile.

His remaining eye rolled once or twice more, like some hideous compass finding true north. When it finally settled on her there was a moment of hesitation, of uncertainty. Maybe he thought he was imagining her. Or thought he had died and she was an angel coming to claim him, or that he had gone over the bend and was a crazy man and she a figment to taunt his raving lunacy. His mouth came open. His lips pursed like he wanted to say something but nothing came of it. Perhaps he couldn't talk, perhaps he'd never talk again.

"Oh God, what they done to you?"

"There, woman, it ain't nothing that bad." When it finally came, his voice was hardly anything at all.

He looked like he'd been to hell and brought a goodly portion of it back with him. She was immediately thankful she had heard him speak, for had she not, she would have thought him crossed over. His face wore the same fevered, drawn look as the others in that cursed town. It seemed the war had taken most of him and what was left lay in a heap before her. On the instant she decided she didn't care. Whatever remained would be enough. She kissed him long and gentle on his forehead. His skin was too warm and it wasn't until just that moment she knew he was still alive. Her eyes misted.

He shivered under his frayed blanket, which looked gossamer in the light. The odor of stale piss clung to him. She took him in her arms and held him, wanting to warm him, remembering the feel of him against her breasts, sensing the life still in him, at the same time noting how small he felt.

"I'm gonna clean you up," she said, and dabbed at the corners of his mouth with the sleeve of her blouse.

The room he occupied in that old mansion had been some sort of library. The walls were lined with hundreds of books. A large brick fireplace dominated the room, though if there had once been chairs and a sitting area, there was not but cots and sick men there now. Cold ashes covered the floor of the firebox, surrounded by more books and pieces of books. The weasel clerk came to mind. He had been crouched over that burning pail on her arrival and she allowed in that instant how she could justifiably kill the sonofabitch.

It didn't take long to rip apart a score of books and get a fire going and the room warming. Whoever had lived there had been a scholar, but Purdy could not read. She boiled water and took it around, encouraging those who could to wash themselves. She broke off pieces of the soap she had brought for Enoch, passing them out to those able to bathe themselves. She rubbed a wet cloth over Enoch's arms and legs and across his back and washed his soiled underside. He didn't look small now—thin maybe, but not small. His fat was gone, he was all muscle and sinew, a tough old bird.

For his part, he never took his eye off her. "I knew you'd come."

She couldn't stop weeping as she worked, not knowing if these were tears of joy at finding Enoch alive, or tears of sorrow at finding him so poorly living.

He reached out and wiped her cheek, his hand frail and trembling, like a twig quivering in an autumn rain.

"Of course I came. Would've come sooner—" Their eyes met. "I'm so sorry I wasn't here sooner. Lots sooner."

"Hold me, woman."

And she did.

They stayed, together, another four days at Falmouth, amid the chaos of a defeated army. In that time the library was turned to ash and the crash of hammer blows was everywhere. Later she would discover all the coffins piled along the road leading to the train station and know what the hammering had ordained.

TWO

Enoch's only wound was the black hole beneath his eye. He didn't know if he'd been shot or hit with a piece of shell and he supposed it didn't much matter anyhow.

The battle itself was a blur. He'd gone down shooting and awakened not knowing if he was dead or alive, as cold as he had ever been in his life. He was cold still—only the burning books and the warmth of so many gathered bodies filled the house. That the body itself burns hot in its death throes, the dying being oftentimes feverish and thus some warmer than the living, was a pure fact he had discovered in the days before her arrival. His cold now was nothing like it had been out there on that field though, when he lay in the dark, buried completely in icy mud and snow. The cold out there had enshrouded him, gone through him like a living thing, a beast that ate the warmth out of a man. Its color was blue and it stank of gunpowder and rooty earth. In the shadowed light of the morning after, the battlefield had lain before him as a frozen wasteland, everything ice and white with smears of red too numerous to count. And nothing moving. Not a goddamn thing moving.

He didn't know how he'd come to occupy a place in the wasted mansion. He told her all of this, that it was only his belief in a greater God, and his desire to see her one last time before he quit this world, that had kept him alive. She made him promise he'd fight to see her tomorrow and he promised he would.

The day after she found him the bonfires began. For days long after she left Falmouth, the sickly odor of burning horseflesh never left her nose. At night, the pyres glowed red on the hillside and the beauty of it made her weep in her dreams, which were always of him, of them, of their life together in the before-time.

Opposite Enoch lay an old sergeant of artillery, much worn. He had a bulbous nose oddly off center of an otherwise pallid face, and his hands were blackened by dirt and gunpowder, the fingers swollen and split. The whole of him looked very tired but he was loquacious and rarely shut up. He went by the very plain name of Homer Smith and claimed to hail from the Illinois back country, where his parents still lived in their old years. He had a brother Wilbur who'd died of camp fever the year before. He said as how Wilbur had been fifteen years younger than himself but thin and sickly since boyhood. He had lain many days in hospital and the sergeant had visited him each one, and every day had been more ghastly than the last. In the end, Wilbur had melted away between the trots and pukes.

"Had 'im buried, and the undertaker he only charged me half the usual so little was going in the ground." Another brother was with Grant in the west. This second brother's name was Johnston Smith and he was between Homer and Wilbur in years. The old sergeant had not heard from him in many months and supposed he too was dead. He speculated on how his end might have come, but the gist of it was he hoped at least Johnston had met a better end than Wilbur. He offered that while nobody got out of life alive, the ways of exiting were not equal. In this and other musings, his manner was easygoing, not at all grim or dispiriting. He made a game of predicting those who would die each day. On the third day he had guessed he himself was doomed and bid Purdy to tell his folks he died thinking of them and God and the good green grass of home. He had spoken so much of them that Purdy supposed she knew them and their ways. By dusk, he seemed keen to see his brothers again.

On their fourth morning Purdy woke to find the old sergeant had indeed passed in the night. In death he didn't look anything like he had in life, being much less substantial. He stared out past all of them, his eyes lowering and unseeing and his grizzled features now just dull has beens.

This old sergeant was neither the first nor the last to die, and other men quickly took his shoes, his blanket, and his place in the ruined mansion. That such a thing went hardly noticed cut Purdy like a scalpel. Her education in the ways of war was advancing fast.

Enoch slowly improved under her nursing and soon grew strong enough to be moved. He and she went by rail and steamer and wagon train to a hospital in Washington, DC. The journey took an entire day, agonizing in its particulars. The last leg was by horse-drawn ambulance. Purdy watched the city approach through the open windows. It came on slowly, like a gathering storm, and just so ugly.

If Falmouth had been one large hospital, Washington, DC was a city of hundreds of them. Endless tent villages ringed the outskirts. Military encampments housing a hundred thousand men or more she was told. From afar, the unfinished dome of the capital building towered over the trees and looked not unfinished, but broken like the town around it. Their train of ambulances drew up alongside a squad of pickets, who stepped forward to check their passes and wave them through.

The crowded, unpaved streets ran with mud. A busy place, thick with people scurrying here and there. The train of ambulances passed a park with scores of cannon standing in neat rows. Their wheels, some as high as men's shoulders, made passersby small. A little beyond, a man in top hat and bow tie stood in the ice and snow. He lacked shoes and she wondered about his tale. She saw many such curiosities.

Somewhere in the middle of all this, the wagons got stuck behind a huge drive of cattle. Men on horseback drove and howled at the animals, wild hoots and catcalls that strained the bounds of propriety. The dust was vile and Purdy choked in the burdened air. This and the stench were near too much, but she made do best she could. She covered Enoch's mouth with her kerchief, as if he were a helpless child, as if he had somehow heretofore escaped the smell of manure all his forty-plus years. He objected with his eyes, but the long trip had tired him and he had nothing left for argument. It was all he could do to follow her with his eyes, and she leaned close by his ear and whispered the names of their children one after another, and after he lay quietly.

Not much later she saw the driver pull something from his pocket. It was a twist of tobacco and paper. He put it to his mouth and lit it. She tapped him on the shoulder and he turned. "You got another?"

"'Fraid I ain't."

She half-smiled and looked from him to her husband. Not quite begging.

"Hell." He took another drag and passed her the hand-rolled smoke.

She put it to Enoch's mouth. He squeezed it between his lips, getting the taste of it, and inhaled. The tip flared red and he blew twin plumes of smoke out his nostrils. Maybe she saw a trace of smile in his features, but she was more concerned with a bit of smoke that rose out of the corner of his mangled eye. Every time he took a toke and exhaled that same twirl of smoke wafted up from his eye. Enoch didn't seem to notice and she was at a loss for words.

The cowboys cracked their whips and put on marvelous displays of agility as they went after strays on the sidewalks or down alleys. They wore tall, wide-brimmed hats and looked magnificent on their dust-covered mounts. They moved with ridiculous ease through the crowded streets, as if driving a herd of cattle through the middle of the nation's capital was their natural calling in life. The thousand head consumed a dozen city blocks and the whole place smelled of manure and after they passed the ground was a churned quagmire of mud and cow dung amidst the settled horse shit.

Near twilight the wagons gave on an imposing building, the granite steps and ledges heaped with dirty snow. At the top of the steps, a dozen large, round columns carried the upper floors like proud soldiers on parade. A pair of thin-shoed negros carried Enoch up the wide steps and into a vast portico, then upstairs to the second floor where they placed him in a grand alcove alongside scores of other injured men. The injured were set down in two rows, heads to the wall and feet to the aisle, so that a visitor might walk the center between them and yet have room enough to touch neither. There were no cots, only beds of straw against a cool, marble floor—which was to say no bed at all.

Several enormous glass cases dominated the portico and were filled with a rummy assortment of things. One could do no better than to call them things, for they were mostly nameless artifacts, and even then largely of a queer and strange sort. Models of one kind or another, be they wood, glass, gutta-percha, or something unrecognizable. A small stuffed bird with blue feathers and a bill no bigger than the nib of an ink pen stared out from behind one case and above it a larger bird, more colorful than the first with an entire rainbow of feathers festooning its crown. This last hung from the top of the case by a twine of rope, its wings spread as if in flight. Beneath it, what could have been the same creature was posed skeletal and skinless on a rock. Another case housed a steam engine of enormous size and a complex pencil drawing of the steam plant it might command, the sort of thing that would give one a headache before too much study. Down the hall was a display of several plows, each less crude than its predecessor, and another entire case was devoted to iron implements of a sort not easily described or recognized. Things. In the twilight, their odd shadows fell across Enoch and Purdy and the others and seemed only to confuse the night.

It made a person feel queer to be in such a place.

Purdy refused to leave his side and together they passed a tolerable night. The building had a peculiar echo—cold, hollow, reverberating, louder than it had any right to be. The granite columns and marble floors amplified every noise in that great hall until it came back at the observer many times over. The next morning Purdy learned the place was the Patent Office, to which all manner of the citizenry came to deposit their clever wares and industrious ideas. The casualties at Fredericksburg were, so she was told by one bystander, so great that every public building in Washington had been redesignated a hospital. The bystander, whom she took to be a midlevel bureaucrat by the clean, sober manner of his dress and unsoiled nails, went on to observe that the peculiar echoes might well be the massive edifice complaining at its sudden sanguinary burden.

"Huh?" Purdy asked, not taking his meaning.

"The wounded, madam. The building wasn't built for them. She doesn't like it."

"Well, I don't know about that. You ask me it's just the men, out of their heads with fever or blood poisoning or whatever. Of course, it could be they breathe in all at once, the whole lot of 'em, and it's like the whole world gasping for breath. That's what I think. We all is wounded by this here war."

The bureaucrat nodded, tipped his hat. He looked about to offer something more, but Purdy had neither time nor interest in such trifling conversation.

Daylight rolled in only slowly and revealed a gallery four stories high and built entirely of marble and granite. On each floor expansive hallways fanned out from a central rotunda, whose wide staircases they had ascended in the dark night just past. The halls were the widest she had ever seen, the walls broken at regular intervals, every ten feet or so, by doors of the blackest wood imaginable. Hundreds of wounded filled the halls, attended by a few men and a greater number of mostly older women. These women were of a singular and inconspicuous variety, plain on the eyes with bland garments to match, always white or gray. All with a sense of fatigue about them, yet none looked exhausted and they seemed to go about their work with a quiet, simple dignity. A score of negroes carried the slops down the wide staircase, returning at intervals with empty buckets. The negroes had the usual wan, carefree look of their kind.

A group of doctors—their dirty topcoats easily set them apart from all the others—made slow, deliberate progress among the wounded. One, a greasy looking fellow, unwrapped the stump of a soldier's arm, splitting the plaster cap with a pocket knife pulled from his bag. He passed the cap around for the others to see—several sniffed it as well—then hastily replaced the soiled plaster over the man's tortured remnant of an arm, reinforcing it with a piece of gauze pulled from a pocket in his once-white vestment. He wiped his hands on his coat as the group conferred a minute, then offered their prognosis, grim-faced to the last man. They moved forward, repeating the scene in one insignificant variation or another many times over.

When at last they made it to Enoch it was late afternoon. The same greasy fellow bent over him. He still wore his overcoat, the whole of it dull and shabby and generally filthy. The several pockets bulged with bandages and lengths of twine or bits of lint or other incidentals. He rubbed his hands together and took Enoch's arm and felt the pulse at his wrist, then placed a thumb beside the hole under his eye. He pressed gently and lifted the lid and looked at that damned eye from many directions, cocking his head this way and that as he spoke a few words to the soldier's ear.

"You had any drainage from that there eye?"

"Nope, don't recall I have. Aches is all, something awful at times."

"Can you see any out of it?"

Enoch closed his good eye and put his thumb up and made like he was sighting on a target. After a moment he reopened the good eye and stared up at the group. "Not a dang thing."

The greasy fellow wiped his hands on his coat again and shook his head up and down, as if he understood what it meant to be shot in the face and blind. He rose to confer with the others. They'd do what they could, he finally offered, but was careful to add that might not be much.

"It's a bad time to be wounded," the greasy fellow said, and allowed how the air about Washington this winter seemed particularly fraught with bad humors. He motioned Purdy away from Enoch. "Try and take him out to the countryside soon's you can. Air might be some better there."

Purdy thanked the doctor for his opinion as well as his prescription, and wiped a tear from the corner of her eye with a finger. The medical men moved on. Enoch looked at Purdy with the eye he had left and she forced a smile. She wasn't ready to lose him. He was her man and she would fight for him any way she could.

***

Enoch had at first improved and the time passed so quickly. The army was slow to release him, wounded or not. The holidays passed with the capital either too weary or too wary to celebrate the new year. A few weeks after their arrival they went out. He was bundled and sat a high-backed wheelchair as she pushed it along the streets. The people greeted them with sincere warmth, as if they might be distant relations.

They took to warming in the lobby of the Willard Hotel, where Purdy placed his wheelchair beside the grand fireplace, where the heat could be felt but was not overbearing. This day she rearranged the blanket over Enoch's legs so his hands were free and reached into her handbag and brought out a store-bought cigar. She put it in his hand and he rolled it between his fingers before bringing it up to his nose to sniff the fine tobacco, exaggerating the act. He put it between his lips and she lit it and he inhaled as if this was the finest moment of his life.

He smoked the cigar slowly, obviously enjoying the taste on his tongue and lips, and she savored the moment with him. He commented how it was without a doubt the best smoke he had ever had. She said the proprietor of the smoke shop, who had rolled the cigar with his own hands and from whose window she had selected it, had allowed he would say as much. Enoch ordered a hot toddy and they sat beside the grand fireplace. He finished the drink and ordered another, and Purdy knew from long experience it would be this way, that the whiskey would both warm and soothe him. They held hands and talked about everything and nothing as the day grew old and passed into night. She finally told him he would be a grandfather soon. Hannah had hoped to tell him herself, but she had had to stay behind to care for the twins, especially Coal, who did not travel easily since being kicked in the head as a young boy. That Hannah, their eldest surviving child, had married during his long absence he had known. That she was pregnant and due in March was joyous news.

It was their best day since they had watched each other fade to memory as Enoch crossed his yard and joined the other men of Adams County and marched away down the long road that had eventually brought them to this place, sitting beside this fire. A future together still seemed possible. Only the extra curl of smoke wafting from the corner of his dead eye argued differently, and this she kept to herself.

That night, she slept alongside him in the narrow bed the army had moved him to at one of the numerous newly minted public hospitals. He wore his bedclothes and lay on his side with her spooning against his back. She dreamt of the last day of their old life.

She stands on the porch at their home, the house Enoch has built for them, with Coal and his twin sister Loli at her side. Loli is crying; Coal is pill-rolling a small polished stone in his good hand. Purdy kisses Loli on the top of her head and hugs the boy, thinks what God giveth, God taketh away. *She wipes Coal's mouth with her kerchief and blows Enoch a kiss. She will not allow herself to cry, indeed makes herself stand tall and confident. Her eyes betray her though, alternating between her man and her boy, as her lips move to a silent prayer. In the distance, seen through a skein of road dust and midsummer blossoms blown on the wind, a ramshackle, hard-muscled gaggle of men and man-boys marches out of step. Thus do they go off to war, to make soldiers of themselves, to do all the great and terrible things soldiers do. They will kill and they will be killed.*

Enoch stirred and Purdy awoke. She rubbed his back and he settled. She rose and went to the basin, where she wet a cloth and wiped her face. It had begun to snow again outside. The frosted pane reflected her image, but as she stared at her face the eyes were wrong. Bigger, not as deep set as they ought be.

Not my eyes.

She saw then how one was a sunken, bruised mess. Not really an eye at all. The other looked too big for her face.

She stepped back, not able to credit what she was seeing. *I'm still asleep,* she thought, thinking how distant and blank those eyes looked. But that wasn't really true, was it? It was only the one eye that looked distant and blank. *Only the one eye, because Enoch only had one eye.*

He stirred again, this time turning over, his face alight in the candle-flame. His sunken eye was apparent. The other was closed.

She was sure in that instant he'd open it, and that when he did it wouldn't see anything at all. She was certain it would stare off past her, looking—if anything—to a world beyond this one.

To the world of the dead, she thought, and began to weep.

The following day was Enoch's last good day on this earth and even so he was a good deal less vigorous than he had been. They walked the city again, a long walk across the capital mall that took them through a large army encampment. Purdy pushed him in his high-backed wheelchair. The day was mild but still the muddy field was mostly frozen and so they had not too difficult a time of it.

On the far side of the mall a photographer was set up on the sidewalk. He hawked his offerings for near nothing, but even so she couldn't afford the three bits he wanted. He offered to do one or the other for two bits only and they talked it over and decided Enoch should be the one. He insisted on pulling off his overcoat and sitting for the image in his long sleeved plain white shirt buttoned full to his neck. He was a lanky man with a long and narrow face, the bottom end of which was obscured by a long and well kept beard and mustache. These of course were bright red, but in the tintype they'd come out looking some shade of gray. He was a proud man, self-conscious about his missing eye and the bullet hole just beneath, which still hadn't healed and from time to time pushed out a rheumy fluid of greenish tinge. Today though the hole was dry and the eye didn't look too bad, if one ignored the bluish discoloration surrounding it. You could almost imagine he'd been punched in a bar fight.

Enoch rose carefully from his wheelchair. He was not used to using his legs and it showed. The photographer suggested he lean against a small post, he'd shake less and the image would be clearer than if he stood by his lonesome, but Enoch was unable to pull it off. Just standing left him out of breath and he took a seat on a chair offered by the photographer.

A small crowd gathered as these preparations were being attended to, and an older gentleman stepped forward and remarked how he would kindly give his coat off his back for the veteran to wear in his photo. He was cadaverous, with a green bowler hat, dressed otherwise in black. There was something irregular about him, outlandish even. Purdy finally decided it was the hat, which he kept lifting an inch or two off his head to dab the skin underneath. It wasn't hot, nowhere near being humid enough to cause that kind of sweating. The old man was ridiculously thin, unhealthy even. Something about him made Purdy…uncomfortable. She tried to think what it was, but couldn't figure it. He coughed every now and again, hiding his mouth with a cloth each time, and maybe that was it. She didn't think so though. Plenty of the wounded men coughed. It seemed a thing that came with being shot, like blood. You got shot, you bleed, you coughed. Coughing had never made her uncomfortable.

Beside the old man stood a negro boy, twelve or thirteen years old Purdy guessed, in a clean but worn denim shirt and a frayed pair of cotton pants. As she watched, the old man bent and whispered something to the boy, who turned and ran off through the crowd. Her gaze followed him, though she couldn't say why.

The old man gave his attention to her, at the same time looking at Enoch. "I believe my coat will just about fit your man," he said, and there was that cough again, along with the subtle action to cover his mouth.

"My husband thanks you kindly, but that won't be necessary." She didn't like his mouth either. Couldn't say why.

"Oh come now. Let's us, you and me, give him the distinguished look he deserves, being a veteran of this infernal war and all. It is the least I—eh, we—can do. He—they, I mean they—have been through so much."

She was about to ask him what he knew of her husband's suffering, then realized it was a pointless question. You had only to look at Enoch to see he had been through an ordeal. But looking at this man, thin and sickly himself, he'd been through something too. Maybe that idea, an ordeal, was common between them.

The old man took his coat off, and Purdy thought that maybe ordeal was not a strong enough word for whatever he had experienced. Even through his shirt she saw his meatless ribs, how his bones poked out against his skin. He looked to be starving under his clothes.

She thanked him kindly again—she could think of nothing else and no way out of it—and the old man handed over his midnight black suit coat, along with the string tie he'd been wearing. By then the negro boy had returned. He carried a matching vest. Together, Purdy and the boy put the vest on Enoch. Then the old man tied the string tie in place around Enoch's neck. The old man's neck was scrawny, but so too was Enoch's and the tie fit like it belonged. In fact, the fit between the old man's clothes and Enoch's body wasn't bad—as if the old man spent his days modeling for the sick and emaciated. The sleeves were a bit long was all.

Once dressed, Enoch stayed seated. He had never had his picture made before and had no idea what he should do with himself. He sat up ramrod straight, like his back was pressed tight to some imaginary board, and stared at the camera with a face as rigid as his back. He looked in every way uncomfortable, like a man going to his execution. Somebody in the crowd pointed out the wedding band on Enoch's left hand and suddenly everyone in the crowd demanded Purdy should be in the picture too. She politely demurred but the crowd would have none of that, whereupon the photographer sighed and motioned for her to join her husband. She removed her winter coat, handing it to the old man's boy to hold, and sat to Enoch's left, their elbows touching but only just. Her clothing, a long-sleeved, dark blue fitted bodice which gave way to an ankle-length dress, looked more stern in the resultant tintype than it had in real life. At the last minute her posture had mirrored that of her husband, so that in the gray tones of the tintype they would forever appear to the world as two strangers dressed in Sunday fine black on their way to their own funerals.

When it was over, Enoch and Purdy thanked the old man, who tipped the green bowler hat at the pair of them. He smiled, not a particularly pleasant smile Purdy thought—but then the entire affair had not been particularly pleasant. Still, she had the picture to look forward to, a tintype of her and Enoch together, and that made the affair, more an ordeal she thought now, worth it.

She didn't find the card in the pocket of her coat until they were back in Enoch's room. It read simply *Dr. Jupiter Jones, Undertaker & Keeper of the Dead.* No address, no contact information of any sort.

The old man, of course. She knew this as surely as she knew what an undertaker was. It fit him, and now she saw again that final smile in her mind's eye. It had not been pleasant, no. It had been ghoulish. That's what had made the whole thing an ordeal. That final smile.

By then, of course, the old man was long gone. She tore the card in half, then in half again.

They made plans to return to Adams County, to follow the prescription of the greasy doctor as soon as possible and get out to the country and its rarefied air. But it was not to be. Enoch's strength ebbed and five weeks after that first meeting with the doctors at the Patent Office, he convulsed and the socket holding the remains of his ruptured eye opened and a black crud spilled out.

A few days later, as the eye continued to drain what the doctors called 'laudable pus' and Purdy thought of as 'a nasty, vile matter,' a small piece of tarnished lead appeared at the opening. It too fell away, but the damage had been done and within a few days more Enoch Gamble drew his last ounce of breath and quit this world. She was at his side when he did so, of course, and as was her way she grieved but did not cry. The two of them had made peace with their parting after all, or so it seemed at the time, and there was nothing to do but bring her husband home. She kissed him a final time, his cheek still warm, and the indentation she left on his lips—or maybe she just imagined such an indentation—seemed to linger. When she decided it had faded, she finally allowed how he was gone beyond her reach.

In the end he had wasted away and his hands, which had always seemed the most part of him, looked now to be the least. They had lost their weight and bulk, and the ring slid from his finger without the slightest resistance.

Sometime later, in the dusk of a falling sun, she thought in her grief about the old man's card. *Dr. Jupiter Jones, Embalmer & Keeper of the Dead.* She hadn't liked the man, but did that matter? Would she have liked *any* man in that profession?

She knew what an undertaker was, of course. But a 'Keeper of the Dead?' And how to find him?

As it turned out, he found her, the following morning. It was early, the sun barely up. She was standing in the yard of what passed as a hospital, what had been a private home in one of the seedier districts of Washington. She had been looking at the tintype, the likeness they'd made just days before. Her breath steamed in the bone cold.

She watched him come up the street, recognized his wasted form, his cadaverous build, that stupid green bowler's hat.

"Name's Jupiter Jones, madam. Undertaker and keeper of the dead."

She realized now she had seen him many times over the weeks, but always in the background. He was like a painting on the wall or a piece of furniture—a person might notice it was there but recalling it in any detail wasn't possible. She'd watched him approach others, simultaneously garish and respectful, never realizing until now how like a vulture he was, how he must smell carrion a mile off.

Did you know at the photographer that my husband was dying? How could you have? How could you not have?

He coughed and she realized something else. He had a peculiarly eager way about him. He seemed to enjoy his work, and that seemed wrong. It turned her stomach to think this, turned her against him, made her feel uncomfortable all over again. And sweaty too, despite the cold.

"I won't have you touching my Enoch."

"I understand, you want the finest for him. That is all any person can ask for a dearly departed, especially one so close. Such a fine man he was. Seen it with my own eyes."

"What do you know of my Enoch?"

"Your love was obvious. Still is."

"How did you know…" Purdy's voice drifted off.

"That he would pass?"

She nodded.

"It is a talent. Not unlike foretelling the weather."

"Are you always…correct?"

"Mostly. Some folks linger."

"They don't die quick enough for you?"

"Your words, madam."

"I don't much like you, Mr. Jones."

"Well, that's okay, madam. Mine is not a likable calling, to be sure. I want only to be of service. You won't find better, I can tell you that. You seem a person of quality. You've a long trip home and he'll need, shall we say, preserving."

There was that, she thought. And now that she thought about it, she'd seen this ghoulish man's work. Peculiar or no, he knew his business. His work had a lifelike quality. She was about to ask him how he did it, but thought better of it. Some things are better left unknown.

"I'll find another," she said.

"Have you a likeness of Enoch?" he said, ignoring her words.

"You know I do."

"Well, all the better. And all the easier. May I see it?"

She wanted to say no, but instead found herself offering the tintype. He took it, holding it at an angle to his eye rather than straight on, as if trying to see the couple in profile in the two dimensional plate.

"It'll do," he said, "yes, it'll do quite nicely."

She suddenly realized Enoch was headed for his last great moment and she couldn't deny him. She didn't like this man, but she didn't need to. "I ain't got much money."

They haggled over price, not much because the undertaker could afford to move on—the old man didn't need her work nearly as much as she needed his—and in the end she hired him despite everything that had come before that moment.

Whether or not he saw something in the tintype image others did not, Jupiter Jones did Enoch up right lifelike. After a few hours work, he returned both her husband and the image to Purdy, who had to admit he looked at least as good as he had on the day that image had been made. Maybe better.

She brought Enoch home, an eighty mile trip by train and buckboard that took four days in the merciful icy chill of late February, the land caught in the grip of one of the coldest winters on record. All the while she sat beside his coffin and watched his face behind the half-inch-thick pane of warped glass. Maybe he had grayed around the edges, but for the most part when it was over and they put him in the ground, that was the same face she'd seen in the window pane the week before: the face of a man laid out in his burial coffin, his eyes open but unseeing.

The remains of Enoch Gamble, the only man she would ever love.

THREE

Enoch came home in the dead month of February, in one of the most severe winters in memory. His plain casket, hewn of the fine but inexpensive white oak common to Southeastern Pennsylvania, lay four days in the front room as a freezing snowstorm swirled outside and turned the world a numbing white. It took another two days with a man working a pickaxe and shovel in the frozen ground before the hole thus made could reasonably be termed a grave and a burying could be had.

The negro wielding the pickaxe, whose name was Moice, was older than the dead man by a dozen or so years, though it hardly mattered, and he dug out of a kindly respect and not, as many would have guessed, because someone told him to. He was big, some would have called him a giant, and he worked bare-chested in the white cold day, building his body's warmth with each strike at the ground. At the end of the first day's shoveling, he retrieved his worn and dirty jacket from off a branch in the willow tree where he'd set it. He snapped it in the air a few times to break the crusted ice from it and pulled it on and worked the collar up around his neck. When he had done this to some satisfaction, he set the pickaxe and shovel to his shoulder and walked off into the snowbound night without a word. Any seeing him would have looked twice on account of first his size, then his skewed gait, a remnant of his past, which caused him to seem to stumble with every other step and thus made him look lopsided. It wasn't the best he could do with half a foot missing, but it took less effort and was easier.

Moice didn't have much use for people, though the dead man he'd dared call a friend, and as he had nothing more he could offer, and having had some little experience in the matter, grave digging had seemed both the least and the most he could do. He returned with sunrise of the second day and completed the digging late morning, the work being easier since the deeper ground wasn't frozen, and thereupon took his leave.

"You could stay," she had said when he knocked on the door. She opened it just enough to let the chill in, which wasn't enough to let him in. He'd never been in their home. "It'd be warm enough in the barn if'n you'd git a little fire to burning. I guess there ain't no harm in spending the night neither. In the barn I mean. With the horse."

He had dared a look at her then, something more than a sideways glance, certain even before the words came out of her mouth he wouldn't spend the night with her animals. "No. Thank you kindly," he said. "If it's all the same, I's be back first light or before to cover 'im."

"I'm obliged for what you done. Much obliged." And with that Purdy closed the door in his face.

He didn't linger on her porch. He turned and walked in his lopsided way to the edge of the woods, then moved in a little deeper. He knew these woods like no other, and making a fire, even a shelter to spend the night was no great affair. He damn well preferred it to breathing horse all night. Not that he had anything against horses. Just her. He made a fire and warmed himself.

Sitting beside that fire, Moice had time to think about the man who would soon go into that hole in the earth. In truth, he had been thinking about him for several days, ever since word of his passing had filtered down to him. Now, with his shovel still and only the crackling fire to soothe him, he had time to miss his friend.

They had known each other twenty years, going all the way back to Korley, Mississippi, or rather almost that far. He had meant Enoch only in the aftermath of that terrible moment, as if their acquaintance had been forged in the fires of hell. Perhaps that was why it had endured.

It was more, had been more, than an acquaintance, of course. Theirs had been a friendship. He supposed the fact Enoch had been white had mattered once, though that time was long in the past, relegated to the 'Mister Enoch' period. It had been a dozen years since he'd called his friend 'Mister.'

Except around Purdy of course. On the few occasions he'd chanced to meet her, he'd been careful to call him Mister Enoch. Still, she'd been suspicious—a wife had to know such things he supposed, and of course she didn't like him. He couldn't blame her.

He had asked Enoch about her once. He hadn't answered, except to say he had told her he was going trapping. Enoch went 'trapping' three or four times a year.

Those had been good times. Not great perhaps, but certainly good. Great would have been in the context of a family, and of course Moice had had a family once. In Korley, Mississippi that was and it had been the best time of his meager and difficult life, but that had been taken from him. Enoch had had nothing to do with that, but everything to do with what followed.

The fire popped. Moice peered out beyond the flames, into the white woods surrounding. He knew most every inch of them, snow covered or not. Enoch too had come to know those woods. They'd known them together.

Two hours later a dozen or so folks huddled in the lee of the willow tree. They stayed just long enough to say the usual words. Moice, at the edge of the woods, held back out of sight. He more imagined the words being said than heard them. He crossed himself when the others did and watched from his hide as two old men, a boy, and the bible talker himself prepared to lower the casket. He'd passed two lengths of rope, one front and one back, under the casket. The four picked up the ropes between each pair of souls front and back, and together worked the casket gently home into the bowels of mother earth.

The bible talker was a big, wide man, fleshy enough for two. He faltered with his rope and for a moment it looked as if he might topple into the hole. Moice had time enough to suppose he'd have to help pull him out if that happened, but then the deed was done and Enoch was safely home in the ground. Purdy, her girls, and Coal looked on. It was the first time Moice had seen Purdy and her daughters up close, or close enough, since the start of the war. The older girl was with child. He saw too how the younger girl was the spitting image of her pa in his younger years. Enoch had been handsome and she was pretty in her own right, even through her tears. And her father had been fidgety and adventurous and he saw that she was this too.

"You was a blessed man, Enoch," Moice said, and then he saw Coal, whose every breath rose frosty and blue-gray in the frigid air. It was funny how he hadn't noticed that fact with the others, not until after he saw it with Coal. The boy stood leaning against his sister, the one not in a family way, and rolled a small stone in his good hand. Drool oozed out one corner of his mouth and over his collar where it froze. He looked blue from the neck up and the wrists down, which were the only parts of him visible. He was the only one of the family not crying.

"You was a blessed man, Mr. Enoch," Moice said again, "and a cursed one just the same. We was more alike than different you an' me. God help me, but we was."

Only after dark, when he couldn't be seen and all these folks had gone, did Moice return to shovel the dirt and make good his promise to his friend. "Amen," he said as he turned the final shovelful and pressed the mound with the back of his spade. He tapped the turned dirt under his half foot and said, "You was better than most," in a broken voice that trailed off unheard by any living soul save he who had uttered it. "And I loved you for it."

For the second time that day, Moice wept.

All of this in late February in the year of our Lord eighteen-hundred-and-sixty-three.

"I am the resurrection and the life, saith the Lord; he that believeth in me, though he were dead, yet shall he live…" They stood dressed in funeral black, in their Sunday finest, the snow falling around them and on them and all it touched became a dusted white.

Purdy stood with her children, her daughters flanking either side and Coal beside Loli. The boy's good arm held a kerchief to his face, which covered his upper lip and mouth as if he might cough something weighty at any moment. His twin, the girl Loli, fidgeted and held Coal's other hand and halfway through the service leaned her head on her mother's shoulder. Their breath smoked in the cold. Purdy's eyes moved from the mound of dirt (below which lay the bones of the nameless breech baby, their firstborn) to the glacial landscape, which was dirty white and more desolate, more cold and barren than she remembered. She couldn't imagine it having ever been otherwise.

She wished they'd put flowers out. A long time ago, back before the war and when she'd had time for such things, she'd had a small rose garden. Enoch had enjoyed that, had liked the flowers she cut for the table. But to look for flowers in the dead month of February was to go on a fool's errand.

She put a hand to her chest and felt the lump of the ring under her coat.

"Man, that is born of a woman, hath but a short time to live, and is full of misery..." The minister droned. He held the Book in one of his big hands and was a head taller and a waist wider than the few other gathered folk. Standing beside him was a boy of fourteen years, Coal's age. He looked a bit like Coal, or maybe not. It had never seemed a right thing to Purdy that the two boys should look so much alike. There seemed no utility in it, only a cruel reminder of what had been lost.

It seemed her life entire was just such a reminder. She let this go and held Hannah and Loli close as they wept. She wept as well and reached down and placed a hand on Hannah's belly and felt the baby kick. Hannah's husband was a soldier in the Union Army and had come and gone on a one night furlough eight months before. *Thank God for small miracles.* Purdy looked out across the hills and into the mist and fog and snow, and for a moment it was as if she could see forever.

"For as much as it hath pleased Almighty God in his Providence, to take out of this world the soul of our deceased brother, we therefore commit his body to the ground; earth to earth, ashes to ashes, dust to dust." Purdy saw again the willow beside which they'd laid their first born. She'd broken his legs getting him out and somehow he'd died. Most of his birth and all of his death was like a washed-out gully to her. Time had made it featureless, a land she knew yet could not describe with any certainty.

The baby's grave was a small mound in the cold earth, alone no longer.

Hannah Gamble Griel gave birth to a baby boy one month later.

FOUR

"It ain't right, the way she clings to that baby an' all," Loli said. "Ain't natural, that's all. Ain't hardly natural."

Purdy sighed and her eyes rolled from her spent daughter on the floor (the one with the bundle in her arms) to the younger of her two girls. Loli, just fourteen, stood in the doorway glowering at her older sister. Hannah had a washed out, blotchy look. She'd been crying, and not just a little bit either.

Purdy eyeballed Loli through a gelid stare. "It's a hard thing, girl, giving up one you love."

"I loved him too, mama," Loli said, and the strain in her voice made it clear she'd felt the sorrow of the night and day just passed as much as anyone in that room.

They were all alone together.

"Ain't the same, honey. Just ain't the same." Purdy put an arm across the younger girl's shoulders and turned her head and looked out the window at the old willow tree. The glass in the pane had begun to droop the way old glass will and the tree stood in the yard looking wavy and warped beyond the usual. The roots of that tree hugged the breech baby close, and someday they'd do the same for her husband. Not yet, though. Enoch hadn't been in the ground but four months. Now he just lay cold in the earth.

A sound came from the front room and for the briefest moment it could have been a baby crying. It wasn't though, just the yap of their thin-ribbed dog heralding his way through the house. Beyond that slight noise, a sort of whispered soliloquy filled the room. Hannah had been singing *Hush a Bye Baby* for hours.

"You best go an' get dawg on outta here," Purdy said.

The dog had been with them for years, but 'dawg' was all anyone had ever thought to call him. Everyone but Loli that is. She had once seen fit to give him a name, except that by then he had been too big and the name had never stuck. "Mama, what we gonna do?"

"Ain't no doing 'bout it, child. Hannah's hurtin'. Fierce, like a part of her's been cut out. Gonna take a long time healing that cut too." She pulled her young daughter close at the shoulder. Her red hair was bright in the evening sun streaming through the window. It smelled of the eggs they'd cooked for breakfast.

"Pa woulda known how to do."

She kissed Loli on the top of her head. "I expect he woulda. But he ain't here no more. You go on get dawg now. Let me take care of this."

"But I can help. You think I ain't but a child, but I know things, mama."

"This ain't the time—"

"Like what happens twixt a man an' a woman—"

"Child, this got nothing to do with that. The day's been trial enough without your foolishness."

Loli sneered. She slid from Purdy's grasp. She called after dawg and he came straight away, wagging his tail like he didn't have a worry in the world. Loli walked across the room and dawg followed. She opened the back door and the two went out into the yard.

Purdy faced Hannah, who hadn't moved save for rocking back and forth. She wore the same off-white cotton nightgown as the night before, the one she'd paced the floor in. The baby, Noah, would have been four months old in another few days. He'd stopped breathing sometime in the early morning. Hannah held him wrapped in a bundle of blankets close to her breast. She seemed not to notice the smell, which wasn't yet cloying but had turned sour. The afternoon was aging, the light still strong for only another hour or so Purdy guessed. She'd have to do something soon.

A movement caught her eye and she turned to the window. Perhaps one of the hogs had gotten loose, perhaps Loli had failed to latch the pen after tending them, or maybe Coal had wandered. Not a hog though. A man, big and burly, making no effort to conceal himself. Before she blinked Purdy saw another and in the next instant a third. Then the back door flung open and Loli came through it, breathing hard.

"There's soldiers, mama, soldiers in uniform in the yard!"

They were pounding at the front door. Purdy's stomach dropped. She wished Enoch was there. But he was gone, deader even than the baby in Hannah's arms. Or at least dead longer. More raps now—insistent—and she thought too late of the flintlock over the fireplace. The front door jamb splintered and she pushed Loli through the back door, out into the yard. The girl nearly tripped over dawg, who had chosen the back steps for a nap at just that moment. Purdy all the while panned the yard for Coal. Not there. She tried frantically to recall where she'd seen him last.

The place was crawling with them, maybe a dozen. They blowed about the yard like fools high on moonshine, made a sport of chasing the chickens. They wore Confederate gray. Secesh. One caught a cackling bird and grabbed it by the head and began whipping it around ever faster in the air until its head spun off and the body flew to the ground, where it ran crazy about the yard spurting tiny fountains of blood. The man fisted the chicken head and looked on with crazed, bulging eyes and others jeered and carried on with like sickening gusto, not particular about what wasn't theirs. They were in the barn too, after her milk cow. After the hogs.

After everything.

She sucked breath. *Hannah.* She turned and looked back at the house, at the kitchen door standing wide. She turned back to the yard. The men were all around them.

The shithouse door opened and Coal stepped out and stood to the wind in his off fettle way, the one side of his body paralyzed and small and making him seem only half a person. His shirt was untucked on the palsied side and his pants canted the opposite way. Purdy's gut came up into the back of her throat and she tremored as if she'd struck her funny bone and it had lit up her whole body. She motioned Loli with her head over towards Coal and the girl moved slow but deliberate toward her twin, who was twice her size but only half her smarts. Coal just stood the ground pill-rolling a small rock back and forth in his good hand.

The soldiers looked snake-bit, hooting and hollering nonstop. Purdy singled out the one she took to be the boss, the one standing his place and not looking the fool. Of slight build, slender, small like an urchin she'd known once as a child. He was shorter than her and stood with a booted foot on the stump of an old tree, which served to make him look bigger than he really was. His face was dirty or crusted with stubble, she couldn't decide which. Either way it had been some time since he'd seen soap or a razor. His coat was road dirty and his boots worn thin at the toes and heels both. He sucked at a piece of straw and looked at the scene around him with detachment. He did all of this without saying a word. When the headless chicken ran by, his gaze followed it and that made Purdy all the more angry.

She pulled at her sleeves, long sleeves rolled up above her elbows. One had come undone and she worked to roll it back. She had on lace up boots and wasn't above kicking a man if she had to. Her gaze shot up in a quick, furtive glance at her hat. Her hair, red like her daughters', was pinned tight in a bun under a wide-brimmed, black leather hat that had been one of Enoch's favorites. She'd worn it most every day since his passing and had put it on that morning after finding the baby.

That hat was all she had of him. That and this place. His. Theirs together.

"What're you people doing here?" Purdy hollered, trying to make her voice heavy.

"Why, neighbor, we just lookin' after ourselves a bit is all."

The boss drew the words out in long, lackadaisical tones, as if he had all the time in the world and all of this was his and Purdy the intruder. He never turned his head, but she could see the one side of his face, the way his lips on that side curled upward. *He's smiling. Smiling at my headless chicken.* The dying bird had fallen over but was still twitching some.

"You've no right. This is my place." She crossed in front of him and caught his eye. "Them birds—they're mine. That there dead one specially."

The rebel soldier crooked his head and eyeballed her for the first time, needing to look up to do so. It wasn't clear if he was studying her or deciding on a response. "Ma'am, we don't mean y'all no harm. Just leave us be."

The drawl made it come out *jes laive us beh,* and she took a second thinking on the meaning. She looked him in the face, a hard accusatorial stare, as if she knew all the sins he was guilty of. "Them's my birds," she repeated, "Mine and my family."

"Well, they rations now. We ain't meaning no harm, but the boys," he reached into his pocket and pinched out a bit of tobacco, "well, they gotta et." He pulled on his lower lip and slipped the chew inside, between lip and gum. He worked his tongue back and forth over it, like a man with a piece of stringy bird stuck in his teeth. "Yes ma'am, we all gotta et." With the same hand, he reached in another pocket and withdrew a roll of scrip, peeling bills and counting as he went. He extended his palm and proffered the money.

"Lieutenant, my family can't eat those. You folks just go on back where you come from and let us alone. This ain't our fight."

A commotion erupted from the barn. Her milk cow was being led out. A big sow began to squeal behind the barn and it came around the corner, waddling and jiggling.

"It's sergeant, ma'am, not lieutenant." Then, almost as an afterthought, "Where's your man?" He looked around again, as if he might have missed her husband previously.

She struggled not to look at the mound of earth under the willow tree. "That ain't none your goddamn business. He'll be here soon enough though. And then you'll see."

"See what, ma'am?"

"See you ain't got no business on this here property." She looked at the cow moving away, at the chickens hanging across the men's shoulders. She counted half a dozen birds. "Damn you. I got mouths to feed."

As if to verify this fact, Loli had situated herself before her favorite mount, in fact her only mount, a speckled brown two-year-old. A rebel soldier had the animal by the reins. "Please mister, she's a good horse. Name's Tillie and I ain't got another. Ain't another like her in the whole big world." Tears streamed down the girl's cheeks and her face was a mess of screwed-up flesh. She had her hand on the animal's mane, stroking it. "Tillie! Tillie!"

The soldier hesitated not at all as he stalked away, half dragging the girl with them.

"Ma'am," the sergeant hardened his stare, "you Yanks don't know nuttin bout hunger. Maybe if'n your bellies go empty a few nights y'all'll understand what this war's all about and put a stop tuh it." He turned to his men. "Let's go boys."

Purdy looked at Loli. The picture of her clawing the air after Tillie was something she was going to remember a long time.

"You ain't gonna eat him?" Loli was saying, though to whom was not exactly clear. "Please. Ma!" She turned to her mother. "They ain't gonna eat her?"

Purdy yelled at the rebel sergeant, "Ain't you people got souls? No sir, none at all. The good Lord, he's gonna strike you dead, strike all you dead."

At her words one side of the sergeant's mouth pulled up. "You think God's a Yankee? That what you think? Don't y'all know I got young 'uns back home myself. We all does. And most all of 'em ain't gonna have full bellies tonight."

He took his booted foot off the stump and Purdy again thought how it had made him look bigger, or at least loom larger.

"Thing is though, they didn't have no full bellies last night neither, or the night afore that. What you have last night to et?" The sergeant looked at Coal, who had gimped his way over next to Loli. The girl stood in the yard, trying not to cry and doing a poor job of it. "What you et last night, boy?"

Coal stared blank-eyed at the man, still pill-rolling a small rock, as if no question at all was in the air.

"I'm talking to you, boy." The sergeant raised his voice. "What you supper on last night?"

One of the soldiers held his rifle butt up, apparently aiming to strike at Coal. Loli stepped in front of her twin brother. "He won't talk. Don't hardly have no voice. He don't know what you're saying anyhow. Leave him out of this."

"By the grace of God—" Purdy began.

"Your Yankee God can go to hell lady, can just go to hell 'cause I don't give a dog fart about what your God says or does or thinks. This my God right here."

He leered at her, at them, and held up his musket, elbow extended. He looked suddenly very tall and mighty. The other soldiers cheered. "And it's all the faith I need. I ain't never yet met a live sonbitch who didn't bow down to it. Met a few dead ones though." The sergeant turned to leave, showing his backside, then looked back. "Now, I suggest you gather up that family of yours and git out our way, else we gonna do some praying right here, by God, in my church."

Purdy reached forward and grabbed at his arm.

The sergeant turned, his hand coming up. He backhanded her across the face, and it was like a shotgun going off. She fell back, cheek stinging. She lay in the dirt and chicken shit, spitting blood, and saw Coal struggling against Loli's hold. Fourteen and a gimp, but he was still stronger than his twin sister and she couldn't hold him. He made a sound with his mouth, a feral noise none of them had ever heard come out of him before. He moved as fast as Purdy had ever seen him move, but of course it wasn't fast enough.

One of the soldiers—a dead chicken was stuffed in his blouse—kidney punched Coal with the butt of his rifle. The boy went down like a spilled stack of poker chips, spreading across the dirt, holding his side and crying something unintelligible, his hands and the fingers on those hands the blue color of bad blood.

The sergeant shook his head. "Tsk, tsk, tsk. Guess we gonna have to pray after all." He stepped forward, the business end of his musket aimed down at Coal's belly. Two others came up alongside him. They had a godless look. Coal himself was blue and puny and just trying to breathe. "This your fault lady. I told you leave us be."

"No! He's dumb, don't got the sense of a horse—" Purdy was shouting. Coal stammered and writhed in the dirt in exactly the gawky way you'd expect of a crippled man. The soldier swung with both hands on his rifle, the butt making contact and the terrible, awful sound of something popping, of wood splintering.

It happened both with all deliberate slowness and with the speed of that first slap. In an instant the sergeant had his own musket in Coal's gut too. The hard, blunt tip of it seemed an inch deep in his flesh. "I told you leave us be. And now—"

"Sergeant, what in hell's going on here?" A new voice. Authoritative.

They turned all together, soldiers and family alike, like oxen at the yoke. A neatly bearded, tall man a few years older than Hannah came round the corner of the house. The pits of his blouse showed broad sweat stains and his hat canted at a jaunty angle over one eye. He wore the same gray as the others and moved toward them at a brisk pace that wasn't quite a run, not seeming to be in a hurry but clearly with a purpose.

The sergeant shook slightly, cussing something under his breath. He moved the rifle off aim and came to attention only slowly. "Lieutenant, we just having a spot of fun is all. Sir."

"These people don't look like they're having fun." He never took his gaze from the sergeant.

"My men, we been on the long march, sir. They was hungry is all. Just hungry. Ain't seen a spread like this in a year and more."

"Sergeant, what unit y'all with?"

He told him and then spat. The spit missed the officer's booted foot by no more than an inch.

The lieutenant held his tongue, clearly seething. When he spoke it was through clenched teeth. "Sergeant. You will get your men together. You will move on outta here. I don't much cotton to Confederate troops beating on women and children."

The sergeant looked at the ground. Coal had curled fetal but his breath was gaining and he had pinked some. His sister had dropped down beside him and cupped his head in one hand while she rubbed his back with the other. Purdy was sitting on the ground a few feet away. The sergeant looked around to his men, grinned toothfully. "As you wish, sir. We dismissed then?"

"You are."

"What about my cows and chickens?" Purdy said.

"What about Tillie?" Loli shouted.

The lieutenant put a hand out to Purdy. "I'm sorry." He turned toward the sergeant, who was heading toward the road. "Give this woman back three of her chickens."

The sergeant stopped, spat again in the dirt, and wiped his mouth on his sleeve, which looked to have seen a lot of spit in its time. "They dead, lieutenant." He said 'dead' like it had two syllables, like the word was a long, meandering path and his tongue could only get around with a great, tired spasm.

"Then give her back three *dead* chickens."

The lieutenant pulled off his glove and put a hand out to assist her, but the farm woman brushed him away and said how she didn't need his help, didn't need any rebel's help. He looked at the boy and knew immediately something was queer. The kid was off kilter somehow, and not just from the gut punch.

"His name's Coal. Got hisself kicked in the head by a mule going on ten years now. Been slow ever since," the young girl said.

The lieutenant nodded, still looking at the boy. Coal's eyes went back and forth in small, jerky spasms, his head unmoving all the while, as if he was trapped behind that face, peering out through the slots of those eyes like a prisoner with a life sentence in hell. It gave pause just thinking on it. The officer looked back at Purdy. A dab of blood blemished one corner of her mouth and her cheekbone was already swollen up a mottled purple. "I'm afraid that'll be a right shiner in the morning. I'm sorry."

The woman ignored him and moved over and rubbed the boy's side. The girl searched the dirt with her eyes and picked up a small, polished stone. She put it in Coal's good hand and curled his palm around it, taking a moment to squeeze her fingers tight over those of the boy. This seemed to calm him a touch and together the woman and the girl pulled him to his feet.

The lieutenant removed his hat and offered his hand again. "Name's Taylor. Ben Taylor. Lieutenant, CSA."

"What about Tillie?" The girl said again. Her face screwed up like she was going to cry. "My horse. She's mine. What about her? She ain't hurt nobody. She's a good horse."

"I can't do nothing 'bout that horse."

"But she ain't gonna understand."

He bent toward her. "What's your name little missy?"

"Loli. And I ain't little. I'm fourteen." She sniffled once and avoided his hand.

"My apologies Miss Loli. I see you ain't so little so I know you'll understand when I say these are hard times for us all. Hard times even for horses. Maybe horses got it hardest of all."

"You think so? They ain't gonna eat her?"

"A horse is good for lots of things. Eating would be the least of 'em. You can take my word on that." He tried to smile but there wasn't much smile left in him and it came out looking just mostly like he wasn't frowning.

Loli's mouth opened to say something but the woman silenced her. "Shush now, child." She turned to Coal. "Come on, boy." The several of them moved toward the house and after a few steps she looked back at him, a pace or two behind them. "My hogs?"

He replaced his hat. "Can't help you there neither. The men, they do have to eat. You understand I'm sure." He stopped at the back steps as the others went up.

"They ain't gonna eat her..." Loli said again. It wasn't clear if this was a question, a statement, a maybe even a plea.

Purdy said, "Damn rebels. What gives you the right—"

"Ever been to Virginia, ma'am?"

Purdy went through the door and into the kitchen, bracing slightly at the sickly sweet air. "Ain't been and got no plans to go."

"Well, I wish the rest of you Yankees felt similarly." The lieutenant gestured with a light, airy upturning of his hand.

She hung out the door looking at him. "I'm Mrs. Enoch Gamble and this here's my house. Mine and my husband Mr. Enoch Gamble. Why should I let you in?"

"I don't guess there's any reason you should, but I feel obliged. I'd like to help if'n I could. They needed the food but had no right to make it hard on you all like that."

"You ain't the only ones has suffered."

The lieutenant opened his mouth as if to reply, but a movement caught his eye in the room beyond the kitchen and whatever he had thought to say left him as his eye fell upon the young woman sitting on the floor there. She held sway just beyond the doorway, looking shrunken and pale, almost ghostly in the fading light. She rocked back and forth with a gentle motion, a small something swaddled in blue in her arms, all the while her lips moving with a stolid sort of energy. "—come on Noah, mama's got you some milk."

The near ghost of a girl put the bundle to her tit but it didn't take her nipple. Whatever was in the bundle lay unmoving in her arms. "Okay, not hungry, maybe later. Maybe when your pa gets home. Your pa's gonna be so proud."

She put the bundle over her shoulder and it plopped down queerly, floppily. She patted the back of the thing, then bit her lip and paused in her monologue and her slow breathing filled the room. She began telling Noah about his father, how he was a soldier fighting for the Union, how he was going to be home soon and they would go picking mulberries and hunting rabbits together in the back woods. "You'll like mulberries. They's just so juicy and sweet. I like the sweet ones. Your pa, he's partial to the tart ones but I like the sweet. It's okay you like the tart ones. You can like anything you want. Here, have some milk Noah. Just suck a little, okay?" She had it back to her tit again, but its head just hung there.

Taylor gasped. "Ma'am?"

"The baby's ripe," Purdy's tone was low and flat and exhausted. "Deserves a proper burial."

He crossed into the kitchen in an instant. "Those men, they didn't—"

"No." Purdy put a hand to his shoulder. "Been dead since this morning. Passed in the night. The fever."

Loli stood beside her mother, nodding, her big eyes doleful. Coal leaned against the wall behind them, holding his side with one hand and not looking anywhere particular. A person couldn't tell what he was thinking, or even if he *was* thinking, Taylor thought.

He pushed the old woman's hand away and crossed the doorway, his step less urgent at the new information, and entered the death room. The odor was stronger here and it made him think of a ham that had turned. He resisted an urge to draw his kerchief and went down on a knee beside the girl. Up close, he saw her pale tit and her nipple where she'd lifted her nightshirt.

She sat indifferent to his presence.

"Holy Mother Mary," he whispered, his lips barely moving with the words. He leaned in close and stroked her hair with an ungloved hand by way of claiming her attention. Behind him, the older woman had brought a candle. It flickered in the growing darkness and the room hung on to the light as if magically lit.

Taylor stroked the baby's blanket. Hannah lifted her head toward him and her lips moved without any sound and he couldn't understand what she was saying. She was young, but there was no youth in her face. Horrid, dirty circles eclipsed her eyes, which looked burnt. Her face had a thin, skeletal likeness and he saw clearly the bones beneath that pale skin, and perhaps even the gaps between those bones. It was the kind of face seen only in nightmares, that would age any man who looked on it. He had to avoid turning away.

He stroked the baby's blanket a second time and Hannah's lips stopped their empty whispering. They quivered and she sat the floor with her legs under her, sat Indian style with her legs knotted about each other. In a weary, lost voice, she said, "Sometimes he don't breathe so well."

Purdy came forward at the sound of her daughter's voice. The candle flickered and the small flame bent in the reflection on the window. Darkness was gathering outside, doing its best to fill the room as well.

Taylor nodded. "What's your baby's name?"

"Noah."

"May I," he hesitated, "hold him?"

She nodded, it wasn't yes or no but just a random movement that showed her exhaustion. He said how it was okay, how he had a nephew who was just a little older than Noah and how he thus knew something about holding babies. He put his hands out. She slackened her embrace and he took the bundle in his arms and she let him have it.

"Mind you rock him now, he likes to be rocked. Likes to be rocked even when he's asleeping. Specially when he's asleeping."

Purdy pulled Hannah's nightshirt down over her tit and took hold of her hand and caressed her palm. She wiped at the loose strands of hair matted alongside her nose. "There now sweet child. Mama's here. It's all right, everything's gonna be all right." Her voice was soft, like when Hannah herself had been a baby.

Taylor had lied. It had been a long time since he had held a baby, but that baby too had been dead and so maybe he knew about as much as there was any need to know about holding dead babies. He rocked Noah, even put him to his shoulder. He nodded at Purdy and slowly, ever so slowly, his face hardened until there was nothing to it but the square, granite look of a life lived hard. Little by little, wrinkle line by wrinkle line, the look on Hannah's face mirrored his own.

"Honey love, Noah ain't sleeping," Purdy said.

"He's dead, ain't he?"

"He's gone to a better place," Taylor said.

She blinked out a tear, but only one. "You think when we go that we can maybe be whatever age we want? That if we've lost an arm or leg we're made whole again? That even babies can eat rock candy and run and jump and play with dolls and ride ponies and pick mulberries? That someone's there to help them comb their hair and tuck in at night? That's what I think."

"I believe that sure as I'm here with you," Taylor said.

Hannah lay back against the wall. Her skin was pasty white and the sweat of it glistened even in the small light of the candle flame. She turned away, burying herself against Purdy's bosom. There was no sobbing, just the low sound of breathing. Slow, relaxed breathing. Hannah was asleep in an instant and Purdy held onto her daughter as if to let go she might lose her forever.

Ben rose and stepped back, the baby wrapped in the blue blanket and the blue blanket cradled in his arms and those arms drawn in close to him. He stepped wordlessly around

Purdy and past Loli who stood at the base of the stairs. The room seemed to darken and close in behind him as he moved away from the candle and toward the darkness on the porch. He stepped through the splintered door and set the blanket and its swaddling on the porch, then shrouded the small bundle with the only thing he had at hand, the coat off his back. He saw Loli watching him through the window even as he knelt.

Please Lord, wrap yourself around these here poor folks and watch over them in the days to come, for they will surely need it. When he stood again his cheeks were wet where they hadn't been before.

He looked at Loli and she nodded at him. He wiped a loose hair from his forehead and adjusted the hat on his head. He had never removed it save for the one moment when he'd introduced himself to Purdy, and walked out into the night.

Loli watched until the dark swallowed him, until he wasn't but a figment out there in the night. So far as she could tell, he never looked back.

The three of them buried Noah beside Enoch and the breech baby. For a time Coal sat off to one side and watched as the others hove their shovels to the ground and dug at intervals. It was done in the dark of the night, which meant at least they didn't have to break their backs in the heat of the day, and neither Loli nor Purdy said much since neither had slept for going on two nights now. Fatigue made them clumsy, but the deed needed doing. They dug a hole, shallow since it was a baby after all and maybe they'd come back later and do it better, though both knew they wouldn't. It was hard enough getting it done once.

They didn't have a pine box, of course. No box at all. When the digging was done they laid their tools aside and bundled the boy in the blue blanket and called it a burial shroud. Loli kissed the cloth over his face and Purdy pulled him close one last time before she laid him in the earth, and he looked pretty much as he might have under the blankets in his own cradle. Loli put in a stuffed animal she'd made, just a puffed out rag of a sock with the end sewn over, but as far as anyone could tell Noah had liked it.

Loli wanted to include a little silver cross her father had given her as well, a store bought thing, but it wasn't anyplace she looked. She improvised on the moment with a cross made from two twigs hastily joined with a strip of thin leather. "It's sturdy enough don't you think?"

Purdy allowed how it was sturdy all right and said a few words over him, nothing fancy, the usual words somewhat abbreviated. What could you say about someone who'd spent just four months on this earth? He'd brought some pleasure and a lot of pain. It wasn't a fair world and that was that.

Whatever remains will be enough. What Enoch had said. Purdy looked around at the looming shadows of her homestead, at the willow swaying in the gentle night. "Take this boy in your arms, Enoch honey."

When it was time to put the dirt back, Coal came forward. To that moment he had leaned against the willow or sat under its branches. Now he rose and the others stopped what they were doing as he crossed to the grave. There was the usual limp and buckle in his step. He kicked at the piled dirt a bit with his spastic leg then sat down and pushed the soil into the hole with his good hand, all the while his useless arm flexed at the elbow, the hand fisted against his heart, the polished stone held fast in his palsied hand. The tips of those fingers blanched. When Loli tried to help he pushed her out of the way. When he was done, his palsied hand uncurled and the polished stone fell to the mud topping the infant's grave, where he worked it back and forth with his good foot. This he did for some time and might well have passed the entire night so occupied had not

Purdy tugged him by the shoulder and bade him come inside.

Purdy herself stood at the door of the kitchen a moment longer, watching the night shadows play across the yard and feeling the creep of time against the place. Nineteen years the first baby had lain out there alone. Now, in the span of just four months, two more graves had been dug.

Whatever remains will be enough. She took the preacher hat from off her head and kissed it.

As baby Noah was laid to rest, Hannah lay upstairs in her bed with eyes vacuous and the world and all its happenings continued without her. She showed no more life than if she herself had died that night, and if she'd never been born at all it might not have been a bad thing.

FIVE

The constant, pell-mell thwacking of the front door against its jamb woke Loli less than four hours after she'd closed her eyes. They'd nailed the door shut after the rebels, but the wind had come up in the night and busted it free again. She stood now in the dark waiting on her eyes, rubbing at them with hands still cramping from the grave digging. She looked down on her sister. Hannah lay in the bed beside the spot she'd just vacated, curled on her side, her form faint and near lifeless in the dark space. She wore the same nightshirt she'd worn four days running now. The bed beneath her was darker than it ought to have been and when Loli touched it the dampness came away on her fingers.

"Eew, pee." She took several moments trying to cajole her sister into wakefulness before she decided the effort was wasted.

Loli made her way across to the window and the chair beside it, where she found the dress she'd tossed aside climbing into bed. She pulled it on over her undergarments and found her shoes and held them up to the moon streaming through the window. In her fatigue she put only one on and carried the other as she crossed the room back the way she'd come. She kicked the leg of a table with her bare foot, said "dang it," and bent over and massaged her toes and put her other shoe on.

At the top of the stairs she stopped and listened, hearing nothing but the thwack of the loose door, a cricket's song, and the wind worrying the trees alongside the faint tumbling of Tischer Creek, a long stone's throw out the back side of the house. Her first memory of anything in this world was of carrying a bucket half full of water from Tischer Creek to this house. It could have been a made up memory though since she'd made that trip twice or maybe three times a day every day she could remember until her father had dug a well and installed a hand pump just out the back door. That had been in the spring of '61 and the war had come that very year. The well had been Enoch's last project.

She felt her way down the stairs, the steps complaining under her feet just as always, and when she got to the bottom she crossed the short distance to the loosed door, which she braced open against a chair. She stepped out on the porch and the bony outlines of several trees were just visible in the mist of an early morning fog. The sun was barely a crack in the east and the sky that way had a smeared, pumpkin-orange slice of glow, while in the west it was still black dark. She sat the weathered stoop and dawg, thin-boned with a gap in one ear from some long ago incident, ambled out the door and sat beside her. She put a hand on his back and sat for a long while feeling the thrum of his innards against his ribs. He fed well on scraps and wild rabbits, but he had never been a sort to put any meat on and she could feel those ribs plain.

After some time, an odd assortment of noises came out of the dark expanse in front of her. Dawg lifted his head, canting it from side to side as if to hear better, and she felt the beat of his innards pick up a notch.

"What is it dawg? Who's there?"

Dawg stood and she followed and dawg stepped out into the yard and she followed there too, as if dawg was the master. They walked along a berm and past several brace of cottonwoods. When she looked back the house appeared ghostly in the fog, thin and near gone altogether, as if a memory she only vaguely recalled. There was a black spot where the door still yawned wide, but no detail beyond.

The air was pearly with misted water and it silvered the landscape all around, stole the particulars. They entered another stand of cottonwoods, the ground wet and slippery and moldy, the underneath mostly mud and worms. The muck slathered dawg's belly and her dress alike and she felt the dampness of the morning close on the skin of her legs. Dawg shivered though it wasn't overly cold and he scratched at a bother on the side of his head, which made him look as if he was trying to take an ear off. Old Dutch Road, the name a holdover from another time and place, was a half mile straight ahead in the light of day by the flight of a crow, but they covered twice that distance getting there through the brush and weeds and felled trees and rotting logs. She could have taken the more direct path from the house but dawg hadn't done so and she'd followed dawg the whole way.

She and dawg stopped short of the road by a good distance, close enough to make out the semblance of men against the silver night come dawn. There were horse shapes and wagon shapes too. The pair drew closer still and the cantankerous sounds of men and horses and wagons going about their business became louder. A body could make out faces here, some long and square of jaw, others pallid like what you might find in a sick house.

There was a little guy with a drum strapped over one shoulder. It was only a little smaller than he himself and as he walked his head lolled lazily from one side to the other and his mouth gaped wide like a man snoring off last night's shindig. He had but rags on his feet, and these bloody. A soldier limped along behind him and his butternut trousers were smeared crimson on one pant leg and it was the same leg he favored as he moved. Still another fellow looked something like a well-fed tinker Loli had seen once, all round and plump and hard to figure how he walked without waddling. His trousers were too short or maybe his legs too long, either way the effect was to show off the pale skin of his plump legs above the stockings that likewise doubled as shoes.

A man dressed in civilian clothes trotted through on a calico horse and the slapdash column of men parted slow and reluctant, several pointing after the interloper and not a few cursing him to hell as he rode by. He kept his focus like a man possessed of a mission and did not dawdle. An old soldier, a veteran of many battles to look at him with his pugilistic jaw, bent nose, and deepset eyes, spat a tan gruel and wiped the spittle on one sleeve or the other. The man behind him had eyes the size of two-bit pieces and something of a nervous tic. His chin kept twitching toward one shoulder as if he was about to convulse generally, though he never did. Another rider drew rein and stopped his horse on the road directly in front of Loli. She could have spit on him or vice versa. The fevered stench of horseflesh was big about her until the pair moved on a moment later. She held her ground behind a deadfall, afraid even to breathe but awed nonetheless. She heard as well a muffled word or two of conversation between the men now and again, but it didn't make sense.

They talked of Yankees. Of killing damn Yankees.

She hugged the gap-ear'd dog and he seemed to sense she needed to hold him just then and he made no effort to wiggle away. He stood with his tongue hanging out the side of his mouth and eyes that were at once oblivious and compassionate. She felt the rapid thrum of pulse as she held him against her chest and it was only later, after he'd run off and her head had cleared from the blow of the club, that she realized the heart racing between them in that embrace had been her own.

***

The Gamble home was a small, weather-beaten two story, a simple clapboard with broken shutters and two steps rising to a rickety porch Enoch had intended to reinforce before time and all else had gotten away from him. The whole affair had been painted a pale yellow years before, perhaps by way of standing it apart from the greenery surrounding, but the dirt of the countryside had grained the siding hard in the intervening years and the sun had bleached what was left until it was a dirty off-white now. Behind it a hundred steps farther up the hill was a good sized barn, which had never been painted and so stood the countryside baring dead sidewalls of a weathered brown patina. The inside of the barn smelled richly of manure and hog droppings and chicken shit. A shed at the back housed a not-too-rusted plow and other implements.

Sometimes, in the dark of the night after she could be sure the others were asleep, Purdy would don Enoch's preacher hat and steal away quietly out the back of the house and cross the wide yard to the willow, beneath which lay her husband. Its trunk canted upward at a slight but comfortable enough angle and it was here she'd passed the lonely hours of a score of nights in the months since Enoch had died. She'd lean into and against the willow, trying to feel its wind rumblings. She'd wait on her eyes to adjust to the dark, conjuring images of him coming in from the fields after a full day farming, of him taking her in his arms and squeezing her so close she could hardly breathe. When the light was right, she'd produce the tintype and look on his eyes, sometimes tracing the outline of his face with a finger. Sometimes, if the air was just right and there wasn't too much pollen about, she could even smell his sweat in the band of his hat. This only made her want him more of course, made her want to feel him more, to feel all of him, to feel him in her...

These were the things that remained.

On two or maybe three occasions she'd actually lain down on the grave mound and let her cheek press the bare soil between her and Enoch. She had cried then, the only times she really had cried, and all the built up pain and misery and woe had loosed itself into the earth. She had prayed and cried and prayed and cried until each time she had known anew that dead he was and dead he was going to stay. She had felt then foolish laying on the burial mound and with some effort—she always wanted to stay—she pulled herself upright and went back in the house.

She had never told anyone about these nights.

Somewhere in the distance a rooster crowed. Under the willow, whatever it was that passed for sleep in Purdy's world dissolved. She rose from astride the grave and ambled back toward the house. Enoch's preacher hat sat her head like a mourning veil with her face lost in the shadow beneath the wide brim, which was pulled close over her eyes as was her fashion. Halfway across the yard she stopped to look up at the morning sky, which was a deep blue, the kind of blue that renews a person's faith in a heaven above, and the yard smelled mightily of trees and green things. It was near perfect, except that already a person could feel the heat of the day coming on. A whippoorwill sang in the cottonwoods fronting the house, and a breeze stirred the branches of those same cottonwoods, as if they too had just awoke and this was a part of their daily ritual on this just another day on God's green earth. Old Dutch Road, a goodly stretch of which she could see plainly half a mile or so down the hill before her, lay as quiet as a baby satisfied to suck at its mama's tit. There was a calmness and a stillness to the place.

God's country, Enoch had called it on so many such mornings.

She entered the kitchen, hollering. "Loli, you and Coal get on down here." She took from off the cast iron stove a dented teakettle, the underside of which was black charred from a lifetime of such mornings. She hollered for Loli again as she opened the back door and stepped out onto a rotted wooden step that sagged as it pressed the mire underneath. Enoch would have fixed it long ago had he been around, but it was just one of a hundred things that needed doing now and it wasn't anywhere near the top of that list either.

"God's country," she said aloud and swooshed the last remnants of yesterday's coffee into the dirt and rubbed her eyes at the brightness of the dawn light. She noted the fresh turned dirt of the tiny grave dug in the night, thought again how it wasn't a fair world. She thought too how she and Enoch had planted that willow tree so many years before. It had gone from scrawny to the keeper it was now. She wondered if Coal would ever be a keeper, if the breech baby would have grown up strong in this world had he not entered it so poorly. That such thoughts lived in her she had not to that moment known and as she bent over and cranked the hand pump and the weight of water deep in the earth pulled against the mechanism, so too did the weight of these thoughts pull on her. She cranked the pump and the water rose and came out cool and fresh and smelling of a sweet, clean river deep under the ground. She played a hand in the pumped water and took Enoch's hat from off her head and put her cupped hand to her face, slapping the cool on her cheeks. When she was done, she put the hat back on her head and went back inside and put the watered kettle on the stove.

"Loli, you and Coal need get us some wood."

When the girl still didn't answer, Purdy went through to the front room and noticed for the first time the open front door. She paused. She turned and yelled up the stairs. Coal appeared at the top of those stairs wearing naught but his nightshirt. "You best go wake Loli. Git on now," and she shooed him to his task with a wave of her hand. She let the door be and returned to the kitchen.

She had the first smolderings of a fire going a moment later when Coal appeared, barefoot in his underwear and not a stitch above the waist. "Boy, what's with you?" He stood silent and unmoving, like his being there was incidental. The spitting image of his sister stared out from his face. "And where's Loli?"

The boy shook his head. The sun was full up in the window. The morning chill, if it had ever been there at all, had burned off and the day was warm and leaden and a person couldn't help but feel it had turned somehow. A promise ruined.

"You ain't gonna need them under things," Purdy said as she adjusted her hat, pushing the brim back enough to brush at the sweat once again. She pushed Coal ahead of her, turning him round in the process. The pair stopped at the propped open door and one side of her mouth drew up in sober contemplation a moment before the whippoorwill's song was broken by gunshots, then even louder, deeper reports. She tensed with each pop, her hands fisting and letting go, fisting and letting go.

"Lordy," she said, teeth clenched. Of a sudden she noted the stream of dust rising off Old Dutch Road, too much for anything less than a very large group.

An army.

"Loli!" she hollered again, more insistent now. Coal, for once, had an advertent look about him. He stared at his mother, his gaze following her around the room as she went from window to window pulling aside the lace curtains, her attention all to the yard and the invidious road beyond.

"Oh Enoch," she said, and the wind went nearly out of her as she spoke to her dead husband, "So they've come. May the Lord have mercy on all our souls for they ain't gonna have none." She moved quickly then, switching the chair from one side to the other, so that now it braced the door closed rather than open.

She turned to Coal. He had come into this world second of two, blue and puny and she had not thought he would live a day. But he lived a week, and another, until finally he'd lived long enough they had to give him a name and by then the dead blue hue of his skin had begun to pink and so they named him Coal, musing on how maybe this boy had some fire in him after all. Fire or no, his skin had never quite pinked enough and even now after fourteen years the dead hue could be seen in his lips and the tips of his fingers, which thus always looked cold but never proved so on touching. At odd moments the peculiar color would flush across his face, especially his cheeks and jowls, ghostlike and not always fleeting. It gave the boy a coffin-bound look that took some getting used to.

"Boy, get on up those stairs now." She pointed and at first Coal hesitated, but she gestured again, with a hard fling of her forearm, her pointer finger insistent at the end of her arm. And all the while she looked him hard in the eyes, those eyes talking loud above all else. A mother's eyes that said *There's trouble coming and you got to get out of harm's way.* "Go on, boy. Get on."

He went, but with a wary, watchful gait, as if he knew something about the day to come. He opened and closed his good hand and inhaled deeply and for once any blue in his lips pinked and he moved up the stairs.

She had no mind to watch him go. She took a knee beside the braced door, leaning forward and pulling the lace askew for the look the window afforded: a dead-on view of Old Dutch Road. The house sat the upslope of a gentle rise and all before it slid away with a certain graceful dignity, as if He—that is, The Lord God Almighty himself—had taken more than a simple interest in the outcome. The cottonwoods, tumbled rocks, and curve of the hillside were of such disposition that an interested observer on the front stoop could note the comings and goings on the road below. And just now that road presented a curious sight: scores upon scores of men marching at the double step, the blown up dust looking not unlike a plague of locusts from the Old Testament. And in the near distance puffs of smoke and things—men, she realized—moving every which way. She let go the curtain and in the same motion took the preacher hat from off her head and worried the fingers of one hand along the sweat band, the much-worn hat rolling in a great circle on her palm and leaving a smear of dirt behind.

"Loli!" she hollered again and again, until her voice gave over to a sob then out altogether—but there was nothing by way of an answer save the hard, dry swallow of her own spit and the dolorous hiss of her breathing.

She slumped down until both knees pressed the hardwood and the hardwood pressed back and blanched her flesh. She squeezed her eyes closed and crossed a fist over her heart and pressed her lips tight together. She bit her tongue and her breath came in quick, shallow digs and her chest barely moved for the better part of several long minutes.

"No no no no no. You got to pull yourself together," she said in a half whisper, "and you got to do it right now. Right this here very minute."

A vision of Enoch came, familiar as if he had never entered the grave. She thought he was wearing his black suit, but as she looked harder she saw the sleeves were a bit long. It was Jones's suit, the one the peculiar undertaker had lent him to have his picture done. Like the tintype, he looked straight-backed and uncomfortable, like his bones had fused rigid.

She opened her eyes and he was still there, in that black suit that wasn't his. The suit that was his she had buried with him. He hadn't worn it to his funeral, what he'd worn was his army uniform with its three gold chevrons on the sleeves, but she'd put the suit in the casket with him because nobody else was ever going to wear it.

She held tight to the preacher hat in her hands and asked The Lord God Almighty to hold them all tightly in their time of need and looked over to the sideboard, where Enoch's Sunday reading spectacles sat on the shelf. Dust covered the lenses and it occurred to her she should have buried those with him as well. They were useless now, no good to anyone.

"You got to pull yourself together," she heard again, only this time it was Enoch speaking. She swallowed big like she was swallowing a lump of lard. The image faded until it was no more than a stir of dust against the light streaming gold through the window.

Loli pulled herself up waist high, sideways to the ground. She'd been lying bent over in the muck and one side of her face was mottled and tattooed with dirt and twig lines. The other was blue and bruised and swollen where the butt of a musket had come down against the rise of her cheekbone. Beside her was a man with butternut trousers and a dirty undershirt, the best about which could be said it was all in tatters. He stank of sweat and a little booze and was sprawled full out, arms at his side and legs fully extended like he was fit to be encoffined, only he was breathing with more gusto than any dead man she might have imagined. The tall trees paralleled him and it was only then she righted her own head and understood the man wasn't lying down at all but standing.

He was a lanky trooper with the makings of a salt and pepper beard and his face was burnt like leather too long in the sun. He was chewing a piece of straw that bobbed between his lips and had one eye open and upon her. A person couldn't say where the other eye was looking. "Ye kindly awake, girlie."

It might have been a question, she couldn't tell by the inflection. Loli righted herself all the more on hearing it though, so the answer was clear enough. "What?"

"Not what. Where," he said.

"Where?"

"Yeah, where. I kindly take it from the looks of you that you from around these parts. Don't figure on a runt like you going too far afield."

"I ain't no runt," Loli said.

"Suit yerself."

"Who're you?"

"Name's Bifford if you gotta know, but I'm guessing it ain't so important." He sucked at the straw and waited like she was supposed to say something but she didn't. He knelt beside her and somehow looked all the more lanky in doing so, like he had to fold himself at the knees and hips. "He the surgeon, yonder," he said and raised an arm and pointed to a fellow standing the other side of a rutted dirt road.

Loli followed the raised arm. The road was guttered by perhaps a dozen and more men. Only one stood and he was bent ninety degrees at the waist, like a mechanical man with only one working joint. The doctor worked with a pack slung over one shoulder, his movements deliberate and purposeful in the same way one clearing a chicken coop of eggs moves ever forward toward that last prize. Still and all, his goal, was elusive. The men kept arriving faster than he could work. The roadside had become a bloody hole in the countryside where men came or were brought. And they were piling up.

All were sprawled randomly in the dirt. Those who were moving writhed about in various states of disarray. Several had bandages about the head, one held up an arm minus a hand, and still another shouted in high pitched tones how he was dying. He kept shouting and the others kept ignoring him and the countryside kept filling up with others like him and them all the while.

The mechanical man, the one who had been pointed out as the surgeon, made his way past the pleading man with hardly a glance. He found a quiet fellow and knelt once again in his peculiar manner. He had about him the look of a preacher and this made Loli think of her father, who all used to say looked the part of a preacher man. The surgeon, if that's what he was, appeared stern and serious and all of one mind. When he spoke it was out of only one side of his mouth. The fellow he helped had a belt tied round his thigh just shy of his knee and he yelled profanely when the surgeon tightened it another notch. He drank lustily from a tumbler the surgeon offered.

"There now," said the doc, "this will warm you."

"You people ain't Union," Loli said.

"And thank God for that, girlie," Bifford said.

"What you want with me?"

"You was laid on our doorstep, girlie. So to speak anyways."

"I didn't ask to be brought here."

"You been out more 'n two, maybe three hours. Been standing here watchin you most all that time. Sort of protectin you, if'n you know what I mean."

"You a doctor?"

He chuckled and it sounded like a chicken clucking. "One of yer damn Yankee balls nearly took my head off."

"You look healthy enough to me."

"Well I's injured just the same." He bent to show her a near bloodless gash on the side of his head.

She had to look twice. "That ain't no kinda wound."

"What you say? That there's a near dead head wound, girlie. Why...you ain't no sawbones so it don't matter what you think." He stood again.

"You best let me go."

"I ain't thinking so. But it ain't up to me."

"Who's it up to?"

"Probably the gineral I figures."

"How do I find him?"

He clucked again and nearly fell over. "You can't find no gineral, and if'n you could he wouldn't have no time for you no how."

"So why would he care whether I'm coming or going?"

"I ain't got no idea, runt."

"I told you I ain't no runt."

The infantryman turned his head and spat in the dirt and dried his lips over the length of his arm, which left a long brown smear. "What they call you then?"

"My name's Loli. Loli Gamble."

"What kind of name is Loli?"

"The kinda name my paw give me."

He grunted. "How old you is, Loli?"

"Fourteen years my last birthday."

"Well that's fine. That's real fine." He smiled and black and yellow teeth showed beyond upturned lips. "You best to be careful. Out here, round these varmints, you best to be real careful." He gestured big, like he was all there was between her and them.

"Mister, ain't you got no work to do?"

"I showed you I'm injured. Besides, I's supposed to be watching you."

"I don't need no watching."

"The doc there said I was to keep a eye on you. Said I can't let you out my sight even one minute."

"That's ridiculous."

"There's a battle being fought out here case you hadn't heard it."

"I figured that much. I ain't dumb."

"No girlie, I didn't figure you fer dumb. Young. Young and pretty. But you ain't dumb." He spat again and repeated the lip wiping gesture.

The doctor came toward them and the infantryman rose and backed away, perhaps preferring to stay out of the surgeon's direct line of sight. The surgeon eyed her. "So, you are okay."

"Yes, sir. A little bruised is all."

"I am sorry for that." There was an odd monotone quality to his voice. "Soldiers sometimes get their ire up in battle. That is all it was. Ire. You were in the wrong place at the wrong time. You must be careful. You will be all right." He started to move away.

"Why you put that man to watching me?"

"I did no such a thing."

"He said—"

"I do not care what he said. Look here, I have no time to be thinking too long on the likes of one little girl. You best get."

"You mean I'm free to go?"

"Just keep to the roads and away from the fighting. And if you got any sense, you'll get inside soon as you can. Get inside and stay there, miss. Only thing out on a day like this—well, you just best stay indoors."

SIX

Purdy Gamble waited in her front room, in a chair by the propped-shut door. Hours before, she'd pulled herself off the floor and crossed the room to the massive work of dry stacked stone laid twenty years before by Enoch. The stones bounded a cavernous fire pit black with years of soot, was surmounted by a mantelpiece of scarred red cedar and this by an ancient flintlock musket Purdy's grandpappy had used as a boy. She had fired it once as a girl and a second time as a young woman. That last had been ten plus years ago.

She sat in the chair with the ancient weapon propped across her knees. Coal sat the top of the stairs, pill-rolling his good fingers over and over again. His bad side quivered now and again. Purdy stared out a front window, her head moving this way and that as she craned her neck at whatever caught her attention. The flintlock was charged and ready to fire. The only time she'd stirred from the chair was to pull the lace curtain back a tad to afford her a better view. She shifted and the weight of her bladder pressed her pelvis. She rubbed herself down there and cursed beneath her breath. The shithouse was a full fifty paces out the back door. Enoch had dug it just over the crest of a shallow rise so it drained away from the house. Too far on a morning studded with close gunfire, a missing child, a dead baby, a ransacked yard, and a daughter catatonic with grief.

She hollered for Coal to bring down her chamber pot.

She pulled the curtain back and glanced out to the yard. All seemed in order, as much order as the day had yet mustered anyway, and she looked up to Coal and spun her hand in the air indicating he should turn around. He stopped waving and closed his eyes and looked to be concentrating with all his might. She ignored him and went about her business.

The noise of something or someone rooting around in the yard interrupted her and she froze in mid-squat, the last tinkle of piss following loudly. Coal opened his eyes. Apparently he'd heard it too. He made as if to say something, but her hand went up quick in the air between them, the five fingers spread wide. Coal either took the meaning or didn't, but he stayed silent. She listened another moment and heard the sounds come around the near corner of the house, close by the back door. She rose and smoothed her dress and picked up the flintlock and held it chest high with her finger on the trigger.

She nearly blew a hole in the wall when Coal coughed. Purdy cursed him and put another finger to her mouth shushing him. As she crept into the kitchen, she saw him come down the stairs out of the corner of her eye. She walked slow and deliberate, as if the floor might give at any moment. She made herself small against the wall by the door, then lifted the hat from off her head and carefully set it on the floor beside her. She looked at the ceiling, then at the floor, as if whatever or whoever had made the noise had branded these objects, then cocked her head and peered out the window. She pressed flat against the wall and used her side vision. She was aware of Coal moving through the front room.

"Can't see nothing," Purdy murmured uncertainly. The noises continued, something rubbing or chaffing the sidings. She made herself taller by way of seeing better, just as Coal limped into the kitchen. He didn't know enough to make himself scarce.

"Jesus, boy," she said with only half a voice through pursed lips. She gestured with her free hand, pointing that he should get down on the floor. He ignored her or didn't understand and went for the doorknob. She rose full upright and so now saw the source of the noise outside. "The sow. Goddamn pig. Thought they took her away."

She set the flintlock on the table and didn't protest as Coal opened the door full. The she-hog raised her head and regarded them. She glanced quickly about the yard and looked at Coal.

The boy pointed toward the barn.

"No," she said without hesitation, "grab her on in here. Ain't gonna lose her again."

Coal didn't understand, just stood looking at her.

"Dumb," she said under her breath. She had to show him by gesture what she wanted, making a big loop with her arms and pointing at the pig and making like she was pulling.

She and the boy struggled with the sow for several long moments. They'd have struggled all the day except it of a sudden gained a mind to enter the house. She lumbered across Enoch's kitchen floor and for a moment it looked as if the floorboards would give way. The whole place shook with each step the beast took, but the house was well built after all and the sagging boards held.

"The root cellar," Purdy said, "put her in the root cellar." She gestured toward a door in one corner of the kitchen. It opened on a narrow stairway that fell away into the darkness below. It was steep, certainly too steep for a pig, but that wasn't something to worry about just then. They pushed and the hog squealed and moved. They got her through the small door and gravity did the rest. The animal tumbled down the steps with a long, awful squeal, then crashed into the shelving at the bottom. She was quiet and Purdy, out of breath, slammed the door. She retrieved

Enoch's preacher hat and put a hand on Coal's shoulder. The excitement had blued his lips.

"Mind you just let her be," Purdy said.

And that was when the world went all to hell.

Hannah Gamble Griel lay curled on the bed she'd long shared with Loli, in the same spot she'd held the whole of the long night. She had all the spirit of a potato-filled gunnysack. But when the shooting started she sat bolt upright and her hands gripped tight the stained bedcovers, her lanky fingers curling hard on themselves. She seemed lost, first within herself and then within the room. Her eyes sank in their sockets. With each pop and bang she jittered like a bug on a hot skillet and her mouth clinched taut as she strained from cheek to jowl; her eyes squinted narrow one moment and became wide the next.

The gunfire receded, or at least seemed to, and Hannah didn't move again for a long time and when she did it was to swing her legs over the edge of the bed and cross the room to the chamber pot in the corner. She sat the floor beside it for some miserable period, intermittently leaning over it with dry heaves. When finally she allowed she wasn't actually going to puke, she rose and sat the bed again. She rubbed her eyes and ran her hands through her hair. She heard a pig squealing somewhere.

She rose and took a meandering path to the door, now and then finding the wall for support. She bobbed unsteadily. Her legs seemed to rebel at holding her upright. She collapsed within spitting distance of the door and crawled the last little bit and pushed it open with an outstretched arm. She was half in, half out when she blacked out altogether. The last sound she heard was a heavy pounding floating up from below and in her daze she wondered if pa—Enoch—might be working on the porch.

***

Purdy heard the front door crash open and ran back to the front room in time to run headlong into the rebel soldier who'd busted it in. He had a gut a hog would be proud of and held his rifle diagonally across his body with both hands. She stopped just short of running into him. For his part, he had no look of surprise or astonishment. He didn't step backward or make any move to withdraw. He stood his ground as if he had a perfect right to be in her front room. He might have been a cousin come calling.

"What in hell you doing in my house?"

There was an uneasy lag between the question and the soldier's answer, during which his expression suggested he was thinking on the issue, perhaps even trying to decide what the issue was. "We taking this here place," he said, and the words came out like the most certain thing he'd ever uttered.

"You go on and get the hell outta here," Purdy said, but even as she spoke others were pushing in. Someone spoke and when she turned a grubby faced man with two chevrons on his sleeve stood there.

"We got wounded, lady. Major guesses this here place'll do as a hospital."

The flintlock lay on the kitchen countertop behind the grubby-faced soldier. Her eyes went from the fat soldier to the grubby-faced one, over to the flintlock, back to the grubby-face again. She cupped one hand in the other before her in a prayerful gesture. "A hospital? Don't think so. By The Lord God Almighty, I ain't thinking so. This is Enoch Gamble's home. My husband built this place of his own two hands and he didn't build it to be no rebel hospital. Hell no."

Grubby face's eyes grew bright. "Where is he, lady? He hereabouts anywheres?"

"He's dead. You killed him."

"I ain't kilt nobody. Least not today. Least not yet."

"I don't mean you special. I mean those like you. He were a sergeant in Lincoln's army. One of you murdered him at Fredericksburg."

An officer had come up the steps of the front porch and come in behind the fat soldier. He moved with a limp and his leg made a curious clicking as he went. In spite of his soiled uniform, which included a gold oak leaf on each shoulder, he had about him a certain polished look. "I am sorry for your loss, but a lot of people got themselves killed at Fredericksburg. A lot of good people on both sides." He spoke slowly and deliberately, his enunciation deep and certain, as if measuring every part of every word.

She addressed herself to him. "My husband was a good man. A very good man."

"I have no doubt of that, madam. No doubt whatsoever."

"Then don't dishonor him with this." She moved an arm in a wide circle.

"We have not been properly introduced. My name is Brody. Major Peter Brody. I am a surgeon and it is my task to take care of good soldiers." He held out a hand. "And you are?"

"Purdy Gamble's my name. And it will be a cold day in hell when I shake the hand of a rebel in my own house, doctor or no."

"Very well, have it your way." He withdrew the hand. "We mean you and yours no harm, but we have injured and your farm is the most convenient."

"That ain't no concern of mine." Behind her, a pig squealed and a man shrieked.

"You will no doubt understand it is every concern of mine just now."

"Major, I ain't understanding any of this. We've nothing and yet you people seem to want it all." The room rocked with a musket blast. "What'd your men go and do now?"

A soldier appeared from the kitchen. "Sorry suh, damn pig down the root cellar. Weren't expecting it."

"You killed my sow?"

The man gestured ignorance with one shoulder.

The major said, "Madam, you have four walls, a good supply of water, high ground, and you are close enough to the fighting, without being too close. This is ground for a hospital."

"My husband, he didn't build this place to be no retreat for rebel heathens, wounded or otherwise."

"We are no more heathens than you." The surgeon had a face every bit as chiseled and precise as the words he spoke. He was of square jaw with a full set of good white teeth and high, proud cheekbones. The skin under his eyes had reddened with the July sun. Or maybe he'd been born with rose in his cheeks. "Madam," when he spoke only one side of his mouth moved, "you only need ask yourself one question."

"You don't belong here," Purdy said.

"One question."

"And that be?"

"Might your husband still be alive if there had been a surgeon available when he fell?"

She had no way of knowing if this was true, of course. If the bullet that had broken Enoch's cheek and ruptured his eye had been removed early on, might he have lived? It seemed a plausible enough notion. Standing in her front room, it even seemed likely.

A vision of the wasted mansion came to her then, of seeing Enoch after so long. So poorly living, smaller and thinner than any had a right to be, all his fat burned away till he was nothing but flesh and sinew and bone. Blind in one eye, he'd still been hard to kill. He had lived two months thus, had seemed to be getting stronger until…until that damn bullet had reemerged out from under that blinded eye. He had gone quick after that, a few days and she had lost him. The damn piece of lead had been the harbinger of his final days. Now she saw him under the coffin glass, saw the neat black hole—bullet-sized, ugly, and grotesque in her pained memory—under his right eye.

Might he still be alive?"the doctor said again.

Yes, she thought, and found herself open mouthed, unable to speak. The idea seemed a very plausible notion indeed.

"God rest his soul," the major said and touched the brim of his hat but didn't remove it. "It is too late for your husband. But there are other husbands out there. Other fathers. Other sons. Would you deprive their loved ones? Have them wear the black veil of mourning? Have them endure that which you have endured? You don't strike me as such a woman."

She found her voice. "Strike you as such a woman? How can I strike you as anything when you don't know me? You're in my house, major. I don't suppose there's any choice in the matter. You people look like you're used to getting your way. I don't suppose you'd let a woman stand in your way, now would you? You don't strike me as the type."

"You are correct in your particulars. This is war, and we do not much get to choose who we may help, only the when and the where. And that when is now. We are both victims." He tipped his hat to her. "Good day, madam."

From that moment she might as well not have been there at all. She made for the stairs and heard the curtains being ripped from the windows. "Bandages," someone shouted, and Purdy thought of the many wounded she'd seen in Falmouth and Washington. Bandages or no, most of them had died.

Not so far away as the crow flies, Loli might as well have been on another continent. It had quickly become obvious her way home was blocked by the fighting. She'd kept clear of the roads and pikes, which were inundated with all the machinery of war, everything a girl could imagine and much she could not. She stood across a narrow road behind a row of trees—tall, ancient cottonwoods—and watched a line of cannons slowly roll crosswise through a parched cornfield. Between her and the rebel artillery an old masonry wall lay half demolished. It sprawled like a picked-over dead snake along the shoulder of the road. Beyond the cannons, maybe a quarter mile in the distance, several men stood in the doorway of an old stone house. They were too far off to make out their uniforms, but they appeared unconcerned at the sight of the artillery.

It was awe inspiring to see the cannons with their wheels half again as tall as a man. The horses pulling them were huge, great beasts bigger than any in her recall. "They won't eat her," she said in a low whisper, then began to cry. She went down on a knee and rested a hand on a rotted log where a mass of termites battled for the few grains of wood still holding it up. The sounds of men at war were everywhere, the vibrations underfoot, infernal and inescapable. She closed her eyes but the dark was less comforting even than the light. Seeing this was not a fit place for man nor horse, she rose, walked backward twenty yards through the brush, then turned and began to pick her way through.

It was a loathsome, scarred countryside. The land reeked of gunpowder, caustic and rich in the way it tore at her throat. The air turned to a fine grit in her mouth and she spat with every other breath. The menacing yells and shrieks of soldiers skirmishing came and went at frequent intervals, sometimes close and sometimes very close. She had to move cautiously and every tree and lump of earth became a refuge against the madness. She never saw any soldiers but those wearing butternut, and she never had a shot fired her way or chanced to see the fighting directly, but this didn't lessen her confusion as the day wore on.

And the day did advance. Slowly, inexorably, in muted moments of horror. A blood filled shoe, a swath of gray blouse, a soldier's cap shot through and through, a smoking ruin that had once been a home. The day seemed to landslide forward in a million little pieces, each no kin to the next, each owing all to the last. She thought of dawg, the thin-ribbed, gap-eared mutt she'd followed down to the roadside that morning, which now seemed a fortnight ago. She longed for the thrum of dawg's innards, the rough of his coat against her palm. She wondered where dawg had gotten himself off to.

She thought too of her pa and missed him all the more in her solitude. The Enoch Gamble she remembered—that memory was the better part of two years old, a considerable chunk of time when you were only fourteen—had been twice the stature of any other man. In her eyes, he was big and powerful and could have bested any on that field that day or any other. She wondered if it had been like this for him in battle—the world a mess of confusion, hope a distant flame smothered by despair. She was afraid, very afraid, and she wondered if her pa had been afraid too. That seemed an impossible thing, her pa afraid of anything. Her eyes misted at the thought of his big hands pulling her close. God how she missed him, longed to see his flaming red hair come over the rise, how she wished he was still alive…

But he wasn't and thoughts of him died as she spied a pile of a man lying supine in the brush a few paces ahead. He was just that, a pile, nothing but limbs bent clumsily one over the other. He lay beside a deadfall and was all twisted up and she was sure he was dead too but when she poked him with a stick he roused and unfurled long arms and legs and said in a lazy, guttural tone difficult to understand how he was thirsty and didn't she have no water.

She didn't. His hair wasn't flaming but was all caught with leaves and a worm had worked its way out from under the dead matter. It squirmed lengthwise on the side of his head and made him look more dead than he was until she brushed it away with the back of her hand. He looked confused and shied back from her touch. She wiped his face and he asked again if she didn't have any water. She told him no she didn't but she knew where there was a hole in the ground not too far off where she had stopped herself not long before. She told how it was under a felled tree and how the whole of it was green and moss covered so that most folks probably never even knowed it was there. She told how her father—his name was Enoch Gamble and these were his woods didn't he know—had taught her to keep an eye for such things. The wounded man stared her in the eye and rubbed his beard, maybe trying to decide if she was fooling or not.

He grinned and there was a bloody gap where one of his front teeth had been knocked out not long before.. He was missing his tunic and sat the ground beside the bushes with nothing more than a worn undershirt on his back. He had on butternut trousers with a gold stripe along the seam of the leg. A pair of suspenders looped his shoulders and tugged the trousers at the belt line. His boots were dusty and worn, the heels thinned out and the soles with several small holes. He looked to have done a long stretch of walking in those boots.

He turned his body toward her and she saw his right arm was busted bad, a piece of gristle or some such poking its way out from around his elbow, which was bent cockeyed and wrong. He took up his busted arm with the good one and set about getting his whole self up to a stand. He was clumsy about it, though, couldn't seem to get his legs under him properly. Every time he tried to raise up he only succeeded in scooting a bit more to his bad side, which in turn only seemed to excite him all the more. After a half dozen such attempts he laid out in the humus stomach up, his chest going double-quick and looking like a man possessed of a fever. He vomited in the weeds.

Loli stood an arm's length to his good side, watching but not helping. Each time he rose he seemed to get a little closer to standing, seemed to get his legs a little more under him. But only a little and in the end never enough. Each time he would fall back with a grunt and then sigh and bounce up again. What came to her mind was a juggler she'd seen once at a Spring festival. He'd been able to move four balls at once between his hands and until now she hadn't seen anything more mesmerizing than that. This wasn't so much a cripple trying to stand as he was mocking a crippled man trying to stand. She chewed her bottom lip and waited for him to tumble to the ground, which he did before too long. She didn't know if she should try to help him or not. What would pa do?

"Sonbitch," he said. "Ain't got it in me to get up, not no more. I'm played out, just played out is all."

"I saw me a crippled coon once. In the woods. In these here woods matter of fact."

"What?"

She told the story like her father would have told it. He had been fond of storytelling. This wasn't one of his stories, but that hardly mattered. "A crippled coon. His back legs was busted or something, I never did figure it out, not for sure. I was out with dawg, that's how we call him, just plain ole dawg, and dawg he starts yapping something fierce, like he got his tail bit or something. When I caught up with him, I could see how he was standing over this ole coon. Those coon eyes was big, big as I ever did see I do believe. He was watching dawg and dawg was watching him and making a racket that's for sure. I chased dawg off and sat with that coon a long spell. He was watching me I could tell. His eyes rolled with me when I moved. Kinda like yours. I guess maybe he was scared I was gonna do something, but I didn't. Not then or ever."

"I ain't no coon."

"Don't matter. You can die like one. That coon sure nuff died. Weren't quick though, weren't quick at all. I thought he'd die that first day, but he didn't. I fetched him some water in a bowl and he drank some. I tried giving him some grass too, but he wouldn't eat it. The second day he looked swolled some, but he took a bit more water. I poked him with a stick trying to get him a-going, but he mostly didn't care. Not so far's I could tell anyhow. When I came back that last day, just after sun up that was, he was still breathing. He looked different somehow though, no spunk if you know what I mean. His eyes weren't so big no more. They was dead eyes to tell the truth. Kinda spooky too. I knowed he was gonna die that day when I saw those eyes. I guess I knowed he was gonna die when I poked him with that stick and he just laid there looking stupid. Coon is a stupid animal. Pa told me that a long time ago."

"I told you I ain't no coon."

"It don't matter. I knowed you was gonna die first thing I saw you. No man what wants to live gonna lay down in a pile like that. Only a stupid coon do that."

He stared her down and slowed the rising of his chest and one could of a sudden see purpose in his movements that hadn't been there before. His face took on the look of one who wanted to hit something. His lips disappeared into a thin line of pink. He took up his broken arm with his good and sat upright, all the while making throaty little noises against his thin lips like he was taking a shit. He scooted butt first to a nearby tree and pressed his busted arm against it. His lips parted and thickened so you could see them again and he cried out as he let go the fractured arm and pushed off the ground with his good hand until he was sitting on one knee and resting the bad arm on his thigh. He was bawling now, blowing hard breaths and snotting out his nose like a sick toddler. He was drenched too, like a man that had been drug out of a river just shy of drowning. But he finally had one foot planted under him and the other foot took almost no effort in comparison and then he stood tall, his busted arm cradled by the good one. He stared at her, blinking the sweat and tears from his eyes.

Help this man.

She heard the words above the din of the surrounding gunfire and artillery shells, more plain than she had any right to hear them. She might have spun around looking for their source, except she knew better. Her pa was dead, and it was her pa who had spoken. She would know his voice anywhere.

"I guess you was right," Loli said. She wiped his brow with the sleeve of her dress. "Ain't no coon here."

"Where you say that water hole is?" His voice was gravelly and lacked substance. He turned to get a better look at her and she saw his face full frontal, saw immediately the neatly kept beard, saw it all the same way she had seen it the day before when this same man had appeared of a sudden and run off the heathens who'd stole their chickens and her Tillie. She'd seen him on the porch, seen him praying over Noah. She gasped at the recognition, perhaps not totally convinced by her eyes.

"I'm powerful thirsty," he said looking right at her, his eyes begging.

She looked again by way of convincing herself. It was the very man who had helped with Hannah, had taken care of Noah. The lieutenant. He had called himself lieutenant.

Help this man. Her father again, loud in her ear. This time she looked up to the sky above. "I will," she said, then found herself saying, "This way, it's this way."

She wrapped an arm around his waist. He was taller than her by a head or more and together they moved off into the woods.

***

Purdy found Hannah face down on the landing at the top of the stairs. The girl's mind was not her own. She had started in with *Hush A Bye Baby* again, except that the words were dirge-like and flat, the melody lost, and her voice a croaking whisper Purdy could only hear by putting her ear close. She sat her upright against the wall, trying hard to maintain her own sanity.

"You got to come round to reality, girl."

She moved matted strands of hair from before Hannah's eyes and ran her fingers like a comb through her hair. She shook her by the shoulders, but the girl was a wet rag.

Purdy got her to her feet and dragged her back through the door and into the bedroom. They fell together on the bed. The light across the younger woman's face revealed a blank, wide-eyed stare; she looked to have aged, as if someone had woven rings around her eyes, as if the days just passed had taken years instead of hours. Spittle hung between her lips in thin, bejeweled threads. Those lips moved slightly and it was clear she was saying something, though this time Purdy couldn't say what. She was maybe praying, maybe not. No, she was saying the lullaby again, a confused version with the words jumbled every which way. Purdy held her and massaged her, and cocked her own head every now and again to better catch the light off her daughter's face, which glistened of a sweaty sheen that made her look some gray and washed out.

Her appearance purely scared Purdy—she'd never seen a person so out of herself, not even Enoch at the worst of his fevered death. She wanted to cry and came near to it, her own face screwing up and dread weakening her. She watched Hannah and yawned out of a bone-weary fatigue and said not a word. Not a time for talking. Later maybe, but not now. She owned her own demons and knew this only too well.

She pulled a blanket over the girl and kissed Hannah's forehead. "Hush now." She went to the window, where she watched the wounded arrive in droves, wagon after piled wagon, others walking or being helped along.

"It's the devil own day, Enoch dear."

She pulled the curtain closed and dragged the preacher hat down over her eyes as she collapsed into the rocker. The sound of it creaking back and forth filled the room and was the only noise beyond their breathing, beyond the jumbled lullaby, and beyond the terrible sounds coming from without the walls.

Twenty-four months before, in the first summer of the war, Purdy Gamble had watched as the only man she ever loved walked the sloping half mile of dirt trail to Old Dutch Road and joined twenty-odd other men from Adams County.

She had stood the porch and had watched them go and had not cried because she had not wanted Enoch to remember her such. And standing on that porch with her had been Hannah and Loli and of course their blue-lipped, dribbling brother, who stood alongside them with his spastic leg and palsied arm. Purdy had hugged the boy to her side and thought *What God giveth, God taketh away.* She wiped Coal's mouth with her kerchief and blew Enoch a kiss and her bright, energetic eyes alternated between them. She said a silent prayer. In the distance, seen through a skein of road-turned dust and midsummer blossoms blown on the wind, a ramshackle, hard-muscled gaggle of men and man-boys marched out of step. Thus had they gone off, made soldiers of themselves, done all the great and terrible things soldiers do. They had killed. They had been killed.

She'd known Enoch Gamble all her life, had been a Gamble herself twenty-odd years come the winter of his taking, and the rhythms of their lives beat upon the same drum. Little more than a year into their marriage, Purdy had gone into early labor with their first born and Enoch two miles distant working the fields. The baby was a footling breech—feet first and all tied up inside her—and she'd pushed the better part of half a day, to the point of exhaustion, before pulling the dead child out with her own two hands. She'd torn herself though, bad enough she would no doubt have died had not Enoch showed home hours before he was due. He'd returned unaccountably early, he said later, because he'd felt called. That's how it was between them. They had a calling, each for the other.

Saturday, December thirteenth, eighteen-sixty-two. A biting, too cold day with the feel of snow about it. In the front room, one of four on the first floor, tiny bits of ash danced in the air and that air smelled of burnt poplar as a fire tweaked and creaked and twisted on itself in the corner firebox. The boy named Coal sat the old stone hearth looking into that fire as Purdy watched him from across the room. He palmed a small rock over and over in his good hand, his other arm worse than useless the way it occupied his shirt sleeve without earning its way. Palming the stone, he from time to time leaned toward the fire, maybe seeing something in it that others couldn't.

Coal had ever been fascinated by fire, would sit for hours and watch how the flames curled this way and that. He liked to stir the ashes and watch the sparks rise. Once or twice he'd tried this with his bare hand. He was a slow learner, sometimes no learner at all. Sometimes he would poke at the fire with a branch. Once he had brought the burning branch to Purdy in the kitchen, where she'd had to douse it in the stew she was cooking lest it burn the house down. She dared not take her eyes off him.

Impossible to get straight wood from crooked timber was how Enoch had liked to put it.

In the better days before the war Purdy had sometimes still caught Enoch weeping in the night. Weeping as he had in the hours and weeks after the incident with the mule. Weeping, she supposed, over the son he'd lost, over the past that was and the future that would never be. One night she'd reached out and felt the bed cold beside her and searched to find him in the barn, considering on putting a piece of lead through the head of that mule.

"Won't do no good," she'd said. "And we'd be out both a boy and a mule."

Enoch had put the gun away, and had come back to bed with her. They'd made love in the wee hours that followed, an impossible urgency gripping them until they had spent themselves in a frenzied passion of sweat and tears. They had lain entwined for a long time after that, taking solace each in the heat of the other. She had laid her head upon Enoch's chest and the thrum of his heart beating within had seemed so mighty as to be unstoppable.

Purdy rose and crossed the room and went to the boy. His fingertips were blue and cold-looking, but he felt warm enough when she put her hands on his shoulders. He squirmed and she felt the warmth rising off the fire and rubbed his neck and he squirmed some more. She held him a moment and whispered a few words his way and wiped the spittle at his mouth and he went back to pill-rolling the polished stone and staring into the flames. Only now there was a piece of a smile on his face. Just a piece though. Any person could look at him and see something was queer.

It was the only way he ever smiled.

That too cold December day moved along slower than most and she spent part of it fretting over the girls. She worried over them the way a parent will when the doings are new and uncertain. But the doings were not new and uncertain, they'd occupied those parts off Old Dutch Road a score of years. It and the nearby woods were as familiar as their thin-ribbed family dog. And the girls, nineteen and fourteen, needed no real looking after. Indeed, the oldest, Hannah, was a young woman, married herself not a year, and her belly already six months in a family way. They all looked forward to the coming baby.

As always, Purdy had cooked up supper on the old wood burner in the kitchen. Boiled ham and potatoes, because boiled ham and potatoes was what they ate every Saturday come suppertime. There'd been bread too, but she'd burned it in her mania and the entire house had smelt of it.

Time had seemed to string out that day, to go on forever like the lazy fall afternoons of her childhood—the ones where she and Enoch had played seek in the tall, rustling hallways of the corn mazes and lost themselves for hours. Such a carefree time was long past though, and the dreary December day paid itself out despite her thoughts to the contrary. Not much after supper she put a pot on the stove to boil water for baths, another Saturday night ritual. A short time later, while combing Loli's bright red hair—all the Gambles had flaming hair—Purdy's mania hit her full force and finally conjured the image that nearly undid her. With the air redolent of burnt bread, her chest tightened of a sudden and the comb caught in a tuft of Loli's hair. Purdy's hand squeezed around the comb, blanching white against the teeth.

"Lordy," she said in a low moan as if the word was diseased.

"Ma?" The comb pulled at Loli's hair and the girl winced, desperate to put a hand over her mother's before her hair came out at the roots. "It's just a tangle, ma."

Purdy's breath caught somewhere between crying and gasping. She took on the look of the stricken, like she'd tumbled down a well and could only hope to ever see blue sky again. Like that damn mule had hoofed her the way it had hoofed Coal.

"Hannah, come quick. Something's wrong. It's ma. Her color or something ain't good." Loli's voice had the timbre of urgency.

Purdy's eyes rolled as if too loose in their sockets and she was on a go-round spinning very, very fast. "Where's he?" she said, and then something that sounded slurred and sloppy and unknowable to the girls.

"Coal's in the corner, ma. You know, by the wood burner. Like always," Loli said. "Like always. You good?"

She took a moment, seemed to be thinking on the words. Her chest felt pressed. Purdy turned her head and there was Coal rocking back and forth beside the stove, back and forth, one arm folded useless as always and his leg stiff like it had never been meant to bend in the first place. The pot of water—*Saturday night, bath night*—steamed above him, hot but not yet boiling, the pot only threatening to whistle. The pressure in her chest became an ache, then a tightness. She said, "No, no," her mouth a big 'O' and her tongue filling it clumsily. She didn't seem able to make herself understood.

"Pa pa," Coal said, his torso moving to and fro in lazy ignorance, the sounds no more than two enthused grunts strung back to back to resemble a word, sounding all the stranger because he so rarely uttered anything at all. He was simple-minded (dumb was the word Purdy usually used, as in deaf and dumb, though he certainly wasn't deaf) and knew maybe a couple or three dozen words. The best that could be said of him most days was that he was oblivious, sweet but oblivious.

"Pa pa," he said again, and for a moment she was of a mind he actually knew what he was saying, and then the pot on the stove began to whistle in little interrupted tweaks and the moment was lost.

He rocked back and forth and said, "Pa pa, pa pa, pa pa." The grunts, for they had lost the sense of any meaning now, came two by two, hard on the ears.

"Ma?" Hannah said, sounding impossibly far away. "Ma?"

Hannah turned to Loli. "ain't never seen a person so pale. Fetch over some water..."

I'm having a fit, that's what. Enoch honey, I'm dying sure. Right in this here old kitchen, right by this old wood burner where Coal near died hisself... And in her mind's eye she saw Coal twitching uncontrollably in the dirt where that floor now lay. She saw the mashed potatoes he'd been eating smeared across his chest by his flailing arm as it seized back and forth—back and forth—and those lips, those too blue lips...

The pot on the stove whistled louder now, no longer interrupted in its shrill warning. The tightness in her chest eased, but it was like the end of a bad dream, that terrible moment just before waking when everything is real and everything—everyone—is doomed. She couldn't catch her breath and feared the tightness ending, feared it in the worst way imaginable, thought: *when it ends, I'll end too.*

She fingered a nail head coming out of the floor and felt herself falling through the air, but it was just the girls coaxing her into a chair. Coal still chanted something blasphemous, the pot whistled menacingly, and the world and the people in the world rushed by her. She thrashed her legs until she found the hand-hewn firmness of the floorboards under her feet. She looked at Coal rocking against the stove, the pot boiling above his head. She saw something more too, something in the boy's face that hadn't been there even a moment before. Something so impossibly real it couldn't have been there a moment before, couldn't be there now.

Except it was.

Of a sudden Coal's head came up and he stared at her through his father's eyes, her husband's eyes—Enoch's eyes. And they didn't just look like Enoch's eyes, they *were* Enoch's eyes. And the look in those eyes, as if they held an entire war's worth of pain.

She slumped as if suddenly boneless. She was suddenly confident of only one fact in all the land: those eyes belonged not to her son but to her husband—and they saw nothing at all.

"Those is dead eyes," she said, the words pitiful, low-spirited, and dirgelike. "Dead eyes sure."

At that very instant somebody screamed. It might have been one of her girls. She doubted it was Coal, but a person in her state couldn't swear it wasn't. It might even have been her. It mattered little.

She had no memory of things after that. Then or later someone had gone after the doctor. When she awoke, it was to a room shadowed in the dim light of an oil lamp. The odor of the place, at once familiar and ambrosial, anchored her. She was in her own bed, had sobbed in her sleep. In the feathers of the tear-stained pillow she could smell Enoch, the scent still not faded despite his long absence. She liked that she could smell him.

She wanted to smell him always.

Three days later, this would have been the sixteenth of December eighteen-sixty-two, another hellishly cold day, the telegram had arrived. A thin note, the paper yellow by design or age she knew not which, creased and folded unevenly across the middle. She played the note between pointer and thumb, as if she could thus feel the shape of the words within. In her whole life she had never wanted anything so much as to open that note. She was a long time opening it though, and when she did she stared at the scrawl another long time, trying hard to discern the meaning of the ink laid there. As if she could teach herself reading by staring.

There wasn't but a person in ten in the country round who could make out words on a page. The girls had learnt some book reading but this kind of scrawl was difficult for them and poorly writ besides. Hannah could make out some of it, like the words Enoch and Gamble and a few others, but she couldn't get the gist. Loli couldn't make out even that much. Who came to mind then was the minister, the girthy Jeremiah Penn. Horses regularly swaybacked beneath him.

As circumstances would have it, Purdy was a day getting to the minister and it was the longest day of her life to that moment. She found him in the church on Main Street, in his office, not at his desk but sawing a piece of wood. Most of the floor was covered with a thin veil of sawdust.

"Pardon the mess, just doing a little work on the ceiling." Minister Penn gestured upward with one finger, it could have been toward God, and sure enough the ceiling was partly bare to the rafters above. "Water leak. Truth is, I'm sort of caretaker, gardener, minister. Whatever the need, I do my best."

He slipped his glasses off and came around the desk and took her hand and offered her a chair. He didn't sit himself. Penn had whiskers across the meat of his large jaw, which hid only partially his abundant jowls. A person couldn't tell if he was smiling or frowning. He asked how she was, calling her by name and waiting for her to answer. She lied and said she was tolerable and took the chair and gave over the note at once for his reading.

He took the yellowed paper and leaned butt first against his desk, sliding an inkwell out of the way with his off hand. On the desk a burnt nubbin of candle from the night before, a bit of caked wax pooled around it. Beside this a pen, a much worn Bible, a sheaf of loose papers, and the pair of wire-rimmed spectacles, which he took from off the table with a deliberate manner. Glasses in hand, he gave the note a once over at arm's length, then nodded to her before donning his specs.

She thought the note looked small in his big hands and that he took longer reading it than it could have required. She didn't know how long it should have taken, just that it seemed generally too long. Maybe he couldn't read it, maybe it was too poorly writ even for him and she'd have to go round to the telegraph office and ask on a new copy. Then she thought maybe he was deciding the best way to tell her. At the thought of this last the sounds of the street outside faded, as if the street and all on it had suddenly moved a great distance away. She stopped breathing.

Your Enoch is dead. These words had floated in her head like spit in a bucket for an entire day. She couldn't read, but that didn't seem to matter. The imagined words, big and red and ugly the way a cow's udder is ugly when the milking's been neglected, vibrated between her ears. It was suddenly all she could hear.

Penn said, "It looks like your Enoch got himself wounded."

"What? What did you say?" *I didn't hear you right.*

Minister Penn looked past his glasses to her face and turned up one side of his mouth, a gesture perhaps meant to soften his look. "He's in hospital, a place called Falmouth. It's across the Rappahannock from Fredericksburg."

"Not dead?"

"Not according to this."

She closed her eyes and watched the bucket spill over, watched the spit wash away. She inhaled deeply, remembering what Enoch had looked like the last time she'd seen him and savoring this new information as if some sweet fragrance that had just blown her way. Cherry blossoms on a just warm enough spring day maybe, or the sweet smell of magnolias.

She rose from the chair, now anxious and wanting answers. "Where? Where did you say?"

"Falmouth."

She had never heard of such a place and the word seemed to come off Minister Penn's lips limp, like a day-old dead fish, sounding disagreeable and smelly, if such a thing was possible in a place name.

"Falmouth," she repeated, and it sounded no better in her own voice. She breathed again, having not realized she had ever stopped.

"Come, let us pray for his recovery," Minister Penn had said then, and he took up the much worn Bible and they bowed together, each to one knee in the sawdust. Penn took her hands and placed them under his, close unto the Book where she might feel some comfort, and they prayed together on the floor of his small office.

She came near to weeping with his words.

Part II:

A Perfect Hell

SEVEN

The girl and the lieutenant clinging to her moved through the tree'd countryside with a faltering, laborious drag. It was all he could do to lift one leg after the other and he had long since ceased to do it effectively. Loli dragged him more than not, and his weight, not quite dead weight, was all the heavier in the stifling heat. The sudorific air did nothing to lessen the fever in his chest and each breath piled hard upon the last, as if he might drown. His arm had early on ached to the point where it seemed he must by one instrument or another—be it the surgeon's hand or the priest's robes—be delivered from the excruciation. For some hours however he had felt nothing at all from it and it hung insignificant and less useful than a piece of dead wood at his side.

They had by the grace of God come this far without getting caught. Now Taylor stooped beside a large tree, the world around him wavering this way and that like it was storm tossed. His throat burned from the bile which kept creeping up just high enough to taste and he was bent over now trying to vomit. Trying but failing in the effort. He put a finger in his mouth and pushed it to the back. He was like a man choking on a chicken bone, a few gags and his eyes watering.

Footfalls close by. Rebel or Yankee? He took the girl's arm.

The world, or rather their part of it, crawled first with soldiers of the one side and then the other. There seemed little rhyme or reason to their actions, except that all were of like mind and that mind was to kill anything that moved. The girl stood at his side, doing her best to support him against the tree. He might go to ground at any moment, and if he did he wouldn't get up.

A pair of soldiers passed just beside them, nothing more than a couple of thick bushes separating them. They had about them a look of devilment, eyes shot with blood and faces tarred with dirt. Their chests were heaving and their words came in short, quick bursts laced with profanities. They'd been running all out, but now one stopped beside the bushes and drew out his member. His friend moved on, but he unbuttoned his fly, all the while his attention behind him, as if he might be overrun at any moment and wanted to see his attackers. He let his water go—"ah gawd that feels good"—and the yellow piss spread across the ground at the feet of the lieutenant. The solider was off running again even before he'd put himself back. If he'd looked where he'd pissed, he'd have found them.

In an upstairs bedroom of what was, or had been, her home, Purdy rocked slowly back and forth in her chair. She closed her eyes amid the numbing sounds of Hannah's grief. She dreamt, as she always did these days, of Enoch.

He comes out of his grave and walks the rooms of his house. And it is his, every last board of it. He's crafted it, shaped it, built it, and lived it the better part of twenty years. His mark is upon every inch. In this dream, the small, black hole under his eye looks not but what it is, a sign. A mark to distinguish him from other men.

Nobody speaks and the house of the dream is oddly quiet. Here the rebels are the ghosts, the ones who don't belong. Vaporous and transparent, their presence mostly an afterthought to the mind. The marked man moves from room to room dispersing their unearthly essence by the wave of a hand. The visitors break apart like smoke in the wind. But when he reaches the kitchen, this room is not his own. The floorboards run with crimson, as if bleeding. And upon the table, there lies the vague form of a man under a winding-sheet, bathed in an unnatural light.

Enoch moves closer, out of the shadows. Closer still—in Purdy's dream sleep this seems to take forever and is agonizing in its particulars—*and the marked man reaches out and draws off the shroud. On the instant, the world spins about and the face beneath is that of the marked man himself, Enoch Gamble. Standing beside him, winding-sheet in hand, is the rebel surgeon Brody.*

Purdy startled and drew in a long, troubled breath, as if lately smothered. Her eyes popped open, of a sudden vigilant and wide. She rode the rocker like a woman possessed, the floorboards creaking beneath her as the chair worried back and forth, the dream enveloping her the way hot wind moves through a room when a furnace door is opened and the fire inside is stoked on high. At first she couldn't breathe—*I really am being smothered*—and groped in the air before her as if fending off an attacker. Only slowly did she come back to her right mind, to the knowledge it was only a dream.

She grabbed the preacher hat and rose. She steadied herself along the wall. She opened her mouth to speak, but no words came. Someone cried out and she jerked as if the cry was a piece of sinew tugging at her.

Another shriek, this one more of a wail, and she ran out to the hall, then over to the top of the stairs. "I'm coming! I"m coming!"

She ignored the several men laid out on the landing, jumping over them and descending the stairs two at a time. Her mind raced ahead, cataloguing the possibilities. A beating? A knifing? A killing? A cry like that, it might—had to—be the worst. She had no hesitation at the base of the stairs, despite how the room was not something she recognized any longer. Like a deadfall she'd come across in her wanderings. *Oh God.* She followed her heartstrings through the kitchen—the floorboards ran with blood but this too she ignored—and out into the yard beyond the back door.

Dusk had come and fires ringed the yard. In the faint, licking light of one of these, two rebels held Coal fast, while a third punched him square in the face, saying something akin to "y'all shut your mouth now boy," in a languid, Southern drawl.

Coal spat blood at the soldier, kicking at the ground with his good leg, like it had betrayed him. One side of his face was a swollen mess. He struggled, arms locked behind his back. His cry faltered to a whimper and when the next blow came, a smack, the sharp sound flesh on flesh makes when it comes together angry and ugly and hard. Purdy's son went mostly limp, his spastic leg quivering and dancing as the soldiers behind him let go and he fell.

"Stop it, you damn Secesh heathens. Stop it!" She rushed forward.

"Lady, ain't our fault. The boy's loony," the one who had struck Coal said. "Crazy as a jumpin frog."

"He ain't right in the head if that's what you mean." She bent to her crumpled son. "Why you wanna do this? He's just a boy. You ain't hardly no older." She framed his busted mouth with her hands, rubbed at his swollen cheek. "Why you wanna do this to him?"

"Hell if I know what got into him. I was minding my own, answering the call of nature I was." He gestured to the others as if looking for their support. They murmured how what he was saying was right, the plain truth. "That sonbitch cripple attacked me. Ever'body here see'd it. He's some crazy. Like a hound dog mad for coon he is." He was buttoning his fly even as he spoke. A dark seam of wetness ran along the inner thigh of his trouser leg.

"Call of nature?" She turned her head and the truth of it hit her. A wet patch of earth under the willow, on the bare dirt of Enoch's grave, where grass had yet to grow in the four months since his death.

Her hands fisted hard and she flew at the boy with deliberate speed, as if she'd practiced this moment, had seen it coming all her life and practiced the clumsiness out of it. She pummeled the man with blows to his face and they went down to the ground as one with her on top. She knuckled his nose and it broke to one side with a snap and bled fast and furious and she didn't care. She'd have hit him again except somebody grabbed her arm and twisted it back and she owned her own pain at that moment. She fell in the dirt and wrestled two men wanting to keep her there. All this in less time than it takes to tell it.

She drew breath and struggled loose and regained her footing, stood at the center of the rebels. "Heathens!" she screamed, and spun a circle, eyeing each in such a way as to mark him, as to leave no doubt she'd seen him. A dribble of blood crossed one cheek where she'd been scratched and she rubbed at her twisted arm. She sniffled and a trickle of blood ran from her nose and she wiped it with her hand, not bothering to look. "So help me God, I'll cut the jewels from the next man what even looks at my Enoch's grave."

Hannah stood at the base of the stairs in a full-length night shirt, looking off into what had once been the front room, the room with the oversized fireplace in the corner. The place seemed to have gone queer, with all manner of strange men about. Soldiers, to look at them. The dead and those who would join them. The room pulsed with a restless and irregular fervor and was filled to bursting with these people, several of whom reached out to her with blood-sodden hands and fingers all trembly. She pulled away and shook her head back and forth like an old spinster who'd wandered into a den of iniquity. She uttered words unintelligible and piddling.

What followed was a bustle of activity. In her insensible grief, Hannah saw it all as if through some curiously warped looking glass. The effect was to shift the real to the surreal, to diffuse the view with shades of misty gray and bleached red. A soldier's mangled hand became a sublime artifact of bone laid bare. She opened a door and looked upon a pain-twisted face and saw the dirt ingrained upon it. Grotesque, every grain a graven image unto itself, each pore showing like the irregular dimples in the hammered patina of a copper mask her father had kept. This same soldier raised his upper lip and the mask twisted into a sneer heavy with hatred. Beside him sat an even more pathetic creature. He had bandaged stumps where both his hands should have been and his tongue lay dry and scaly in the depths of a mouth open wide to the room. When he moved, which was not often, it was pitiful to see—like watching a three-legged mule pull a cart. Fascinating and repulsive in the same instance. Her mind twisted at the sight.

She forced herself to look elsewhere, to the shadowed corners of the rooms. These were thick with the vermin of war and were, she realized quickly, nothing more than places to be avoided. A candle flame flickered slower than it had any right to and by its awful light she saw the clotted remnants of dead gut loosed on the floorboards, and beside these the ugly, bloody drippings of the too numerous to count wounded. Everywhere she stepped was tainted with all manner of such incidentals and her footing was clumsy and unsure. Her hands fisted at her sides as a sour nausea rose high in her throat and she tasted her breath, which was vinegary and fermented. Not unlike curdled milk. Spoiled.

She swallowed hard the awful taste, the urge to upchuck, and watched a young man in a plain gray uniform pour from a small bottle into the mouth of one of the wretched men. She stared after the worker, observing as he went from man to man offering a taste of whatever it was the bottle contained. They strained their necks and gulped and gasped and fell back with their tongues on their lips, gumming the aftertaste. They seemed to imbibe the nostrum with a gusto they otherwise lacked and it was plain to see the bottle contained the best medicine available.

The young man came within earshot and she hollered, "What's that there you got? What're you giving these men?"

He held up a silver flask. "Whiskey. It dulls the senses."

She understood immediately. Her husband Levi was himself a soldier in Lincoln's Army of the Potomac. Over the many months he had been gone—nearly a year and only a single furlough home—he had written often. He'd had much to tell, though she suspected he'd spared her the worst. One detail he had shared was that of the reviving effect a shot of whiskey could have in most any situation. He had personal knowledge of this, having imbibed it once or twice himself, for medicinal purposes he claimed. He tried to describe the taste: sharp, exceedingly bitter, the slightest bit burning, unexpectedly dry. All of this and utterly soothing besides. A taste that could cure a man of what ails if only he could get enough.

She became possessed of an idea, an engine driving her back through the rooms of the house and up the stairs, ignoring the men and the slop as she went. She'd seen her father drink of a similar flask, in the dark of night after he'd thought everyone else in bed. More importantly, she'd seen him stash it under a loose board in the second floor hall. She found the spot and pulled a winded soldier to the side by way of gaining it. He tumbled over face first, begging not to be moved. She pulled at the board, suddenly afraid it was the wrong one, then there it was hard gripped in her hand. Beneath it lay the flask as she remembered. She gathered it up, feeling how it was nearly full by the weight of it. She loosened the cap and swizzled a quick drink, which ran fire-like down her throat. She coughed and sputtered, then looked about none the worse for it and was maybe even a little better.

She thrust the flask under her nightshirt, descended the stairs two at a time, and was out the front door and into the dark in another instant.

EIGHT

Coal sat beneath the willow, rocking back and forth and chewing on his busted lower lip. He spat blood from time to time. Purdy sat beside him, framing his face in her hands whenever he would allow it, looking at his teeth. One eye was blackened and would probably swell shut, the other wasn't much better. "What they done to you..." she said, her words trailing.

The willow tree shook in the wind. She'd always liked the way it moved, always felt the tree's vibrations to her very core, and she tried to take solace from them now, tried to ignore the intruders all around her. When Coal regained his wind, when it was clear he would be ok, she rose and pulled him with her. The boy made his way across the ground like it was rock strewn and uneven. She pulled him along by his spastic arm. It was all he would allow, or maybe all he could muster.

They came to the steps at the back door and she would have reached for the knob, except it wasn't there. The door was one of many things that no longer existed. She stood transfixed, looking in. The place was lit with several coal oil lanterns and the light washing the walls was a warm orange-yellow. It gave on the people and they flickered as if insubstantial in the world it illuminated. Coal sat down in the dirt and she stood dumfounded, not quite recognizing the room as her kitchen.

The wall separating the front room and her kitchen had been torn away. That front room was steeped with the mangled and mutilated. And they might as well have tumbled from the heavens so randomly were they tossed—without order or plan of any sort. A person couldn't tell where one ended and another began. The odd and predominant illusion was of too many parts: some men had three legs, others an extra arm or just a hand. Awful, simply awful.

She averted her gaze from the front room and her view opened on the kitchen itself. By local standards, the room had been expansive: wood stove at one end, dining table at the other, the pantry door to one side in the middle. It was expansive no more, even impossibly close, as if the rebels had somehow shrunk the place. The surgeon, he'd given his name as Brody she recalled, stood at the center of the action, facing her. A second man stood to his far side and a third across the table from him with his back to her.

Brody was a taller man than she had at first allowed. His square chin and thin jowls made him look melancholy. He didn't seem melancholy, however, not the way he was working: fast, even furiously, and with deliberate purpose. The brace on his leg didn't slow him down one iota. He had rolled his sleeves up above his elbows and his shirt was open at the collar, but only barely so. Sweat stained his armpits and those of his assistants, and blood speckled his forearms and front, where an apron had captured most of the vital crimson blots, dots, dashes, and smears.

A torch, she hadn't noticed it before and maybe that's why the room seemed so brilliantly lit, washed the table with a hard light that softened at the edges and blended into shadow. The table was the best lit thing in the room; a near constant stream of blood came over its edge and pieces of bone and muscle and gristle and God-knew-what littered the floor beneath. Brody ignored all of this, his naked fingers buried to his knuckles in a man's neck. That worthy, who by a few fragments of shell or grape had been reduced instantly from soldier to patient, was somehow not quite unconscious and squirmed vaguely and with a little utterance now and again under the surgeon's hands. Those hands were mostly a blur, the fingers dancing rapidly through their practiced strokes, tying stitch after stitch as his assistants struggled to hold instruments of one sort or another against the walls of the wound by way of allowing the surgeon to see what he was doing.

Brody pulled his hands free and a weighty stream of blood shot up and struck him in the chest. His fingers went instantly to the source and the geyser stopped. "Clamp."

At once the device appeared in his upturned palm. He replaced his fingers and without looking up said "ligature." The tie was passed to him as well and his hands went to work again. Smooth, furious, no energy wasted. He pulled his hands out again and this time they came away with no drama.

Purdy watched all of this, perhaps not wanting to see, perhaps not quite believing, but both seeing and believing nonetheless.

Brody stepped back from the table and leaned against the wall, taking most of his weight off the leg with the brace. Covered as he was in entrails, he looked like someone had operated on him. As his assistants closed the neck wound, he lit a cigarette.

"You'll have to leave," a skinny soldier said from behind her.

"This here's my kitchen," Purdy said.

"It don't matter," the skinny soldier said.

"Well, it matters to me."

He looked as if about to say something but his eyes deferred and Purdy heard the surgeon's brace click behind her.

"What is this?" Brody asked.

Purdy faced him and he took a long pull on the cigarette.

"I was just telling her she has to leave," the skinny man said.

"Is that true, major? You gonna make me leave my own house?"

He took another long pull on the cigarette. She couldn't tell if he was looking at her or not. His eyes were directed at her, but they didn't seem to be connecting to anything.

"You will forgive me, madam, but tobacco is one of the few pleasures I have left. My time is mostly spoken for these days."

She said nothing to this, but thought instead how much Enoch had enjoyed smoking. The hand rolled cigar she had obtained for him in Washington had been one of his last pleasures in this world.

"It is a busy place," Brody said finally. "More wounded coming in every moment." As if proof of this, his assistants removed the body from the table behind him and replaced it with another. "I would be obliged if you would keep out of the way. We do not mean you and yours any harm, but we have serious work to do. We are fixing good men here."

He had that very deliberate tone of voice again. It might have sounded arrogant from most, but it seemed his natural way and she found she could abide it. She thought she would be angry with him, in fact she wanted to be angry with him, but she couldn't bring up any emotion.

"I see what you're doing. I can't hardly stand that it's happening here, but it is what it is I suppose."

"I am obliged for your understanding."

"Don't be fooled, sir. This ain't no understanding. I'm mad as hell. First chance I get, I'll have the lot of you gone."

"Yes, well, and we will be happy to depart, I am sure. Now, if you please, I must get back to work." He smoked the last of his cigarette and pressed the butt out under his shoe on the floor. Her floor.

Enoch's floor.

Purdy looked down, saw anew how the floorboards had worn uneven over the years. A weathered, bronze patina now sodden in blood. She wanted to go down on a knee, to run her hands over the polished boards. She wanted to feel the square nails Enoch had driven through those boards.

It gave her strength to know he had both made and pounded those nails himself. A long time ago that'd been but she could still hear the hammer driving the piece of iron home, still feel the floor vibrating with each pounding swing. Such a strong, handsome man...

Another image now. Coal twitching uncontrollably on the floor. No, in the dirt where that floor now lay. She saw the mashed potatoes he'd been eating smeared across his chest by his flailing arm as it seized back and forth—back and forth—and those lips, those too blue lips...

She wavered, would have fallen but for Brody steadying her with his hand on her shoulder. "Don't do that," Purdy said, and pulled away.

"I am sorry. I thought…are you all right, missus?"

"Okay? Okay? Fine. I'm fine." She wanted to tell him how hard her husband had worked at putting in that floor. How he'd planed every board himself and how when he was done his back had ached for a week and his hands had bled from the blisters. He hadn't been able to hold so much as a fork for two days. But she said none of this.

"Don't do that," she said and picked the crushed butt up from where it lay on the bloody floor. She tossed it out into the yard. "I'd be obliged if you'd not sully my home like that."

Purdy wanted to scream, could have screamed till the very life ebbed out of her. And it wouldn't have been any ordinary scream either, rather something just this side of hell. Her wail would have broken ears and brought folks to their knees. Instead, she pursed her lips and counted her breaths and the pause between them was long and awkward.

"Is there anything else?" Brody asked.

"My daughter Loli. She's fourteen. Seems to have wandered off. Ain't seen her since early this morning."

"I fear I know nothing of your daughter."

"One of your men maybe?"

"I doubt that. Doubt it very much." He was looking her in the eyes now and she thought he wanted to end it there, but added, "I will talk with my people. I can do no more than that, woman."

"All right then."

He returned to his table and she stepped around one of his assistants and crossed the room and squeezed past him. Brody looked up, but it was more to work his neck than attend to her. He popped his spine with a grimace.

She opened a drawer and withdrew both a small tin box and the tintype beside it. When she looked up, the major had taken a saw in hand. His assistant gripped hard at the arm of a man on the table between them. The arm was bent wrong. The contraption on Brody's leg clicked again as he shifted his weight, and she crossed to the back door, or rather where it had once been. There was not but a doorway there now and it looked out of place. As if out of square. A whole world existed out beyond that doorway but no doubt it too was out of square. It occurred to her that nothing inside that kitchen was any better and besides, she had seen enough. She hurried through and out into the yard, leaving the kitchen and all it contained behind her.

Purdy pushed two fingers under the wide brim of Enoch's preacher hat and rubbed her forehead. She didn't smoke, not much anyways, but watching Brody had made her think on how Enoch used to sit the porch and smoke in the evenings. He hand-rolled his own cigarettes and smoked two or maybe three a given night. Sometimes she would take a drag off his smoke, but mostly she just sat the porch beside him, inhaling the tobacco as it came off him and looking out over their piece of God's green earth. God's country Enoch had called it. Sometimes she would lay back and look at him, at how he looked handsome in his preacher hat even after twenty years of seeing him so. She thought maybe he never looked better than on those evenings, with a cloud of smoke around him and that preacher hat on his head and those big hands that had done so much work over the years resting in his lap. Over the years that smoke and his smell had permeated the leather of his hat, which meant if she closed her eyes and took a deep breath while wearing it or maybe held it up to her nose at just the right distance, she could still smell the tobacco, which meant she could still smell Enoch. Which meant...

The dim light of a quarter moon cut the night sky. Several campfires burned and the air smelled of cedar or oak or some such wood. A half dozen tents stood the ground. Small affairs, odd triangular shadows. They interrupted the land, even pockmarked as it was with the silhouettes of post-ops convalescing in the open.

God's country? More the look of death's waiting room, Purdy thought, shaking her head.

At first Coal stayed hard by Purdy's side, but before long he pulled away and she had to keep at him. The flames of the fires reflected in his dark eyes. She knew what he was thinking, writ as it was all over him. He'd always had a thing for fire.

"We got to move, boy."

But he was transfixed, drawn to the largest of the fires. Four or five men had gathered around it. They alternately stood or sat, using the fire only as an afterthought. It wasn't a cool night and its light was more useful than its heat, except that one of the group was turning a rabbit or chicken on a spit. Probably one of her own chickens. Her stomach grumbled. She hadn't eaten in hours.

"What you want, boy?" The soldier spoke through clenched lips and his hand rubbed the stubble on his chin, which was peach-like and young looking. He couldn't have been much older than Coal himself.

No answer.

"Ain't you never seen chickens roasting?"

"He's hungry," Purdy said.

"Yeah, well this here's my bird. You want some vittles go find yer own."

Coal reached toward the chicken. The soldier moved to strike his hand away, but Coal reached past the chicken and stirred a log on the edge of the fire. Little sparks flew skyward and he pulled his hand back quick and licked his fingers.

"What the Jesus?"

"He don't mean no harm," Purdy said.

"Yeah? What's wrong with him?"

"He's just a boy what got kicked by a mule."

"He gives me the creeps."

"Well maybe you should leave then," she said.

The young soldier chuckled. "That's rich, lady. There's a hundred and more men here, and you and this here boy gonna go 'round telling us we should leave. Like we got any say in the matter. Like you got any say either." He stopped smiling and his expression turned serious, even droll. "I don't wanna be in this shithole any more than you want me here."

Purdy grabbed Coal by the elbow.

"But long as I gotta be here, I sure as hell can choose who I eat with. And I don't hanker to eat with no yankees."

Purdy rolled her eyes. She could stand her ground, it was literally her ground of course, but this wasn't a fight she needed, wasn't a point she wanted to argue. She tugged on Coal and the two of them moved away from the little circle of light.

She held onto him and found the mound of earth over Enoch. It was neither more or less substantial than it had been that morning, or the day before, or a month. She had resisted a headstone because to place such a thing could only be a daily reminder and she had all the reminders she wanted. She pushed a few men out of the way; this was a fight she would take on, though they protested only weakly.

Purdy and Coal sat the grave mound, the branches of the large willow swaying overhead again. Coal's stomach made odd noises and the boy slapped at the stinging insects, which seemed everywhere around them. A body could see the blowflies were well fed.

Coal worked a walnut-sized rock out of the ground and began pumping his good fist open and closed around it. Purdy opened the tin and withdrew a bit of tobacco and put it to her nose and sniffed. It brought Enoch closer. She fumbled for a paper and licked the edges and watched a fly get caught as she rolled those edges together with the tobacco inside. She lit a loco foco and it was the only time Coal looked at her. She lit the cigarette and drew the smoke into her lungs in several quick drags, as if it might escape otherwise.

Coal reached over and squeezed the match-head between his fingertips, apparently ignoring the pain as the flame died. She shook her head and leaned back, exhausted. The sun was long down and she settled into the blackness. She sat a few feet over her dead husband, smoking his tobacco and looking at her dull son, wondering what the boy might be thinking. She could see only half his face in the dim flicker of the nearest campfire. The ground still held the day's warmth and the air, which all spring had been light and breezy, was sulfurous and smothering, the opposite of breathable. Indoors, a man she detested had turned her home—Enoch's home—into a festering pesthouse of blood and butchery. Even now, the screams of the maimed and soon to be maimed filled the blackness and it was a noose around all their necks ever tightening.

The flying bugs crossed her line of vision now and again, but mostly they buzzed her ears and it was a nuisance to keep after them and so after awhile she stopped bothering. She closed her eyes and waited for the night to pass and for a new day to bring what it would.

Coal pumped his fist around the rock and the fires flickered in the whites of his eyes until they died sometime in the deep night for lack of stirring.

Only then did Coal sleep.

A fly walked over the lieutenant's lips and into his open mouth and out again. He seemed to pay it no mind and Loli saw in his eyes he was used up, a thing to be thrown sideways with the trash. A body possessing such a dog would put him out with the heel end of a booted foot, not seeing the use in wasting table scraps on such a niggardly critter. But she'd seen Taylor before he was all of this, when he was more than the sum of his now fetid parts, and she couldn't abide the idea of putting him out. He'd befriended her mother after all, chased off the gang of thieving rebels, and perhaps most of all, coaxed Hannah into giving up the dead baby. Such a man might be a useful. Loli was young, but she had to suppose she knew something of the scarcity of good men in war.

The pair stooped together in the darkness, he once again trying to find his breath or puke or whatever and she trying to hold on to him. She had scrounged a few roots in the woods earlier in the afternoon but whatever fill that had put in their bellies had not lasted long. Now she reached for berries amongst the thorns beside them and as she did so the lieutenant grabbed her arm and shushed her. He looked like his mind had bent. His eyes and head kept flicking in unison to one side and back again. He could have been Coal having a seizure, or possessed by the Devil. It got her attention.

Mud creased his face on one side and he looked all over to be a thing that had turned. She gathered herself and looked about, smacked her tongue against the roof of her mouth. They rested against a large tree on the edge of a bog. In the distance, a hundred yards or more as the crow flies, a grassy hillside shimmered. Something bad had happened there that day and it occurred to her she'd be able to smell the bodies if the wind changed. On that hillside, three soldiers, their allegiance not immediately apparent in the dusk, moved through and among the remnants of the battlefield. They stopped every now and again to rifle remains or lift a canteen from the ground. They looked small against the corrupted hillside. Or maybe the hillside looked especially big against them.

She watched them as they moved from body to body, it being their apparent business to loot the dead. Their breathing carried over to her across the hillside unnaturally, perhaps a trick of the bog. Not too many years before, Loli had joined her pa on a day hike through it and then too it had seemed sound carried unnaturally; as if the stunted grasses and fetid water could not capture it. The breathing of those on the hillside was like that. She could hear it plain: heavy and momentous and more than a little distressed.

Not the distress of the injured though. She made out voices too. Odd utterances, incomplete thoughts. Things the mind put together in whatever way it wanted to.

She stood with the lieutenant between her and the large tree, ankle deep in bog water, which was brown and cool and soothing. She pulled a shoe off and squished her toes in the muck. She wished she knew which way to go. She knew the bog only well enough to know that going the wrong way might disappear them forever. There were things out there what couldn't be explained. Boogy things. In the light of day she supposed she could find her way well enough. But at night—

"Ye Yankee son bitch!"

Loli's eyes went big and she gave her attention all to the hillside. A few more words she couldn't rightfully make out, something like "You'se burn in hell" and then gunfire. Bright muzzle flashes, two or three she thought but they blended. White light. She saw them before she heard them and in their daylight saw a man fall. He hit the ground with a heavy thud, like a potted plant knocked off a shelf. And this too she saw before she heard. Another gunshot, this one apparently aimed at the ground itself; the man on the ground apparent in its flash.

She gasped, "Oh God," and the pace of her breathing picked up.

"Who there?" one of the men shouted. "You best make yourself plain so's we can see you." His words ran impatient and quick.

She shook her head no, a pointless gesture since the men on the hill couldn't see her. The lieutenant groaned beside her, maybe awake, maybe not.

The hill men continued their hollering, talking over one another and creating a caterwaul of sound. "What 'n hell?"

Another, "You come out here now ye hear me!"

The first again, "Git on out here, don't ye make me come after ye. You don't want me a having a come after ye."

The words were cacophonous, raucous and impelling. They didn't seem like voices one could reason with.

Ye Yankee son bitch! The words echoed in Loli's head.

"There. Over there." A pressing, insistent voice.

She ducked to replace her shoe and the wood overhead splintered with the thwack of a lead ball aimed too high. She lost the shoe in the muck and, without coming up, grabbed the lieutenant by his shirt and pulled him away from the tree, pushing him before her, urging him onward with outstretched palms. He understood, or seemed to, the need for haste. The two of them lurched clumsily forward along the bank.

The odor of spent gunpowder overshadowed the smells of stagnant water and rotting leaves. They moved over the wet ground and the mud oozed between the toes of Loli's shoeless foot with every other step. She paid not a whit to the cold water as the ground became less reliable. Now and again the crack of a shot or the whizzing of a ball by their heads urged them on. The trees, which had been as big around as a man's thigh, became thin like a woman's spindly forearms, and more numerous. Before long, they could move only by groping from one to the next.

The lieutenant was alert now, as if his training and experience had suddenly come into play. His arm was still dead weight, dragged at his side, but he didn't let it slow him down. His mind seemed to have bent in the other direction now, perhaps channeled by pain to a greater place. It all ran to their advantage.

The hill men came on. Their cries and shouts were more audible as that distance slowly closed.

Loli stopped in her tracks and stood stooped, as if the sky might come down on her at any moment. *Lost.* She had never known this place anyway, and now she leaned against a dead pine ankle-deep in the quag. Her eyes watered and her breath came fast and furious. She glanced furtively this way and that, needing to make a decision on what to do but unable. Now it was she who couldn't go on, who couldn't be urged forward.

The night was an eerie blue-black in the nothing light of the quarter moon. She saw a man move out of the corner of her eye, but there was only a tree when she turned. It writhed as if the branches possessed soul. There were voices, too. Hollow and echoing, the words not quite there, as if drifted over not from a nearby battlefield, nor even from the hill, but from another time entirely. She hugged a lifeless willow, but it too teased her with its rocking in the dead air of the swamp. Her skin goosed up and she backed away, her steps faltering. A low branch scratched her cheek and it was like the Devil himself stroking her. She wanted to run, needed to in the worst way, but it wasn't something she could muster. She fell back against a tree, its branches all dead and stiff like some sort of skeletal remains, and the lieutenant, at her side all the while, grabbed her with his good hand over the meat of her arm, steadying himself too against the dead willow. That tree, which might have stood thus in that spot a hundred years alive and fifty more dead, did the good work of their legs for several moments as they fought to keep upright and took in great chestfuls of air. Taylor squeezed her arm hard.

"We got to get moving now," he said, "ain't no two ways 'bout it. Those aren't the sort of boys you want to wait around on."

She just looked at him, the blood on her cheek mixing with her tears looking purple in the moonlight. She stepped out, moving too slowly, from one tree to the next. Taylor dragged after her, unable to do more himself. The ground was mushy and as they went the trees on either side of them quaked under their weight. Only a thin crust covered the waters of the bog and the ten thousand years plus of dead matter piled underneath it all. The water was cool, but the summer night was hot and humid and the still air of the bog only intensified the effect. All at once, it stank more of decay than gunpowder.

The hill men were still there, still coming. By their rants and raves they had gained on them.

Loli began to run again, this time nearly losing Taylor, who seemed to be fading again. He lost his grip on her and now it was her turn to hold him, which mostly meant dragging him along. When she could do this no more, she felt a hunger for breath and a want to survive she hadn't known existed. She and the lieutenant sank to the mucky ground. The din of croaking frogs filled their ears and fireflies burned the night, lighting up for a moment here, two moments there. Mosquitoes buzzed and she slapped her neck and swallowed a bug as she sucked in great gulps of air. When she looked up, she allowed how her mind had gone wondering. When it didn't right itself, she supposed the vision before her might be real enough.

She started to say something but the giant of a man before her put a big hand out quick to cover her mouth. It covered her entire face and she stood looking at him through the slits between his fingers. She looked up the length of his dark arm, all the way to his face, which was hid some by thick whiskers fanning in all directions. Her eyes met his—big yellow-white orbs—and in that instant she wondered if maybe she should be scared, if maybe this was one of those boogy things. Maybe *the* boogy thing. He was certainly big enough.

Only she wasn't scared. Not of him anyway. He put a finger to his lips and she understood to be quiet.

The lieutenant had no fight left in him. He reached out for the giant, but it was with his bad arm and it did no good. The arm dangled, or more to the point he himself seemed to dangle off that arm. He was used up, would have been dead in any other place and maybe would be yet here. He collapsed to the wet quag floor and the big man had to turn him face up so he wouldn't drown in the mud.

"I counts three," the big man whispered, his hand still at her mouth.

Loli nodded and her eyes bobbed up and down, as if stuck to his face. Maybe she should run, but where? It wasn't possible anyway.

"Wait here." He drew his hand back, leaving a cold splotch of mud she could feel on her cheek. She reached to wipe it away and it proved to be a leech. She screamed.

This time his hand went in as much as over her mouth. She tasted the mud on his fingers. "Wait here," he repeated. "You'se be safe." He pulled his hand away, slowly.

"Those men—"

"You ain't gotta worry 'bout them."

He wore an oil slicker from shoulder to knee. He pulled a large knife from beneath it and the blade glinted in the nothing light of the bog. The big man took a step and was suddenly out of her sight, had simply become the night itself. He vanished as quickly as he'd appeared.

She stood in the dark more alone than the lieutenant's presence would suggest and her breath all the listening there was to be had. She took air quick, but by and by she slowed and now she heard her heart squeezing and then other things too. She turned one way and then another, the way a person will when frantic to see what's around him, aware anything could be out there.

Her ears perked and the world revealed itself in layers of sound, like it was being peeled open for her onion-like. Somewhere in the near distance, an owl hooted and went silent and hooted again. Frogs croaked and a thousand thousand crickets whined. A wolf or some such animal howled. She was aware of the sound of water lapping against a log and then of a sudden the brackish bottomland gave up a scream followed by a long-suffering moan and a splash. Something that sounded like "no, no." Someone said "Oh Gawd," in a pitiful, all too clear tone and the words echoed in the pitch like the night was taunting their owner.

And then only the goosebumpy sound of something moving slow through the brackish water.

Loli did well not to scream.

NINE

The big man frowned and his forehead wrinkled. He stood beside what passed for a doorway, the hide of a long dead bear strung up so as to mark what was in and what was out. The pelt hung all leathery and cracked and in life that animal must have been a thing to see because it filled completely that doorway. On the man's forehead a large vein pulsed for all the world like a worm burrowing deep into his own dark hide.

He stood the step with half his face yellowed in the meager light of a lantern mounted to the wall, the other half swallowed entire by the black and fetid night. The girl and the soldier beside her were mere shadows in the backdrop. The quarter moonlight encircling them bleached the color from their persons. Their chattering teeth were the piteous rattle of an unburied bone box. They'd walked a long stretch in the wet dark, hours during which their protector had said little except that if she couldn't keep up he'd just as soon leave the both of them behind.

"You killed those men?" Loli asked at one point.

"Never you mind 'bout that," he'd said and kept walking.

When she asked again sometime later he sounded perturbed. "What needed doing is done. Don't ask no question what you don't want no answer to."

"You gonna kill us?"

"I don't espect I'd be workin this hard I was gon kill you."

And that was most all the talking there was. The swamp man dragged the lieutenant on a hastily made litter of twigs and branches, dragged him with his head waist high and his boots rutting in the mud behind him. Even so weighted he moved fast, possessing a knowledge of the landscape that could only be gained over years of trudging through it. He moved them over trees twisted queer by years of growth in the rich swamp water, through tangled and spiny thickets that left Loli's legs cut and bleeding, and along a stream bed that sucked at their every footfall like quicksand. She came to know the leeches well as she picked them from her flesh repeatedly.

They clambered up a rise and down into a depression where the racket of crickets was enough to wake the dead. No light reached this place in the dismal night. Loli couldn't tell if her eyes were open or closed.

It occurred to her more than once how he was leading her farther into the bog, in so far she'd never get out on her own, but she couldn't figure a way around this fact and so put it out of her thoughts.

Now he pulled aside the bear skin and she understood she was to enter and when she had done so he stepped around her and into the dark. There was the scritch of a match struck and it flared bright in the dark and its light fairly blinded her. Next thing he was up close against her, the match burning beyond his fingertips, eyes squinted, his breath hot on her face. His smell was gamy and strong.

"My name's Loli Gamble."

He remained silent and stepped back a pace or two and kept looking at her, or rather in her direction. He chewed his tongue, or moved his jaw like he was chewing his tongue, and shook the match out before it burned him. She held her place and he backed to the far corner. Their eyes adjusted to the darkness until he finally nodded like one come to some decision. "You and he cain sleep out there." He motioned out beyond the bear hide.

"I'm all wet," she said.

"You cain take that there blanket. Mind you give it back come morning. I ain't one for charity."

"Ain't one to take it no way." She stood her place a moment before adding, "We ain't had none to eat neither."

There was a pot hanging over cold ashes in the fireplace. He nodded toward it and handed her a bowl that looked to have been carved out of a single piece of wood. She dipped the bowl and scooped out a lumpy gruel of whatever sort the pot contained.

"That bowl mine too come morning."

She took the bowl and picked up the blanket and stepped past the skin that did for a door and moved out into the night. She stepped down into the mud, where the lieutenant was propped against the side wall of the cabin. She sat in the mud and pressed against him so they were propping each other and spread the blanket over them both best she could. Taylor lay mostly unaware and she could not wake him beyond a few paltry grunts and groans.

Loli fingered the contents of the bowl into her mouth. It tasted lardy and otherwise like nothing she'd ever had in her mouth before. Bits of gristle popped between her teeth and there was a bone or two as well. Maybe some radishes, but she couldn't tell with any certainty. She didn't much care anyway, except she was still hungry when the bowl was empty. After that she just concentrated on the sound of Taylor's breathing and heard the man when he got up to piss sometime later. She pulled the blanket up over their heads and they lay like dead folk awaiting the undertaker.

Morning took a long time coming.

Hannah Gamble Griel came out of the woods at the junction of two roads. It was dawn on the second of July, the sun barely over the horizon, and a dead mule lay not ten feet in front of her. It occupied the middle of the smaller of the two roads, and looked about as out of place as anything she'd ever seen. Hannah stared at it a moment, trying to decide what it was about the thing that bothered her so. She'd seen dead animals before of course, and why this one should be any more disturbing eluded her. Perhaps it had something to do with her baby boy.

She withdrew the small flask from under her shirt, close to her bosom. She'd needed no excuse to sip at it all the long night and now she again unscrewed the cap. The whiskey burned her throat but the brew found its way. She took a second swallow, more used to the taste than a girl ought to be probably, the whiskey a dry hot fire in her belly. Despite the hour, she was not in the least tired. She hadn't slept well since the baby had come—hadn't slept at all in the night just past—but she hadn't one tired bone in her.

"Why?" She cried the word aloud. She imagined Noah as he had been just a week before, sucking at her tit, smiling, playful. He'd been born with a single tooth just breaking the gum and it had made nursing him a chore. Her nipple was still scabbed where that tooth had cut it raw. She squeezed her nipple through her nightie, but it wasn't the same. There was pain, but it wasn't the same. She did it again.

She needed Levi. They hadn't been together since the night they'd made Noah. She needed to hold him, taste his sweat, feel him against her, feel him in her. She needed to tell him about his son, what kind of boy he was, what he might become. She spoke these notions out loud, as if Noah was still alive. She cursed the war, cursed Mr. Lincoln.

"Don't he know he's keeping pa's from their boys? Don't he know he's breaking up families? He's killin' us all. Oh God. What if my man's dead? What then? What do I do then?"

She took another pull on the whiskey and realized she was talking to the dead mule. She laughed and pointed at it.

She put the flask to her lips again, a spill of it run down her neck and not bothering to wipe it away, not wanting to. A fly walked across the bloated hide of the mule's ass and she followed it with her gaze. She imagined the animal humping its ass muscle and flicking its tail at it and there it was.

Suddenly she knew why the rotting remains bothered her.

Where's the crows?

They should have been picking at the carcass, of course. Should have made a fair effort in picking the dead thing clean by now. In fact, there were no birds about at all. She thought back on the night just passed, on the long hike through the woods, and couldn't remember so much as a single hoot. She should have heard a few barn owls at least. She tweaked her nipple again, hard this time, and wondered what the birds knew that she didn't. As if by way of answer, the distant boom of cannon thudded the air and she understood. It was the battle that had scared them off. Not a fit place for anything that wanted to live.

"It's a bad sign when even the damn vultures clear out," she muttered. She stole another sip and replaced the flask against her bosom. She ran her hands through her hair and turned away from the mule. She began to walk north down the larger of the two roads, toward the town she knew to be several miles distant.

Hannah walked all through the queer morning. It was her habit to rise early, before the sun and rooster both, and morning was like an old friend. She knew well the cold dew of summer grass; the morning croak of tree frogs and the whir of katydids and the feel of the wind as it rushed off the unharvested spring wheat and kissed her face. And all of it, on this morning, somehow different. As if the very soul of daybreak had been lost, as if the lack of birds had thrown the rhythm of the day off kilter.

She walked and in the walking recalled a time far in the past. A long ago day when she and Levi had come upon a dead cow lying on its side in a field. She must have been five or so at the time. The memory was one of her earliest. Levi would have been a year older, of course. She recalled buzzards circling high in a gray, looming sky; the reeking air as she and Levi came over the hill and found the dead thing. He had touched the carcass, teased her that she must touch it too.

She got close enough to see worms crawling everywhere over its putrid hide—almost close enough to touch it, certainly close enough to be pecked by the vultures that tore at the remains. They were giant black birds, mostly just shoulders with scrawny but powerful legs and beady heads stuck at the end of swooping, snake-like necks. The whites of those eyes—terrible things those eyes and all the more terrible in memory—were crisscrossed with fine, veiny lines of blood. They had seemed interrupted by the black pupil. She'd bawled at seeing that. Sat right down and bawled till she could hardly breathe through the snot. Had puked and ruined a dress and her mother had tanned her backside with a hairbrush. That pupil was the worst thing she had ever seen and it had haunted her on a thousand nights thereafter. One of the birds had looked at her as if sizing her up for a meal—God himself couldn't have told her otherwise—its pupil suddenly zeroing out, enlarging to fill that damn, veiny white space completely, as if a black void had suddenly opened in that terrible, beady head…

"I said, ye got business bout these parts, missy?"

Hannah did a double take. A man in a dirty uniform stood before her with a rifle slung over one shoulder. He was roly poly with a shadow of whiskers and one eye bigger than the other and he smelled of a hog. He repeated himself, or appeared to. She hadn't heard what business he was up to the first time around.

"I ain't asking again—"

"Yes, business, in town."

"What sorta business?" His bigger eye fixed on her.

Of a sudden she wanted to puke. "Uh. My husband. Levi. Need to find him. Got some news bout Noah. He's with the 115th Pennsylvania."

She rubbed her forehead. Two others stood behind the hog smelling man. Probably came out of the trees and she hadn't seen them. *What else I didn't see?* She turned about like she was seeing the road for the first time.

"Never hear'd of the 115th."

They stared at her and she realized she was three days wearing the cotton nightshirt she had on. It billowed around her in the morning breeze, flopping about her knees, and she was conscious of her nipples poking against the fabric. The urge to puke stayed with her, like a bad smell lingering in the air. The pebbled ground pressed hard against her bare feet. She felt naked before these men.

"You poorly, miss?"

"I told you it's missus. Mrs. Levi Griel. He's a soldier with the 115th Pennsylvania."

"Okay, little lady. Don't get all outta sorts now." The hog smelling man turned to the others. "Hawkins, Tweeter, either ye ever heared of the 115 out of Pennsylvanie?"

"Nope," Hawkins said, licking his lips. They glistened in the morning light, as if dew-laiden.

The one called Tweeter had about him a hungry look. His pesky looking, unfortunate face reminded Hannah every bit of those vultures. He stared at her and a lit segar hung from one corner of his mouth and he talked around it. A long bit of ash fell away from the tip. "Been a long time since I seen a berry so fine as you is."

She shook her head back and forth in a tiny gesture of 'no' and made a conscious effort of pulling her nightshirt away from her chest.

Tweeter stepped toward her and he too she could smell. A combination of stale tobacco and vinegary sweat. Likewise he had a rifle slumped on his shoulder. He blew a column of smoke her way. "A fine looking berry, eh Billy?" He guffawed.

"Now you men," she said, as if what she smelled was their arousal, "you best be leaving me alone." She looked at the first, the one called Billy. Fat but sane, more calm. She hoped her fate was in his hands, not with the others. For a long moment the issue hung.

Tweeter gave her his eyes and they crept over every inch of her body. She stood in the middle of the road like a tom turkey at banquet time. Ripe for the plucking. She felt those eyes trace over her and wrapped her arms across herself and her throat burned with bile.

I'm gonna puke right now.

But she didn't. Her fingers tapped the whiskey flask at her bosom.

Tweeter glanced at Hawkins, who nodded slowly and not quite in the affirmative. He appeared emboldened and raised a hand. He touched her hair. She thought to pull away but didn't.

"What you doing out here looking like that?" Hawkins called out from behind Tweeter.

"Ain't it obvious?" Tweeter said over his shoulder, still talking around the segar, never taking his eyes off her. "No proper woman be out here dressed like that."

He grinned and she saw how crooked his teeth were. It made him look ugly. "Lessin, of course, she was looking for a man. For a soldier." He strung out the last word so that it came out sounding like *sool-dier* and did a little two-step jig and grinned even more broadly at her. It did nothing to improve his looks. "I got me two bits," he said and his eyebrows bounced up and down in a quick, furtive gesture. He took a long drag on the stogie and it glowed red hot between them. He blew the smoke in her face. "That enough to sling the hog?"

"You'd a made a Goddamn good vulture," she said, then turned toward Billy while still watching Tweeter out the corner of her eye. Billy remained silent and she understood she'd been wrong. Fat Billy wasn't the chivalrous type. Her fate was in her own hands. She decided she wasn't going to puke after all. "I told you men. Looking for my husband."

"What ye say?" Tweeter had his blood up, like a hound going after a bitch in heat. "Maybe you don't even want the two bits, eh?" Now he had one hand on his crotch, cupping it for all to see.

"Tweeter, leave her be," Billy said.

"You come near me, I'll kill you. I'll kill every damn one of you."

"Feisty, eh? I do like a hussy what has spirit."

"Tweeter, we ain't out here for that."

"What you say, Hawkins? You of a mind?"

"Naw, I ain't doing this, Tweet. You on your own with this one."

"You boys sure ye still got balls? Maybe you left them with that whore up Cashtown way, cause you sounding awful limp. Me, I'm a git me sumpin. Lady, when I'm done with you, you ain't gonna wanna go back to no husband." He spat and the cigar tumbled away in the wind.

"Wait," Hannah said hastily, putting her hand up. "We, eh, we gotta do this right. Not out here." She motioned to the side of the road. "Over there, them bushes." She hoped she sounded lusty enough.

"Now that's better. I knowed you was my kind the moment I spied you. I always been good 'bout picking 'em." Tweeter walked toward the bushes, unbuttoning his trousers.

Hannah followed and stood beside the bush, eyeing him and pulling his mind to her sex with the tilt of her pelvis.

"Pull that nightie up, let me so what ya got." He couldn't wait and tore the neck part instead. One of her tits fell out, swollen and plump. Noah's toothmark was visible. "I knowed I was right 'bout you."

He dropped his trousers to his ankles. He wasn't wearing underwear and his hard dick jutted out before him. He came in close and cupped her tit, moving his mouth down over the nipple. His dick brushed hard against her. He bit down on her nipple and for just an instant, no longer, she savored the pain. "I'm a fuck ya so hard I'm a ruin ya."

"I don't think so," she said and in one motion she produced the flask from her nightshirt and brought it up hard. She struck Tweeter in his left cheek and the skin split over the bone like a ripe melon and a gout of blood spun across her nightshirt. She quick-knee'd him in the groin and he went to the ground holding his balls and spitting profanities. His dick shriveled and dribbled a little piss.

"You bitch." He moaned with the last of his breath as he lay hitching and grabbing himself in the lee of the bushes.

"I guess you got balls," she said.

"Jesus Christ, you see that?" Hawkins said. He and Billy were still standing the other side of the road.

"Just get Tweet and let's get back to doing what we suppose to be doing. I swear, you dumb asses gonna get us killed some day." Billy said, "I'm sorry missy," he pulled his handkerchief out and wiped his brow, "I'm truly sorry. He got his blood up is all."

"That ain't all he got up. And I done told you it's missus. I ain't to be messed with, mister. Not today specially. Just buried my baby and now I'm going to find my husband. You got problems with that? Any problems at all?"

"No, miss."

"Missus."

"Missus." The three moved back into the trees, the two supporting the one. Hannah stuffed her tit back in and ignored the smear of blood on her nightshirt. She unscrewed the flask and took a gulp and didn't waste time watching them go.

"I blame this on you, Major, on you and your men."

Purdy stood in her kitchen, the family Bible steadfast in one hand. The major had a knife in his teeth and a bleeder between his fingers. The soldier on the table squirmed under his touch. "You people killed my husband, you take our land, I'll be goddamned if I'm goin' give you my daughters too."

Major Brody tried to slip a ligature around the bleeding vessel, but it slipped as he did so and there was a gloppy sound, like a boot sticking in the mud, and a rush of new blood hit the floor. The wounded man tensed, and his eyes opened a degree and canted crossways to each other. Brody held all his attention to his patient.

Purdy moved round to the other side of the room, hesitating only slightly when she saw the soldier's eyes slip open and roll back in their sockets, where they came to rest cock-eyed and staring at nothing in particular.

"Jesus in heaven," she said, then regained herself, "You bastards got no right being here. Don't you know that? Know you ain't wanted here? Whatever harm comes to my Hannah or my Loli, I aim to come after you, Major! You hear me? After you!" She punctuated her statements with excited thrusts of her book before her, like she was preaching a revival meeting. She wrestled past the grip of an assistant. "Leave me the hell alone!"

"Christ almighty." The surgeon clenched his teeth and his fingers slipped in the muck somewhere deep in the wound. He seemed not to hear Purdy at all.

She slammed the Bible down and it thumped on the table and splashed little tear-dropped clots of blood on the sleeves covering her forearms. "Goddamn you, answer me!"

Brody looked up, the scalpel still gripped between his teeth like a dog's bone. He was dead calm, his hands yet wiggling inside the man as he spoke around the blade. "Madam, as I believe you can plainly see, I am occupied at the moment. Perhaps we could discuss this at a more opportune time?" He looked down at the man on the table and added, "Besides, I do not much like extra folks around when I am operating. They have a certain retard on the healing process."

"I don't give a Goddamn hoot—" She glanced about the room, suddenly aware the others were staring at her. She wiped at the blood where it lay bright red against the black leather cover of the book. The blood stained her palm and made the creases stick out unnaturally. She made a great show of drawing herself up before exiting, as if her point had been made.

"What in hell is with that woman?" Brody said.

"Not totally sure, doc. Something about her daughters gone missing. A trifling. No matter for us."

"Well, do we know anything about it?"

"The girls, they're Yankees, sir. That's all I know." Those in the room broke into chuckles. Brody went back to the task at hand.

The surgeon cut on another dozen men, swishing his hands in the bucket of well water outside the kitchen door between them. He smoked after every fourth or fifth man, though he didn't find it necessary to remove himself from the operating room to do so. He ran out of the cotton thread he used for suture and substituted hair from a horse's tail, boiling it first to soften it, which worked nicely. He dressed the wounds with whatever was at hand, though he insisted it be clean and never of a used sort. He was educated, he liked to refer to himself as a man of theory, and one of his theories pertained to hospital gangrene, which he believed had more to do with the filthy conditions of the sickroom than the foul humors of the air.

When the last of the morning's acute cases had been dealt with, Brody removed his surgeon's apron. Walking the grounds, he found Purdy tending a wounded man under a peach tree behind the barn. The man had shat himself.

"You do not have to do that, madam. I can get my men to attend him."

"Don't bother. I'm done." She rose to her feet. "I ain't so proud I can't clean a man what has soiled himself. Or is it you're afraid I may retard his healing, Major? Those was the words you used, I believe."

"I have instructed my assistants in how they are to handle the wounded. I believe cleanliness is important. Yes, madam, it is possible you may retard their healing."

"We ain't barbarians, sir. I assure you I'm thoroughly knowing in cleanliness."

"I did not mean to opine otherwise. It is simply that hospitals are uniquely dirty places, in my humble opinion."

"Well, this here's a farm, not a hospital. Not that one is any cleaner than the other, in my humble experience."

"It is a hospital now, madam. The Army of Northern Virginia appreciates your hospitality."

"My hospitality? Damn you. And damn your army too. You came here uninvited. I would never have allowed you here except you gave me no other choice."

"I assure you we shall vacate your premises—your farm—as soon as humanly possible. I do not wish to discomfort you or your people beyond that which is absolutely necessary to the cause of these good men. I am told your daughter is missing. Please, what is her name?"

"Daughters. Hannah and Loli. Hannah's nineteen, Loli just fourteen. Your men—"

"—would not harm them."

"You and your men drove them away, at the least. Hannah's baby died. My grandson. The girl needed peace and quiet. Instead, you happened. Loli, well, she's just a foolish child but she looks every bit a woman five years older. She's an innocent."

"My apologies, madam, but the world does not stop its machinations at the fated circumstances of a mother. If it did, perhaps we should all be the better off. As it happens, all of the poor fellows you see around you have mothers who are no less loving of their boys then you of your girls. Now, if you will excuse me, I have work."

"Major. I don't believe for a moment in this damn war. It's taken so many good husbands and fathers. Both North and South, I'll allow that much. I count my own husband in that tally. But you're here, and I suppose you'll be here until you can go. Whatever my children and I can do to help your wounded, we'll do, if only to get you out of here all the sooner. But if any harm comes to my girls, God himself won't be able to save the wretched souls of the men involved."

"Let us hope it won't come to that."

"Look around you major. Hope's not in bountiful supply just now."

"On the contrary, Mrs. Gamble, hope may be the one thing we have in abundance. You in the North might be surprised at how far a little hope can go."

TEN

First light and a mist across the land, like all the world entire had burned except this one place. In the obscured distance, indistinct and gray, the barren, bony trunks of trees like ribless spines crooked to the sky. Closer in, the spines brown and leaden, solitary monuments to what had once been. Nature's graveyard. Bursts of evergreens here and there, the ground a carpet of lush yellows, greens, and browns. A stagnant creek, its still waters a mirror so that all is doubled, with a finger in heaven and a toe in hell. And then, too, the mosquitoes. Thick as maggots on a dog three days dead.

Loli Gamble stirred and crooked her neck to one side until it popped then twisted it back the other way until it popped a second time. She had sat propped against the cabin wall all the long night and the lieutenant had fallen over and his head rested in her lap and she could smell him, acid and sour. Warm to the touch and wet everywhere. Both wet everywhere.

She pulled at him and he groaned but it wasn't anything sensible. He'd vomited in the night and the upchuck trailed off her clothes and pooled beside her. She had put her hand in it while she slept and she wiped her hand across the lieutenant's thigh now, which was hot to her touch even through his pants.

She pushed him aside, laying his good arm out for his head to rest on. He opened his eyes as she moved him and said something she couldn't make out. He laughed or seemed to laugh, but it wasn't a hearty chuckle by any measure. She touched his arm under the blanket and he moaned again. That arm was swelled bigger around than a muscled thigh and the skin hard like cowhide. When she pulled the cover back (the smell was rancid meat—acute and awful) she saw how the arm entire had turned an ugly blue-black. At the sight of it she pulled back and retched.

In the clearing, a blackened ribrack, like a marker to the ages.

Loli got to her feet and stepped away from Taylor. The sun was just up and burning through the mist and in the light of it he looked red and drawn, like a boiled man. His teeth chattered and as she watched his crotch turned dark as he made water. Her face squinched like she was about to cry, but then she turned away and stood with eyes clenched and hands fisted and pulled great clean gulps of air into her lungs and let them out again.

The wind blew cool against her skin and tickled her tiny hairs and she was aware of buzzing insects which seemed to come of a sudden. She opened her eyes and ran them around their hollows, taking in her surroundings without moving her head, as if it might fall from the perch of her shoulders if she did. She pursed her lips. Out front of her, the mist thinned enough to make out two crosses run through the ground at the far edge of the clearing, a fair forty or fifty yards distant. She noticed them only because they were white, unnatural to the land. The earth under them was slightly mounded, but it wasn't anything new. They had stood that spot, those crosses, a long time.

She turned about and there was the cabin. A dilapidated thing built of whatever had been at hand. Logs chinked with mud, a few stones here and there laid irregularly. Maybe some animal skins stuffed in at a place or two. No rhyme to any of it except four walls and a roof. An opening large enough to walk through, the bear skin covering it. A trace of black smoke wafted from a tumbledown stone chimney, which teetered at an angle hard to look at but didn't fall. A hint of sulfur in the air, enough to remind a person what sort of world was out there.

"Mister? Mister?"

No answer and she pulled the animal skin aside and peered in. Darker inside by a fair lot than she'd imagined. The two windows were covered by hodgepodge curtains so they lent to the room little daylight, and the room revealed itself only slowly as her eyes sorted the shadows. Light streamed in in little dimples through gaps in the thatched ceiling above her head, where weedy earth was to be found here and there. The lone furniture a hand-hewn plank table and bench in one corner, a huge cot made of willow branches in another. The cot was wide enough for two, long enough for a man and a half. A roll of blankets and several animal skins lay on it, alongside a lumpy looking pillow. A large axe hung on the wall above. Between the table and cot a mud and stone fireplace black with soot. Well used. The cooking pot of the night before hung to one side of a smoldering pile of ash.

She stepped forward and picked up the pot and brought it to the doorway and in the daylight saw the bones of a small animal mixed with the last of a stew of potatoes or roots. She brought it to her nose and sniffed and turned her face away. She took the pot back to the fireplace and hung it on its hook. The whole place smelled of animal and dirt and burnt coal and there was not the mark of a woman anywhere.

Above the bed was a shelf, a piece of plank that ran the length of the wall head high off the floor. One end of it seemed to act as the pantry and held a cast iron fry pan, a few plates, a cup or two, and several utensils. In the middle a near used up candle was melted to a tin plate. The wax had run over the edge of the plate in places so that the plate was in turn wedded to the shelf. On the far end of the shelf, off by itself and close to the wall with the fireplace, was set a dried, shriveled piece of...what? Meat? She moved for a closer look. The thing had the look of a dried out ham-hock. She picked it up. Black, the covering hard and leathery. One side cut cleanly as if by a very sharp knife, the innards both bone and meat. A mummified ham-hock.

Except not. She was turning it in her hand, thought *toes,* just as the big man appeared in the doorway. She set the ham on the shelf and stepped in front of it. The man's back was to the light and at first she couldn't make him out beyond the sunlight streaming through his abundant hair, which made him look near incandescent. He was taller than she, in fact a giant, and had to stoop at the door. He cut a sight standing in it once she recovered from the shock of him.

He wore buckskins and stank of leather and animal matter and sweat. His feet were sheaved in moccasins of a sort a savage might wear. One foot was smaller by half compared to the other, as if it had been somehow shortened. A beaver was flopped over one shoulder and it had bled down the front of his oil skin jacket but either he didn't care or hadn't noticed or both. He had a big nose and surprisingly small eyes, one of which kept all the while twitching. A scar ran across this twitched eye and disappeared into his bearded cheek. The hair over his face and head had a nappy, untamed look, like a field gone fallow. It appeared black with gray highlights but might have been the other way around. Either way a streak of hair the color of bleached corn interrupted the middle of his head and chin, like he'd been stained. But it was his skin she noticed most. She hadn't seen it the night before, not so much as to notice it anyway. Now she couldn't help seeing it. He stood before her with the mark of Cain upon him.

She couldn't recall ever being alone with a nigger before.

***

The man lying in the dirt behind the Gamble outhouse had red hair nearly the same as Enoch. A piece of lead had passed clean through him at the midsection and there was no telling what it had wrought inside except that he hadn't moved his legs since. Shivering in the morning light, one with such a wound had to know he wouldn't see another sun-up. Such a one had to know it was his last day on earth. Whatever this man knew, he kept to himself.

There was a wisp of blood at his mouth. He kept swallowing. Big, easy swallows of mostly nothing. Swallows that moved his apple up and down and made him look like he was suffering, made him look like somebody coming in for his first drink off the desert. That's how he looked, Purdy thought, like a parched man in a field of plenty. He looked too a lot like Enoch had looked on his last day, what with his red hair and all. Or so she reckoned as she dabbed his forehead with a cloth wetted with creek water.

"There now. You'll be all right afore long." She didn't mean it as a lie, but as a small comfort.

Purdy Gamble had given twenty years plus of her life over to Enoch and now Enoch was dead. It seemed only yesterday he'd kissed her for the first time out back of the Willard place, in a deadfall of willow branches. They'd made a summer clubhouse of it, that deadfall, hollowing out a space big enough for a sixteen hand horse, if they'd have had such a creature. Enoch was twelve or thirteen and she a year younger, as she always was. Sitting around under the dead branches, leaves browning more everyday as the sun burned the wet out of them, he had of a sudden leaned over and sparked her, kissed her true on the lips. His mouth and tongue were stained red and it was a quick kiss that tasted of the raspberries he'd been eating all morning.

She still tasted those berries even after all these years. "What'd you do that for?" she'd said in the first moment after the smooch. He'd fumbled something back, she no longer recalled his words but the look on his face told the story. He was embarrassed and climbed up and out of the deadfall in an instant, leaving his raspberries behind, and she took all day finding him again. When she did he was up in a hayloft at the Colton place and said how he was busy and couldn't come down no way, not even to walk her home. Especially not to walk her home. She'd walked home alone eating the last of those berries, thinking how she'd saved them all that long day in hopes they could share them, and wishing he would kiss her again. But he wouldn't for nearly three years.

The red-haired man gurgled and a lump of clot appeared at his lips. Purdy swept a finger past his teeth and cleared his mouth and flicked the clot in the grass. The redhead looked at her the way a dying Papist might look at a priest, with eyes seeking redemption or salvation. There might have been a tear there—probably not, but there might have been.

Purdy was no priest, that was plain enough, but of a sudden she had a revelation and passed a hand over those eyes and pulled the lids shut. She couldn't provide redemption, but salvation might be another matter. Salvation might be within her reach, though it wasn't a thing she could do if he was watching.

She felt robbed. Not about the three years. They were just kids then and kids need time to grow into themselves, to learn their minds and shape themselves to the world. Or by their way of thinking, shape the world to themselves. Those were the loosest years of their lives but they'd been good and necessary. Now Enoch was dead and there wasn't anything good or necessary about that. He was just one more soldier, dead too young of one more battle, and leaving one more family without a husband and father. She couldn't see anything good or necessary in that. Nobody could and nobody would.

"Your pa was a right man," she said of a sudden and mostly for her own benefit, though she could imagine she'd said it to Coal who was sitting beside her but wasn't paying her any mind. His pockets bulged and she guessed he'd filled them with rocks again. He had a thing for rocks and was always filling his pockets and she was always unfilling them after he took his trousers off at the end of the day.

She looked up now, up into the blue, near cloudless sky. The ceiling of the world stretched on forever, majestic and ignorant of all that went on beneath it. The only cloud turned a burnt orange as the sun lit it. For a moment it could have been bleeding.

The redhead swallowed anew, then again. She thought maybe there was another tear in his eye but this too she might have willed. His chest moved slowly up and even slower down but it seemed to her he had outlived himself: a dead man breathing.

Coal turned a rock over and over in his hand. He sat behind her, crouched Indian style except he couldn't bend his spastic leg that way and so he sat looking awkward to the uninformed eye. *Always it's the same with this boy.* In the snow or the rain, come night or day or hellfire and brimstone, always it was the same. She had a bad moment imagining what he might have been like save for that damn mule. The moment didn't last though, she'd had her share of such moments and had learned to capture them at the outset and put them away. She stroked his hair and he smiled at her, which at least was something any boy might do when his mother stroked his hair. *Thank God for small normal things.*

She said "Bless you," then "Go on boy. Fetch me some water." She had to repeat herself but after a moment Coal rose from where he had been sitting and his thighs looked all lumpy with those rocks in his pockets. She watched him go away and turned to the redheaded soldier lying before her and pressed the cloth, the one wet with water from

Tischer Creek right over yonder back of the barn, to his nose and mouth and held it there with purpose a long time, held it there long after he finished his meager protests and his arms stopped jumping and his fingers stopped quivering and fell away from where they had tried to grab her hand, saying all the time "Bless you. It'll be all right. Quiet now, quiet," over and over in a trembling, little voice nobody save Jesus God himself could have heard.

Loli and the big man—the negro, she kept thinking, wondering how long he'd lived out there and why—had laid Taylor out on the cot, a bunching of cotton under his head and a few dusty hides between him and the thick burlap that did for a mattress. Every now and again he trembled in a manner that made a person want to look away. In between such fits his eyes would come open wide and roam about the room queerly unyoked, and with a languid sort of effort as if the lids had come apart of their own doing and there was nothing more to it. He seemed everywhere to sweat dirt from the pores of his skin and, hot as he was, he shivered. When he spoke, which was not often, it was only to repeat the single word 'water.'

"One thing we ain't short of it's water," the negro said.

Loli pushed Taylor's head up and tilted a cup to his lips but most of the water dribbled down his chin. He gagged on the rest. "How long can a body go without no water?"

"Long's he need to, I suppose. The flesh 's a way of rightin' itself, if'n it ain't too far gone a'ready."

She eyeballed the negro. He wore patched trousers and an old work shirt beat thin from many washings. Pegs did for buttons. On his feet were moccasins and he held an unlit pipe between his lips and he looked to puff on it every now and again, like he was pretending to smoke it. When he spoke his lips worked around the stem and a person could see his teeth clinched behind those lips. She tended to watch his mouth when he spoke because he wouldn't look her in the eyes. *He ain't a savage, not exactly.*

"He seem hurt real bad but I seen men worse off git better. Ain't always a way of telling bout these things though," he said.

She was down on her knees, wiping Taylor's brow and chest with the cold water, which maybe seemed to do more good than trying to pour it down his gullet. There was a stink in the room—at first she'd assumed it came from the negro—but down there close to the lieutenant she realized otherwise. It came from him, from his arm to be precise. It lay at his side, half on, half off the cot. It dripped a cruddy greenish matter which pooled on the floor. "I ain't never seen nothing like this. Don't look like no blood I ever saw."

"That there's the laudable pus I espect."

"What's that?"

"The insides of a man gone runny. Like the trots."

"He ain't got the trots."

"That arm do. It gonna poison the rest of him like as not." The negro sat down at the table.

"What happens then?"

"What you think?"

"Ain't there nothing to be done?"

"It is what it is. That arm's dead a'ready and he just a shoefly behind. Like as not be better off witout that arm."

"Take his arm off," Loli said. It was a flat statement, no emotion. She said it the way one might say 'we could open a window.'

The negro looked at her for the first time. "What you figurin?"

"You got a apple what's rotten, you toss it."

He nodded.

"You toss a bad apple soon enough, you save the barrel."

He smiled at that. "We ain't talking 'bout apples little girl."

"It's the principle what matters. My pa used to say that. And I ain't no little girl."

"You right smart that sure 'nuff true."

"So you think it's possible?"

"Didn't say that. No sir, didn't say that a'tall."

"What're you saying?" she said.

"I say this ain't none of my affair. None of my goddamn business." The vein in his forehead pulsed and his eye twitched in time with it.

"You gonna let him die."

"Ain't up to me."

"You gotta help."

"Ain't gotta do nothing."

"Sure you do."

He looked past her again. "No I don't. Caint."

"Why not?"

"Cause it ain't none of my affair. I quit that world long time ago."

"How long you been out here?"

"All your days and then some."

"I don't aim to do you no harm."

"Don't aim to, but you will. Your being here harm enough." He looked down like he was studying the wood planking. "I cain help you, Loli Gamble, but not him."

"I don't understand."

"You ain't gotta understand." He looked off, out beyond the doorway, and in the near distance the two little crosses stood out stark and bleached against the rich woods and bogland beyond. "You got to git. I caint have you here. I thought I could, but I caint. Especially him."

"Why'd you bring us here if you weren't gonna help us?"

"On account of your pa."

Loli give him a quizzical look.

"My name's Moice. Your pa, well, he done me a favor once. He and I, well, we was friends."

"You know my pa? I didn't know we knew no niggers."

"Was afore your time."

"That don't tell me why you just didn't let those men get us."

"'Cause I know something 'bout those kinda men." He hollered the words at her and there followed a silence between them, the kind of silence that is still to the ear but hardly tolerable to the mind. In it the other sounds of the cabin became amplified and it seemed Taylor was breathing through a megaphone. His chest heaved up and down in a harsh soliloquy.

"It's 'cause we're white," Loli said when she could take the silence no more.

"You is what you is. You caint help being white no more 'an I can change being black."

"What you think? That we're just gonna go away?"

"You caint stay here."

"What in tarnation's wrong with you? He's dying. Can't you see. And not dying easy neither." She had thought she was about to cry, but didn't. "His name is Taylor and he showed my family a kindness. He saved us from just the kind you're talking about. Ain't that worth something? For God's sake, ain't it worth nothing?"

"You don't know folks like I does. White folks specially."

"I know it was white folks what took over our farm. And white folks what killed my pa."

He backed away and sat down at the table, at the sole chair in the room. He closed his eyes and rubbed the back of his hand across his forehead. He looked generally tired, suddenly older. Loli looked down and saw a curious thing. His stunted foot, the one half the size of the other. Her eyes went to the shelf, to the mummified ham-hock. She had a sudden revelation.

"I'm sorry what they done to you."

"You don't know nothin' what they done to me." He rose from the table and stepped in his odd, crooked way through the doorway and out into the daylight.

She followed. His eye twitched and in the better light a person could see the scar running across it, how the lid lagged the other a bit in closing.

"You don't know nothing," he said, and the words came out like he was spitting at her.

Inside, the cot creaked under the restless lieutenant. He thrashed back and forth and uttered a few words, but whatever he had a mind to say either wasn't coming out right or hadn't been right in the first place. He seemed always on the verge of choking. Loli peered in at him then looked at the negro, at his black skin and all the scars that seemed now to show in the light. She wondered if negro skin scarred worse than white skin.

"I ain't never known me a nigger, but if this is how your kind is I guess I don't ever wanna know me another." She turned and went back inside.

The old man stood outside and passed his hand across his face and kneaded his throat between his thumb and pointer finger. His lower lip quivered and he stood a piece of time staring at the two crosses yonder. He lit a loco foco on the wall of the cabin and touched it to the bowl of his pipe and walked slowly out into the clearing and stood beside the blackened ribrack. He puffed on the pipe for a long time, all the while looking over toward the crosses. He returned to the cabin and peered inside and watched the girl and the fevered man she seemed to care so much for.

"What you say his name is?"

"Ben Taylor, Mr. Moice."

He stood a piece more, looking back and forth from the girl to the crosses. "Ain't no one called me Mister in a long time." He swallowed and looked at her like a man seeing a thing for the first time. "The last what called me mister was your pa."

"My pa knew a good man when he saw one."

"Yes, yes I believe he did." Moice looked away again, out toward the crosses. "Yes, Sufee, that's right. These folk killing each other now." He turned and faced Loli." "How old you is?"

"Fourteen, Mr. Moice."

"Sufee, it is what it is," he said and closed his eyes for a long moment during which nothing much passed between him and the girl except the labored breathing of Lieutenant Taylor. After a while a person tuned out even that disquieting noise until the only thing to be heard was the wind moving through the trees and the gentle fall of water over the rocks in the near distance. A woodpecker pecked a tree somewhere close.

Moice shook his head slowly back and forth like a searcher who had come upon something but not what he searched for. When he finally opened his eyes he said, "My wife wants me to help you, Miss Loli. You best fetch up some more water."

"Mr. Moice, you gonna help my friend?"

"Yeah I is. And God help us all."

The sun showed high noon and Hannah Gamble Griel lay in a small depression alongside of a rutted road she'd followed for some hours. The road itself meandered back and forth through wooded country and over rolling, grassy hillsides. She had grown increasingly fuddled as she walked, which might have been the first signs of heatstroke so hot was the beating sun, but more likely was on account of Enoch's whiskey. Even now she licked her lips and took another small swig from the near empty flask. She turned her face to the sky and put a hand up by way of blocking the bright light where it streamed through the trees. Her arm kept wavering back and forth, as if refusing the effort. Amused she couldn't quite make it do exactly what she wanted, she giggled and burped. She tried to get up, but the ground didn't seem to want to hold still. She spun feebly, round and round like she was corkscrewing into the ground, and set the flask in the dirt, nearly falling over in the process. She laughed and stood and propped herself against the knobby side of a tree. She hiked her night shirt and spent several very funny moments—she was almost in tears it was so damn funny—pulling her undie things aside.

As Hannah squatted and peed in the dirt by the knobby tree, she of a sudden heard shouts, then shots, behind her. She twisted hard to look over her shoulder and fell on her ass. She laughed again, didn't see any commotion, just the rough and irregular rails of a fence and the trampled, sun-parched field beyond. She turned first one way and then another, the shots seeming to come from every which direction. The musket fire grew louder by the moment and with no warning save the shooting, a group of hell-bent soldiers came dashing out of the woods a long stone's throw in front of her.

The men hollered encouragement to one another, saying things like 'move on Henry,' and 'git them britches moving Tom,' and ran through the grassy field on the opposite side of the road. From her concealment, she watched and listened as the troops—they wore Union blue and this too was funny—knelt chaotically and fired back of them, then up and ran for their lives. She counted six—but her eyes were clumsy with the alcohol and so it could have been more or less—and as they approached the road they had to slow and negotiate a substantial split rail fence. It had weathered black with the years and along the base of it clumps of sumac and Queen Anne's lace weeded the roadside. The soldiers seemed caught at the fence like fish in a net.

A dozen or more rebels came on fast behind them through the woods. They appeared better prepared, or at least ran faster, and crossed the hundred feet of grassy field with greater confidence. They stopped short of the Union troops, exchanged a few words Hannah couldn't make out, and began to use the Yankees for target practice. A man's head came apart as he sat atop the fence, where he teetered as if the issue—life or death—was in the balance. His body slipped bonelessly over and came to rest topsy-turvy in the dirt beside the road. Another was shot through the back and parts of him flung out before him and he fell dead as a stone. Still another put his hands over his face as if they could stop a piece of lead. They served only to shield his dead eyes from the sun after he too fell. A fourth lay on the ground and his fingers crawled feebly over the gravel and dirt. He called out something like Abby or Tabby, a girl's name anyway, and the final shot went through his neck and his hand clasped hard in a fist that only very slowly gave open again in a clump of Queen Anne's Lace.

Hannah should have screamed. It was the natural thing to do. But in her drunken stupor the scene played out more like an act in a play. She remained concealed in the gully as the rebels came forward after the spoils. She wanted another pull on the whiskey, but she'd kicked the flask over in the melee. She rolled onto her back and lay for some time with the empty bottle in her hands before it tumbled the several inches to the mud beside her and she slept.

She awoke to the sound of nothing and the insistent ache of her groin: she needed to piss again. She squatted, then stood and rubbed at her head and felt at the ground tentatively with her foot, as if to check its firmness. The sun was still near mid-sky and hot, maybe an hour, maybe two, had passed. She gathered herself best she could and rose out of the gully. All was quiet save her own footfalls and for a moment she couldn't remember where she was.

Then she saw the fence.

On the edge of the rutted dirt road, a road which now seemed to arise from nowhere and disappear off into the distant horizon, a split rail enclosure bordered a field of trampled, sun-parched wheat. The rails were rough and irregular, broken in places, missing in others. Here and there a trace of their original bark, weathered black over the years, was yet visible. At the base of the fence, looking no more animated than the rocks and twigs among which they lay, were half a dozen men. One was leaning against the fence. Others lay prostrate with faces in the dirt, still others belly up with eyes open or closed—it was all the same. The sumac and Queen Anne's Lace between them was soiled with the black red of crusted blood.

The dead men greeted her as only dead men can. Silent and still, they lay each no comfort to the next, oddly similar in their death poses—right down to their bare feet, for not a one wore shoes. There was too a look of haste about the place, with haversacks, canteens, hats, and cartridge boxes tossed randomly in the weeds. She stopped at a rut in the road where a long, narrow stream of blood had pushed forward against the dirt. She followed the red stream back to the reclined body of the young soldier whose last words had been the name of some girl back home. He lay on his back with eyes wide to the sun and the expression on his face—mouth open, tongue out—suggested the letter Q. His neck was blown open and the meat of it had dried some in the hot air.

Hannah looked back the way she'd come, swore the Lord's name, apologized, swore it again, and looked up to the heavens. "I know you're mysterious in your ways Lord, but what sort of business you engaged in hereabouts?"

She looked down and the soldier's eyes were still wide. She closed them and studied the several dead a long while making her mind up on what she must do. She found the one nearest her size but his trousers and coat were bloodied beyond what she could bear and so when she finally donned pants, coat, and a cap, they were too large for her. She tied the trousers with the same length of rope the soldier had used, for they had apparently been too big for him as well. As she stripped him she said over and over "forgive me," and looked about nervously, as if expecting more soldiers to come out of the woods at every moment.

The canteens were empty. She might have found something she could use, but she didn't want to touch these men anymore than she already had. She felt like an intruder. There was a loneliness here, as if these folks beside this road from nowhere were as far from anywhere as it was possible to be—except perhaps, the end of the world.

ELEVEN

Some few miles west of the massacre on the road, and not far from what had always been a ready supply of fresh water, the weathered remains of Enoch Gamble's barn stood the crest of a small hill not unlike the aged withers of a declining ox. Scarred and out of plumb, not a true straight edge or right angle could be seen from any which way an observer cared to take it in. The peak of the roof sagged from one end to the other and looked like the sway back of an overworked mule. The oversized doors had long since fallen off their hinges and lay tumbled to one side, home to wild flowers, weeds, field mice, and spiders. The siding boards were the dingy brown of age and some so splintered a squirrel or other rodent could slip between them without exhaling. The barn creaked in a good wind and came near to collapse in a gale.

Inside and out of this damnable place, the maimed waited to advance through the line of promotion to the tables. Enoch's kitchen hadn't been able to contain all of the operating that needed doing. More help had arrived and with it more tables set up in the yard. Nothing so much as a curtain obscured these bloody slabs so all within earshot were frequently within eyeshot as well. The appearance of the surgeons—Major Brody and his colleagues—bending at their unsavory but necessary tasks was not for the faint of heart. Men who had spent the previous two years schooling themselves in the glorious and perverted ways of war—who would not have blinked at the passing of a comrade-in-arms on the battlefield—fainted at the sight of these men of Hippocratic sanction elbow-deep in gnawing through mangled limb after mangled limb.

The constant rasping of the surgeon's saw as it ground through one bone after another was a discomfort that kept Purdy on the verge of nausea all day. She watched Brody and the others only at intervals and then only with the utmost revulsion. One table lay upon sawhorses and the other a few boards laid over moldy hay bales. The ground underneath both had long since saturated with gore, which seemed to dull the footfalls of the surgeons. They worked two, sometimes three to a table, bending to their tasks like butcher-gowned ghouls gathered around the recent dead. They went about them with a certain organized efficiency in an otherwise chaotic mess. Their routine varied but little from patient to patient. The wounds were what varied, and many were terrible to see. Arms and legs broken and all askew; holes the size of peaches or small melons blown through shoulders and thighs; jaws unhinged, busted cheeks, missing teeth by the handful. Yards of exposed, shit-filled gut that could never be put right again. Here and there, with no sense of urgency, men bled out and quit the world.

One lay face down in the middle of this torment , all the while moaning. The noise that came from him was both raspy and guttural, and would have been unpleasant had it been loud enough for anyone save those right upon him to hear. He had lain prostrate, as if a supplicant, for some terrible and indeterminate measure. Purdy stumbled on him only by the merest chance, almost falling over him. She thought at first he was dead, and when he moved it startled her. She had to get on hands and knees to make out what he was saying, which sounded like "wa'er." The word was whispered over and over again, as if he knew no other. She turned him onto his back, but he began at once to choke and so she turned him face down again and the sputtering stopped almost as quick as it had come. She was dumbfounded by this. His plea continued, however, and she finally understood.

She turned him up his side and put a canteen to his lips and he took some, but it seemed to cost him dearly. He started to sputter again and this time turning him face down did no good. A spasm racked him, twisting through every ounce of his being, and in the next moment a pink froth bubbled from both his mouth and nose, followed by gouts of blood. Three days before, she'd have run from such a sight. Now she only turned away.

"As the Lord is my God," she said, and kept up a sort of languid conversation with herself all the day. It had to be that way for when she closed her eyes the things she heard seemed worse even than the things she saw. She didn't want to close her eyes then, and as the time wore on, she talked around all she heard by way of not hearing any of it at all.

If a soldier was lucky—not the best word but there was no other that fit better—the surgeon's probing began after the chloroform had taken. This wasn't always the case though, or even usually. The ensuing cries warned her and the others the surgeon had been premature with his knife. "Oh God," she would say at such times, feeling her stomach slide away into some unimaginably black and murky place, and then from her lips a line or two of verse—*Weeping may endure for a night but joy cometh in the morning* was one such phrase.

These men, butchered first on the battlefield by the enemy, lay all the day and night awaiting this second woeful butchering. Each died a little more with every passing hour, and even those who weren't wounded came away less whole.

***

Moice knelt on one knee in the thin grass, his hand fast to the cross before him.

"Sufee," he said, and one could hear the break in his voice with her name even after so many years, "I'm gonna do this thing 'cause it's what you'd want me to do, but you gotta give me strength." He went on to say a few more words that were just between him and her. "It is what it is," he said and when he had spoke his piece he stayed knelt there in the mud, his palm tracing the shape of her burial cross like he was feeling for something in it. A gnat or two buzzed his ear but he paid them no mind. He was used to such distractions. He was a long time rising and when he finally did he stepped to the second cross and touched his fingers to his lips and then to the marker and turned and walked back down the creek to the four walls he'd called home all these years, since the day he'd put her in the ground beside this creek. The ground below the second cross was empty, of course, holding only the memory of their boy. Something he'd put up so she wouldn't be too lonely.

Loli stood at the door of the cabin and watched as he did all of this. In the bog, she had thought him older than he now looked in the sun. She found it curious how at times he seemed to limp as he moved, other times not. He was limping now, favoring his half foot. She moved out to meet him in the middle distance between the graves and the cabin.

"I suppose we best move him out into the day. We'll be needin' the light," he said.

"Who's buried over yonder?"

Moice stopped in his tracks and looked back over his shoulder toward the little cemetery. He turned back to her slow and deliberate, like it hurt his neck to do so, once again avoiding her eyes. His voice was austere. "That ain't no business o' yours. No business at all Miss Loli. When this here's all over, you got to go away and don't never come back. You hear me?"

"I hear."

"On your pa's grave you hear me?"

She did her best to look him straight on, the way she imagined a friend would. "On my pa's grave then, Mr. Moice." She turned and left him standing in the sun.

Moice did not follow her. Instead, he moved over to the burnt rib rack and the circle of rocks in the dirt around it and knelt. He poked about in the ashes, raking them to one side. He placed a bit of kindling in the pit and chased this with pieces of cut pine. By dint of long practice, he had a fire going in less than five minutes.

The day had gone hot and by the time they had Ben Taylor in position Moice and Loli were sweat covered and all but heat exhausted. The lieutenant lay face up on the cot in the out of doors, shaded by an old lean-to. It was too hot for the mosquitoes, but not for the flies, which had found his spoiled arm and were making little meals for themselves. His face was drawn and haggard and his skin dry and leathery. Earlier his skin had been hot and wet, like a boiled rag, and the sweat had rolled off him till he seemed to be floating in it. Now the hot was a dry hot and he seemed more to be baking from the innards out.

"He got the sickness in that there arm fer sure. The devil," Moice said, wiping at his own forehead with a piece of rag. "We best git on wit it."

"How we gonna do this?" Loli swiped at the air, being a nuisance to the flies.

"Ain't nothing much to it I'm thinkin."

"You seen this before?"

"Not esactly. I seen a man get his foot cut off once."

"How was that?"

"Never you mind."

"Oh." She gave up chasing the flies.

Taylor lay naked from the waist up. A person could see how he had a handsome build, not a bit of overhang at his gut. He was all sinew and no fat though, like he hadn't had a full belly in a long while or maybe the fever he now had had ravished him quick. He was tremulous, with little and various parts of him moving and jerking at separate and odd moments. All but his busted arm, which lay still and departed looking. His eyelids fluttered up periodically but never popped open altogether. In short, he had the look of one recently in his prime who was now down on his luck and short on his health.

Loli stood beside Taylor, his good hand in her palm, feeling it squeeze every now and again. His other arm below the elbow was an ugly, purple, festering thing that stank of the rot it contained. The skin of his forearm had burst open in several places and the juices within bubbled to the surface. The flies were having a field day. That arm was swelled three or four times normal and the skin was pulled tight like a drumhead with a sheen like the moonlit surface of a tranquil pond and all of it looked heavy the way a dead hog looks heavy before being pieced out. She had seen a hog or two gutted and wondered if gutting an arm was like gutting a hog. She wondered if the innards of a man looked like the innards of a hog. She didn't think so, but couldn't exactly say why. She wondered if she'd be able to look when the time came. She swatted at the flies again. She wondered if Moice really had only half a foot.

"Ain't got nothing for the pain. He should have something for the pain but I ain't got nothing."

"That's okay, it's okay. He'll understand," Loli said. "It is what it is."

"If he lives, could be he don't remember. A body has a way of forgettin' the worst stuff."

"I think you're right."

Moice stood to Taylor's bad side. He had a collection of knives from the cabin, mostly hunting knives and blades of one sort or another a body might use to peel the flesh off a kill and pare the bones. They were spread on a little table beside Taylor. Moice eyeballed the swelled arm, matching knives to it in his mind and apparently trying to decide which might be right for the work. "We should tie him, I'm thinkin."

"I can hold him," Loli said.

"Not for what's coming you caint."

He limped back to the cabin and returned with strips of rawhide. He tied Taylor's legs to the cot, then tied Taylor's good arm to his torso and lashed his torso to the cot, pulling the ties as snug as he could get them. The flies seemed to be multiplying.

Moice went back to his examination of the arm. He poked at it with a finger and squeezed it just above the elbow where a piece of gristle stuck out. He pushed on the gristle and it moved in a way that seemed unnatural to Loli. She didn't know exactly how, just that it was. Taylor himself did not so much as squirm with the poking and prodding; his eyes remained closed, his breathing something only a dead man would be proud of.

"It seems like maybe he don't feel that so much," she ventured.

Moice grunted like a man who'd not heard whatever had been said. He appeared deep in thought, gaze switching between the swelled arm and the table of knives. Once or twice he glanced over at the fire, which had burned down mostly to coals. "Best stir that."

"What we need a fire for?"

The question seemed to pull the negro from whatever place his mind had gone. He looked her direction, sort of through her at the countryside beyond. "I knowed this ole man a long time back. Name of Prosper. He could do things. I guess you'd call him a healer. Had a boy what fell out a tree once, breaked his leg about here." He indicated midway between his knee and the ankle above his stumped foot. “Bad broke too. Could sees the bone out the skin. That boy, Tommy he was called, he shoulda died. Yessir, as God my witness, shoulda died. But that a hard way to go and Old Prosper, that how we used to call ‘im, Old Prosper, well, he just wouldn’t abide that. We laid that boy out under a big cottonwood and I ain't never gonna forget what happened next. Tommy was all a hollering and carrying on like you’d espect. That boy’s mamie sat down on his chest and Old Prosper gave a yank on that foot and that bone popped and Tommy he just stopped screaming sudden-like, like he had of a sudden been walloped upside the head.”

“He didn’t die?”

“No, but that weren’t the all of it. Once that bone popped back in him there was a hole big enough I could of put my fist in it. Old Prosper say’d there was only two ways to close a hole like that. One was to sew it, but we daint have nothing to sew with.”

“What was the other way?”

“T’ other way was to burn it. Worked too. He put a hot poker to that leg—”

“Oh my Lord – “

“Best you not think too much and put these on the fire.” He picked up two of the knives with long thin blades and passed them to her and she went over to the fire and set them on a rock so the blades were licked by the flames.

“You gonna be able to do this?” he asked.

“Is there any other way?”

“I ain't no healer. This all I know to do.”

“Then I don’t see we got much choice, Mr. Moice.”

He nodded. “Then I don’t guess we gotta wait no longer. Light be fading soon. Ain't a thing to be doing come sunset.”

“Yes sir, I expect you’re right.”

“Wish I had some whiskey.”

“He’ll be okay.”

"Ain't for him." Moice took a deep breath and told Loli to grab the swollen arm at the hand and to pull. "The ball musta busted the bone here." He indicated just above the elbow. "We cain take it off here and not have no bone to cut."

"You sure?"

"Ain't sure of nothin. You just pull when I say and don't let go no matter what happens."

He retrieved the smaller of the knives from the fire, using his kerchief against the heat of the handle to keep from burning himself. He positioned himself over Taylor's arm, looking like a man about to tussle with a rabid dog or a poison snake. He ignored the flies, which mostly traveled the juicy part of the arm below where he was going to cut. He barely put the knife to the putrid skin and already the smoke started to rise.

"Pull," he said, "pull like you ain't never pulled in all your whole life, girlie."

She glomped on to Taylor's hand with her fingers fisted about it. The hand felt spongy, with more give than a hand should have. She pulled then, hard and steady like he had said, and tried to breathe through her mouth, which only meant she tasted rather than smelled what rose off the lieutenant. Her fingers slid as his skin gave and she had to re-grip. The sound reminded her of a dog licking her fingers. She thought she could puke without much more provocation.

Moice saw and felt the hollow under the skin where the broken ends of bone pulled away from each other. He pressed the knife along the skin and it sank through the rotten flesh, searing as it went. Smoky curls wafted upward.

If Taylor had been near dead, he showed no signs of that now. He came alive, his eyes wide and boiling like a damned, cursed animal. He guttered an obscenity and hollered and thrashed with every piece of bone and sinew his brain commanded, and the rawhide straps pulled taut, relaxed, pulled taut again. The one on his left leg, kitty-corner to the swelled arm, broke and it was as if his leg had been launched into the air. It flailed about with aimless gusto, like the proverbial headless chicken running about the butcher's shed. His shoeless foot kicked this way and that, punching Loli in the belly. She gagged, but her grip on Taylor's hand didn't slip. She held on as if her life depended on it.

Moice cut though the arm as quickly as he could, the smell of burning flesh not unlike last night's spit-roasted varmint. He'd expected more blood and of a sudden that was exactly what he got. The searing stopped but the knife kept going and cut through a vessel somewhere deep inside. A thick stream of bright red blood leapt out then, pulsing over his hands. Moice had only seen that kind of bleeding once in all his life, and he'd passed out in the next instant.

But he didn't pass out now. "Git me another hot knife!"

Loli heard him or didn't, either way she looked half lost. She stared at the arm, at the knife halfway through it, at all the blood. A damn lot of blood.

"Miss Loli!"

She looked at Moice. Her eyes said *Oh My God.*

"Let him go and git another knife so I cain burn him!"

She let go the hand and the arm fell over the side of the cot, where it hung grotesquely by a piece of skin the size of her little finger. She picked up the knife, gathering it in the bunch of her dress, and brought it over to where Moice was holding pressure on the artery.

"You have to do this while I hold the pressure."

"I...I can't." She was crying.

"You has to. I caint do both. Cut the skin what remains, I'll move my hand and you sear the knife against where it's bleeding."

"Oh My God."

"Ain't no God here. Just us heathens doing for ourselves." He looked her in the eye. "It is what it is. Do it now or he gonna cross the river sure. Now!"

She cut the fingerlike band and laid the knife against Moice's hand before he could move it. He inhaled like a man thankful for one more breath and jumped and moved his hand and the blood poured out and she laid the knife square against the vessel and the sound of the sinew and muscle boiling was more than she could take. She fainted.

Moice took hold the hot knife with his own burnt hand and kept it pressed against the stump of Taylor's arm. Taylor, who all this time had been thrashing and carrying-on like a man convulsing, arched his back hard and the cot gave out and they all went to ground as one. Taylor relaxed after that, either passed out or dead.

Moice sat in the dirt, inching over to the shade of the lean-to and trying to catch his breath. He propped himself on Taylor's legs and took up the pieced-off arm and tossed it sideways out the lean-to. He picked up one of the rawhide straps and tied it around Taylor's stump as a tourniquet. What little bleeding remained ceased.

"That woulda made things a piece easier," he said, cursing himself for not thinking of it sooner. He tried to recall if Old Prosper had tied anything around the boy's leg before branding it with the hot poker, but any such memory escaped him. He looked at his own crippled foot then at his burnt fingers and saw already how they were gonna be scarred. It didn't hurt, not yet anyway. He had done well enough all things considered.

After all, he was no healer.

Now came the end of another day and dusk falling and the shadows lengthening. Hannah had spent the entire afternoon putting distance between herself and the dead soldiers at the split rail fence. A long, hot, agitation, that walk, the plentiful dead outnumbered only by the endless minutes, which seemed to pass not at all. Time, like the dead, had become eternal, with the road and everything upon it designed exactly for the purpose of discomposing a person's mind. As if to hike this road was to march to the end of all things. And now dusk, the sun setting, and no promise of a new day to come. It gave a person cause to think it might be the end of the world, come not in a bright ball of light, but as a snuffing out, a great and gathering darkness. Terrible. Terrible.

Hannah had twisted her ankle somewhere between there and here and it ached with every footfall. But mostly it was her mind that ached:

How the rebels had slaughtered those men on the road in cold blood. Union troops. Union dead.

What if Levi had been among them?

What if Levi is, even now, moldering somewhere under the dirt?

She limped along in the dusk and such thoughts had physical weight and pressed her shoulders until she bent as if filled with the arthritis. As the darkness gathered around her, she was no longer a living, breathing being but a bag of bones fit to blow away in the wind. Ashes to ashes, dust to dust.

She came, finally, to the end of the road and the town marking the end. An old signpost, which had for all time straddled the road and announced the name of the town to those who came calling, lay splintered and broken in the dirt, all save the first two letters which dangled overhead and moved back and forth in the wind—a thing that was broken and didn't yet know it. Ray Miller's buckboard wagon, she recognized the brand painted on the side, lay tumbled and worthless in the ditch. Beside it a near-dead ox bleated and raised its ugly head and blood trickled from one of its oversized nostrils. The rotted egg smell of sulfur suffused the air and the ash floating in it gritted Hannah's teeth and made swallowing a chore. A fire smoldered in the ruins of a building and she tried to recall what the building had been but couldn't cull the memory.

She entered the town and it didn't recognize her. She had walked these same streets a hundred times and more, had prayed kneeling in the pews of the church on Main Street. But as she moved among the shadows at twilight, she was as much a piece of wreckage as the cracked bell lying in the middle of the street.

A person, then another, passed her and they paid her no more mind than they would a stray dog. She didn't recognize them nor they her. Perhaps, by her scavenged clothes, they thought her a soldier gone wandering. They no doubt had their own worries.

A dark town. One could count the lit lanterns on a single hand. Occasionally, a lucifer flared for an instant or the glow of a candle passed ghostlike behind an otherwise dark window. Battle implements littered the ground: knapsacks, broken muskets, cartridge boxes, an overturned caisson, unexploded artillery shells, much more besides. There was a dead mutt, too, and this caught her mind. She wondered if it might not be her pa's thin-ribbed dog. Enoch was four months dead but that was how she still thought of the dog, as Enoch's. It looked more the size of old Mr. Hound Dog though, a bastard animal that had wandered into town a decade before and called home ever since. It was too dark to make out any detail, and the thing too corrupted by death in any event. A cloud of flies engulfed the remains and she let it be and circled wide around it.

A block further on and the street narrowed and a shutter banged in the wind. The bugs were a nuisance as ever and dust devils danced before her. She heard the patter of feet over wooden sidewalks. A child, from the sound of it. She turned a corner and it was as if the three story brick building passed her and not the other way around. The glass at the front, which had proclaimed *The Granger Hotel* in fancy gold script, lay shattered. Bits of trash and paper bumped along the street and the wind tinkled a chime and caught an old door somewhere—it clanged over and over but never latched. She squinted and rubbed at the pitted masonry beside what had been the front door of the hotel. A score of bullet pocks.

A child giggled and the sound carried up the dark street and echoed off the walls.

"Who's there? Show yourself or be moving on, else I'll put a hole in you where you stand." She had no weapon, but she couldn't see them and so neither could they see her she figured.

A head poked out a second floor window only long enough to know it was there, then disappeared.

"I seen you," she hollered. "I know you're there."

The town moved around her and her eyes darted to and fro in the darkness. She felt herself watched. She sat down on the burned out remains of an old fainting couch.

After a time a boy appeared in the middle of the street before her. Maybe ten years old. He came of a sudden, out of nowhere. Dirty and worn looking, his face and chest smudged black the color of coal. No shoes, trousers held up by suspenders crisscrossed over his shoulders. "You one of those Gamble girls, ain't you?" the boy said in a sure tone.

"Hannah. Only it's Griel now. I been married a year."

"Yeah, I know. I was at your weddin.'"

"And you be?" He stood ten feet away and neither of them moved.

"Jeremiah Penn, but folks call me JP. You best to come with me."

"The minister's boy?"

"Yeah."

"He said some words over my pa just not long ago when we put him in the ground."

"I recall."

"Where is he, your pa?"

"My pa's dead."

Hannah said nothing.

"Best we get off this street."

"Yeah."

He stayed always to the shadows and blended to his surroundings better than she had imagined a person could. She followed, her movements not nearly so fluid. They stood across from the large church on Main Street within a few minutes. Under the quarter moon and against the chasing clouds, the damaged steeple stood stark and tall and inflamed and perhaps not a little foreboding. Having been struck by at least one shell, the side facing the street had splintered and crumbled so that the inner studs were plainly seen. Several of the supports were busted clean through and the empty bell tower leaned queer to one side. The entire building seemed about to heave over, like a ship listing too far. But it was the granite steps that caught her eye. Even in the dim light a person could see something had happened there. The middle part of the gray stone was soiled dark, a splotch which seemed to have run downhill from step to step.

"There, that's what happened to my pa." JP pointed with an outstretched arm.

Hannah looked at the spot, didn't speak. Her mind registered the steps, the dark spot. But there seemed nothing beyond that, no import. She knew what he was saying, but she couldn't credit it. She looked to the boy, who had continued on and stood beside a large door.

"We go in here."

She hesitated, then stepped into the poorly lit nave. Once she was inside, the odor was pungent and unmistakable. Smoke curled through the rafters from a fire in one corner and in its iridescent light, the place looked more a sick room than a church, more a slaughterhouse than a hospital. Most of the pews were stacked to one side and puddles of vomit or shit or whatever were scattered about and blood marred the place everywhere—fingerprints on the walls, streaks on the floor where sufferers had been dragged or perhaps dragged themselves, large blots where they'd rested for any period of time. The shape of a man, long and lanky with two legs and two arms, was outlined in blood on the floor in front of them.

At first, the walls seemed to want to close in on her. The air was so thick she could taste it and she choked. She drew breath and wanted to run but it was as if her legs had gone dumb all at once. A leaf fell from above and she watched it flutter all the way to the floor, all the time holding her breath as it curled and looped on the unseen air. She looked up, retracing the leaf's path, and saw a yawning hole in the ceiling, the sky above.

She took a breath, then another.

A dozen or so men grouped on the floor in the middle of the room and the sight of them was not a thing to bring comfort. An elderly woman kneeled beside the group, supporting a man's head as he sipped water from a tin she put to his lips. There was a dirty, red rag tied around his skull and his eyes were listless holes in his face.

The old lady barely looked up, speechless. She seemed only to be looking at Hannah, her eyes washed out and mute. She could have been blind. She stood only very slowly, the way a person bad with the rheumatism will stand, all the while rubbing at the worst of his or her pain. Her tattered dress testified to her efforts over the previous day and more. The pattern was a brown weave of cotton, same as the rag on the man's head and several others besides.

The old lady eyed the boy, who shook his head up and down in quick, jerky movements. "I brought someone, Gramps. Like you wanted."

The washed out eyes turned back to Hannah. "You here to help?" She wasn't blind after all.

"Help?"

"Could use it," the woman said, extending an arm and motioning around her. Her hand was knobby and crooked, the fingers twisted and bony and useless looking. Hannah had never imagined such a hand.

The men breathed loudly, if at all, and one or two shook with chills. Those who cared or those who could turned their heads and stared. A man with both legs splinted and a dark circle of some unmentionable on the floor around him extended a naked arm toward her. The hand shook with a coarse tremor.

Hannah came forward and knelt and took his hand. His skin was much warmer than she'd expected and she knelt farther to feel his forehead. "He's hot with fever."

"Yes, yes. They all is. They all are."

"How long you been here?"

"A night and two days near as I guess. Could be longer. Ain't less."

"These men, they belong in a hospital."

"Yes, a hospital." The old lady rubbed at the small of her back and her eyes took on that blind look again. "Now, you going to make yourself useful or just stand there jawing?"

TWELVE

Purdy Gamble sat half-silhouetted, one side of her face flickering orange in the light of the fire, the other dark to the night. In a plate of mostly cold beans she stirred a near raw strip of bacon with a hard-tack biscuit. She stopped every now and again to pick a blowfly out with her fingertips. These flies, drawn by open wounds, were as big around as her knuckles.

Her eyes adjusted and she stared out over the yard. Small campfires dotted the ground and men congregated around them, perhaps by way of avoiding the insects, which were a nuisance even so. A group at one fire had a deck of cards and one of the players doled them out while the others sat close-mouthed and waited. A soldier with torn trousers and a bandaged leg leaned against a wagon a dozen paces in front of her. He, or somebody in his stead, had fashioned a crude crutch out of a tree limb and when he placed it under his arm he hobbled about better than one might have expected. The wagon he leaned on was the cook's and Purdy could hear the small words of easy conversation between this hobbled man and the cook, whom she saw only in outline. The cook was big at the chest and bigger at the waist, and waddled rather than walked. He spat in the dirt and ladled out plates of beans and bacon fat from a large iron pot set on rocks over a wood fire. The hobbled man poured coffee from a scorched kettle simmering beside the pot. The smell of that coffee reached her only fleetingly, at such moments as the breeze was right to push away the stink. The wood for the fires had come from the fence behind the barn, and perhaps from the barn itself, or from anything else that would burn. Another trace of Enoch gone to the ages. She spooned a mouth of beans and wondered where Coal had got himself off to. The boy had been scarce for several hours or maybe several minutes, she couldn't recall. For a wicked moment, she couldn't remember what Enoch had looked like either. She trembled.

The click of Major Brody's brace preceded him. The surgeon appeared out of the shadows and stood with his braced leg before the cook and the hobbled fellow, holding out his own hand like a beggar. Only he didn't look like one. No, he had the same impeccable, polished manner about him as he'd had in her front room the first time they'd met. His sleeves were rolled up above his elbows and his forearms slick with sweat and here and there dried blood stuck to his front. Wet blood too. Even so, he wore exhaustion well. A man no doubt familiar with guts and glory and all the innards of war. He held out a hand and in it was one of Purdy's own coffee mugs. "I could use some coffee," he said, the words coming plain and bold and no exhaustion at all.

It was more than she could take and she flung the plate aside and rose all in one motion. She crossed the several feet to the wagon as the hobbled man poured the mug full and hot. "You oughtta try dese beans," the cook was saying as she came on.

"You don't gotta take it all, goddammit," she said.

Brody either hadn't noticed her or hadn't cared to notice her to that point. She stood before him at arm's length. A thick strand of hair had fallen down before one eye and her face was smudged with dirt.

"Beg pardon?" he said at last.

"That's mine. Dammit, that cup is mine."

"I would be obliged, madam, if you would just let us be."

"I bet you would. That's my cup and I aim to have it."

"Corporal, I believe I will have some of those beans," Brody said as he looked very deliberately at Purdy. He took a sip of the coffee, careful-like so as not to burn his tongue, and tossed the rest in the dirt with a flip of his wrist. "Your cup, madam."

She took it and held it with both hands, like she was pulling the warmth from it. "Damn you people."

"Perhaps you would care to join me at my tent," Brody said.

She looked at him, not quite sure what he had in mind by the invite. She wiped the hair from before her eyes. "Why in hell would I wanna do that?"

"I would like to talk is all. It is just there." He pointed.

The hobbled soldier poured another coffee, this in an army issue tin cup, and passed it to the surgeon. He grinned as if he and the surgeon shared an unspoken secret.

"Talk is all," Brody said as he took the proffered cup. With his plate in one hand and the coffee in the other, he walked past Purdy. His brace clicked and he walked with a slight limp and didn't look back to see if she followed.

His tent was of canvas the color of dirty snow. Tall enough along the middle for a person to stand in, it sloped down at the sides. A single cot, a folding chair, a small writing desk of the sort that could be folded easily for travel, and a trunk filled out the space. It smelled heavily of the countryside and of leather. He sat down on the cot and reached to slip his boots off then perhaps thought otherwise and gestured for her to take the chair. She remained standing. He sipped the coffee and played at the beans with a fork, apparently deciding to work his boots off after all. "I apologize for the boots but I have been standing for a long time and, well..." His voice trailed, then picked up again. "We do not wish to inconvenience you."

"Ha ha."

"I did not imagine this to be a laughing matter, madam."

"Nor I, sir. But Goddamn you people."

"We are only trying to survive, same as you all. I am sorry."

"You got a damn funny way of showing it. What're you sorry for, major? For the murder of my husband? Or for thieving my farm? Or I suppose it could be about my missing daughters? Is that what you're sorry for, Goddammit? You sorry for these young women what never had a care in the world to hurt any folk, who for all I know been damned to hell by your people?"

"Is there any word about them?"

"Hannah. Their names are Hannah and Loli. Loli's only fourteen." Purdy stopped, looked away, looked back. She could feel herself going mad in that small tent. See herself grabbing that bastard of a surgeon and squeezing the life out of him. "Damn you people. Why'd you have to come here?"

"I am sorry. Must be hard for you—"

"You've no idea."

He took her gaze and returned it. The air boiled between them and he set the coffee down on the trunk, spilling a bit along the way. He set the plate beside the coffee and stood up. "That is just it, madam. I have every idea. You see, this war, whatever you think it has done to you and yours, I have seen it a hundred times over and a thousand times worse. I have seen boys die like dogs in fallow wheat fields across this fair countryside. Saw a woman birthing in the midst of battle, saw her baby shot through the head before he could take his first breath. I saw another woman—no older than your Hannah she was—smother her own child while trying to hide. That one, she never said a word after that and threw herself in front of a train two days later after getting word her husband was killed fighting with Jackson in the Shenandoah. Was not a piece left big enough to bury.

I have seen boys no older than that one you got die more often than I care to remember, though I do remember. I remember that always the last words on their breath are for their girl back home, or maybe they cry for their mothers. I have seen every kind of ugly a man can do to another man. That is what war is all about, doing ugly. You want I should go on? I can, madam. At length. Of that, I assure you."

"Goddamn you."

"It is just your turn in the barrel is all."

"You've killed my family. I'd be obliged to have you rot in hell if'n it was up to me."

"Madam, I am already in hell."

Hannah sat the edge of one of the overturned pews. The church creaked in the clear night and the stars twinkled down through the rent in the roof. She watched the old lady move between the soldiers. Despite her crippled hands and bad back, she made herself useful in many small and not so small ways. She spooned gruel into a soldier's mouth and tightened the tourniquet about another's thigh. She adjusted the bandages over a man's belly and held his member as he pissed red in a bucket. Hannah couldn't bring herself to do any of these things at first and so she looked for other things to occupy her mind, small things like the roach making its way over the worn plank floor, or the peculiar shape of a blood spot on the wall (which looked decidedly like Levi in profile). She found herself crying in little whimpers.

But the wretched men huddled together at the base of the altar wouldn't go away. They stayed in her thoughts and sights despite anything she could do to the contrary. She'd have left except the one thing that troubled her more was the night, and what might be out in it.

A filthy, unkempt bunch, they ranged from a fellow whose only visible wound was a busted and offset lower jaw, to a shirtless soldier whose chest whistled with each breath. This last youngster had a distinct blue hue about his face and neck and seemed to be failing, albeit very slowly. Another was unconscious and when he moved it was only to tense his arms and legs in rigid, board-like tantrums. Pieces of ugly looking gray matter bulged out his skull behind one ear every time he tensed. Hannah had never seen brain before, but she thought if a person could imagine what brain might look like they'd do well to imagine the gray slime she saw now. In fact, there were all kinds of innards here she'd never seen before.

She began to move among the men and learned that exposed bone glistens white, not unlike gristle chewed clean; that some open vessels spurt, while others only leak or dribble. A sergeant shot through the pelvis and unable to pee moaned incessantly. His lower belly grew big as the night progressed so that he might have passed as six months with child. Near midnight, she let a boy lay his head in her lap for a while. She stroked his face and thought of Levi, prayed he had somewhere to rest his head. The boy's breathing was raspy, the air oozing laboriously in and out of lungs that were all but used up. It seemed a sputtering kind of existence at the fringe of life.

"Please," the boy said after a long interval. His features were gaunt and hollow, eyes glassy and wandering, skin a dusky gray. Tiny, dirt-filled globules of sweat rose over his skin. A sour odor not unlike rancid vomit came off him. Hannah wondered if he might be purging himself in preparation for death. She had not known a body could do such a thing.

"How can I help?" she asked.

The boy's throat bobbed up and down with a long swallow and his hand, which had been quiet at his side, quivered and crept toward his breast. Hannah moved to help and clasped the hand. “There now, I got you.” She reached into the boy’s soiled jacket and withdrew a hard lump.

She held a flat case, smaller than her palm, with an ornate pattern of whirls, leaves, and flowers molded into the hard exterior. She undid the clasp and it opened to reveal an ambrotype. The woman within was seated with arms crossed, one elbow propped on a table. Her plain, dark dress was full length, with long sleeves and a lace bodice. The glass was cracked diagonally across her bosom.

Even in the washed out dullness of the picture, her beauty was plain.

Hannah turned the picture toward the boy’s eyes, which focused for the first time. He reached out for the ambrotype. She directed him and the boy took the case, his thumb pressing against the woman. Perhaps he felt for the crack, like a touchstone. A tear appeared big at the corner of his eye and rolled down his cheek. He stiffened and whispered: “Skin the fair color of peach blossoms, hair soft as the finest silk.” The color ran out of him and he wilted. “A beauty I would die for. Oh Carrie Mae, know that I died for you, that it was all for you.”

The boy’s hand clasped tightly around the glass, reluctant to leave. A moment later he was gone.

Hannah gently pushed his head aside and laid it on the floor careful so it wouldn’t knock, as if that might disturb him. But he was beyond disturbing now.

She closed his lids with a timid hand. Then closed the case and placed it back in his pocket. She rose.

It was the middle of the night and the old lady lay asleep in the corner. Her twisted hands, stilled and deformed, lay in her lap. Hours before, Hannah could not have imagined such hands good for anything. Now she knew better. They could still comfort, could still press a cool cloth to a poor unfortunate's cheek. For the first time in days, Baby Noah was far from her mind.

It didn't last though, and she couldn't sleep. She paced the nave and her footfalls echoed in the darkness. She thought of Minister Penn, JP's father, standing in the pulpit. A heavyset fellow with long salt and pepper burnsides and a lisp that made his t's roll into r's whenever he got his ire up, which was every Sunday. She hadn't known him well, but he'd always seemed prayerful, if conspicuous, and why he should have been shot down like a dog in the street troubled her. JP was now an orphan. It was common knowledge the boy's mother had died a few years before.

The stink of the slop buckets permeated the close air and finally got to her. This was one thing she could change, but it seemed JP couldn't sleep either and he met her as she went about this task. "Here, let me do that," the boy said. He knelt beside her, taking the weight of the bucket.

"Thank you," Hannah said. "I'm sorry about your pa."

"It was rebel soldiers what did it. He tried to stop 'em coming into town and they killed 'im."

"God be with you. God and all his mercy."

"I seen 'em do it. Didn't see no mercy in that bunch. Damn secesh."

The boy had no tears. His face took on a peculiar expression. Later she would think he'd looked rancid—*looked the way a piece of turned meat smells*—but just then she didn't know how to credit it.

"I'll just go empty this," he said, stumbling over the statement. She watched him go and he didn't turn back.

She made her way to the back of the church. The window there was sooty and cracked and a large piece had fallen away. She looked through and saw the boy in the alley, saw him dump the slops. He turned to come back in, but something just out of her view seemed to grab his attention. She rubbed at the dirty glass and saw a man's legs revealed, just visible beyond a woodpile. One foot was shoeless and a sickly blue-black. The other showed a dingy, gray trouser leg. The toes were wiggling.

A late night mist had settled over the alley, dense enough to obscure her vision by half or more. But she saw enough to note a change in the boy, see his shoulders square and his back straighten. She watched, uncertain what to make of it. She couldn't see his face clearly, only that his lips were writhing with hard, grimacing movement. That's when her heart whomped and the idea he'd turned popped unbidden into her mind.

He reached into the pile and took a piece of wood and held it high overhead.

"No!" Hannah rubbed hard at the glass, as if she could wipe what she was seeing clean away.

It took her thirty seconds, no more, to get through the back door and out into the mist. When she reached the woodpile, she saw the boy was speckled with blood. He could have been bleeding, but she knew better.

Too late. Oh God.

She turned to the soldier on the ground beside JP. He wore frayed butternut. He was quivering—his arms and legs danced in jerky, coarse movements—a death spasm that made her think of a turkey at slaughtering time. His face was a pulpy mess and teeth lay in the dirt beside him. A wet crop of blondish, now bloody, whiskers stood out amidst his busted, jutting chin. The dying man's face—and he was dying, no doubt about that—was an unrecognizable piece of hell on earth. Save for the uniform, it could have been Levi lying there.

Hannah shivered.

Beside the woodpile, the soldier stopped quivering. The dirt under him puddled red and the stream of blood from his torn scalp gave out to a trickle, then nothing.

It was not a thing she wanted to see and she looked away. To JP, standing in the alleyway, the piece of wood still tight in one hand, stained red."What have you done, boy?" she whispered.

"I seen 'im, seen this bastard shoot my pa."

"I ain't a part of this," Hannah said, her head up and speaking more to herself than the boy.

"He asked for mercy. I showed 'im the same kinda mercy he showed my pa."

The air went out of her lungs. She could only breathe in great gasps and these were an effort. She felt a rising panic, but it wasn't for her, wasn't even for the boy. It was for all of them. No, she thought, that's not true.

It's for Levi.

"I gotta go." She turned and there was the old lady at the broken window, her face only quarterwise visible.

She wondered again about Levi, whether he was alive. She thought about all the dead she'd seen on the way into town, about the armies marching against each other, killing one another. She wondered if there were different kinds of killing—different kinds of *murder*. She finally decided there must be, else how was it that in one time and place a man shot or knifed or clubbed his fellow and got a medal, in another the hangman's noose?

She walked past the old lady, who was standing at the door now and holding her crippled hands out to her, and down the alley. JP stood alone beside the woodpile, still hollering something about mercy as she turned the corner and walked into the black night toward God knew what.

Loli opened her eyes. In the darkness she could just make out the weedy earth of the thatched roof above. Somewhere in the space around her, the night creaked and she soon saw it was the rocking chair moving back and forth. A dark figure rode it. A negro man sitting in darkness.

Moice rose and came to her.

Her head rose off the pillow and she said, "Mr. Taylor, my friend—"

"He still lives. I ain't sayin how long though. He's some tough."

She fell back. "How long I been sleeping?"

"Some hours. I made a stew. Ain't much, might help some though."

Moice lit a candle and the small room brightened. He brought her the stew and she slurped it half sitting, half lying down. It was only lukewarm but that was warm enough. Taylor lay in the corner by the fireplace, looking as if he'd been disguised as a pile of rags or old blankets.

"Fever broke. He'll sleep the night through I'm guessin', maybe longer."

"Thank you."

"Y'all cain thank me by leaving come first light."

"Mr. Moice, why don't you come with us?"

"I be taking you to the road. You'll find your way okay from there."

"No, I mean why don't you come back with us?"

"There ain't nothing out theres for me. This here all the home I got, Miss Loli. All the home I need too."

She could tell he was looking past her as he spoke, out yonder. "Who's buried out there?"

"I told you I would take you to the road. You best git your rest fer traveling." He blew the candle out and returned to the chair and its back and forth creaking filled the room again.

Loli closed her eyes. As she descended into a dream filled sleep, she thought she heard her father singing to her.

After a while, Moice cleared his throat. "It is what it is," he said in a soft voice, and the room fell silent save for a few creatures stirring in the ceiling thatch. And the creak of the rocker.

THIRTEEN

On the Gamble farm, morning announced itself as the harsh screech of the surgeon's saw against bone. Awful to hear, impossible to ignore. As the sun came over the horizon, haloed by a dawn mist, Purdy realized she had gained an ability to sort out which bone the surgeons were sawing on at a given instant. The large thigh bone produced a low hum, not unlike the rumble of far off cannon. The whine of the less bulky lower leg bones was higher, like a horde of bumble bees coming on fast. The upper arm warbled higher still and the forearm highest of all, a taut violin string as played by the surgeon's saw/bow. Purdy cursed herself to have such knowledge, a useless and wholly unsavory bit of learning. She wished she could forget it and would have lived the rest of her days deaf in the exchange.

A mizzling rain began to fall. For a brief time at least, it would cleanse the air. In it creatures great and small, from the tiniest insects to the wounded soldiers yet peopling the battlefields, found the stuff of life. It was a small gift from the heavens, a momentary respite from all that had preceded it.

A lull before all that must follow.

Hannah passed a bad night.

Sometime in the wee hours cramping started low in her loins. She tossed and turned in the rain-swept darkness, the ground soggy and saturated and everywhere a skim of water. She lay with two strangers at the stumped remains of a tree and the fire which had warmed them and others in the early hours drowned in the storm and so the three curled round one another seeking warmth.

She woke shivering in the wormy hours after midnight to the rough feel of a hand cupping her tit, squeezing and not squeezing, then squeezing again. The only warmth the sickly-scented breath at her neck, which came hot and guttural, a feral animal in heat. She squirmed but the stump blocked her and the man thrust against her.

"Move away!" She elbowed his chest and he of a sudden let go and rolled backwards. His hair lay ragged and slick with muddy ooze, his face appearing half-rotted in the slop of rain and whiskers. She lay staring at him, what she could see of him anyway, and he lay not quite staring back, hands busy at his trousers, finishing himself what he'd started. He had a gamy look, eyes blazing and foul, hand going all the while.

She breathed and said not a word, kept her eyes on him the whole time.

He finished with an intake of breath and a groan—he was missing several teeth—giving her that look the whole time. He wiped his hands on his underthings and arranged himself, pulling his pants square and buttoning his front. He wiped his forehead with the back of his hand and the skin showed white where the mud peeled away like a laceration opening up. He cursed her now he was done, a single word that came out low and throaty, then spat out the side of his mouth, repulsed or disgusted, she knew not which. He rose and muttered how she wasn't worth the trouble and moved off.

She sat upright against the stump. The other fellow, whose complexion resembled in some altogether clear but unutterable way that of a toad, and who might have been sleeping through all of this sordid business, brushed her leg in his stupor and she tensed and kicked him in the stones. He grunted and came up swinging clumsy like a boozer and she pushed him face down in the muck and kicked him in the ass, then his ribs. He stayed down and might have drowned like a bug in a slop jar had she not grabbed him by the hair and twisted his head sideways, whereupon she punched him with a closed fist and his nose began to leak bloody snot.

She stood and made her way to one of the army latrines, which wasn't hard to find for the stench of it. Four walls of dirty canvas and a hole dug in the dirt and a splintery plank for a seat. She eyeballed the board and squatted without sitting and did her business trying to hold her breath, all the while being rained on. Not too much later she found a corner beside a sutler's wagon and shivered the rest of the night through, sleeping in fitful little moments here and there.

Come sun up the air was misty and wet. Her jaw and teeth were sore from chattering. The sound of stirring roused her and she opened her eyes and looked out on the compound and there wasn't a single soul she knew among those either gathered or passing through the clearing. The men, and they were all men, passed by as nothing more than nameless faces in the crowd, the best of them bloodied, mud filthy, or generally looking mussed and rumpled. They paid her not one whit with her tangled mess of hair and dead soldier's shirt for a blouse, baggy enough to hide whatever girlish shape lay underneath. She wore as well a dead man's trousers and these too were filthy. She had become one of them, part of the walking wounded.

She smelled of sweat and sulfur and something that might have been hog droppings she couldn't otherwise place. Not all her; the camp reeked. She washed her face in the skim of water that everywhere made the ground a misery. What looked back at her in the puddle was unrecognizable. She watched a lizard scurry at her feet and wondered that it hadn't drowned.

A man passed her, his chest bared save for the swath of pink bandage wrapping his torso. He was bald with a sunburned head and he moved slow and deliberate as he approached her with a look like he was fixing to say something. He got right up close and though he grimaced once or twice, he went right on by and never did say a thing. He looked back though, and on his face was the first smile she'd seen in seven days that might not have been rancid or lustful. She couldn't bring herself to smile back.

The sun was a long time coming up through the mist, or perhaps the mist was a long time burning off. Either way, the morning dragged like a day that never was meant to be in the first place. Her cramping continued and she counted the days in her head, or tried to anyway for she'd lost track.

"Damn," she said, feeling the moisture buried within and the twist of another cramp as she looked about for something she could use.

There weren't any women about, not even townsfolk women. Too early or the day too awful or they were too far from town or maybe there were just too many wounded. Maybe the town wasn't there anymore. Or they had their own problems, which she decided had to be the case. She thought of her mother and Loli and Coal. Then of baby Noah and she felt as lonely as she'd ever felt in her whole life entire.

Lonely but not alone. The world a too close place and never less alone in her life. Men standing around everywhere, some half-naked, some crouched or sitting on the ground. A mishmash of boy soldiers and old men lying supine or prone or turned one-side-up as if waiting to be basted. Men leaning against trees. Men in the trees, young soldiers who'd climbed to the lower branches and straddled or sat side saddle like they had maybe done before the war. A sutler beside his wagon, some kind of small furry animal scurrying about beside him, tethered on a rope. Like a darkie boy but too small. The thing danced around peeling peanuts between its teeth and perfect little fingers. A crowd gathered to watch.

Hannah wasn't fascinated with whatever the creature was. Not a damn fascinating thing in all the camp. Something squeezed deep inside her and she closed her eyes, willing it to go away, needing it to go away. It passed and she felt the first stirrings of warm dampness at her crotch.

Loli Gamble followed Moice as he pulled a litter through the final remnants of swamp. They'd lashed the still unconscious Ben Taylor to the makeshift stretcher hours before in the dark and had been picking their way along ever since. Moice apparently knew the bog better than Loli knew her own yard. Despite his burden, which she recalled included only half a foot, he moved with a deliberate speed she found exasperating. He seemed to have in mind getting to some place in particular, some place well away from where they had started. By sun up she supposed they'd covered two miles.

They rested just long enough to eat a biscuit and drink powdered dandelion coffee mixed with a bit of roasted chicory. Taylor was ever out of his head, mumbling something only he knew. As she had in the early morning, she parted his lips and poured a cup of the dandelion drink down his throat. He coughed but the liquid found its way and he seemed satisfied with the offering. The swelling in his stump had gone down by half or more overnight. Less stink too.

They walked without talking. Every once and again Moice would raise his hand by way of cautioning her. They would stop and he would survey the trees and the land before them. They might turn a step or two in one direction or another before moving on. But always they moved and gradually the ground began to dry out, to feel more substantial under foot. At last they came in sight of a road of sorts, nothing more than a cow path.

They halted still within the trees and Moice let his burden slide to the ground and sipped something from a pouch unslung from his shoulder. "Your pa, he were a good man."

"Much obliged."

"You follow this here road a long piece, tills you git to a old willer tree, the likes of which you caint forget once seeing it. Big thing, was there a long time before you or me or even anybody we ever did know in our whole lives entire. Burnt some on one side too."

"I know that tree."

"Good. You cain find your way then?"

"Ain't far after that. I guess I can. Whyn't you come with us?"

"I done tole you that ain't gonna happen."

"But you saved his life."

"No I ain't and don't you go telling no one I did. You hear? Far as anyone else knows, that arm was blowed off by a cannon."

"Why?"

"Cause that's just how it gotta be. I ain't looking to git dead."

"Well, I can't carry him on my own."

"Then he ain't goin nowhere."

Loli thought on that a moment. "How come my pa didn't never tell me nothing bout you?"

"Why for? He knowed the way of things. Look, don't fret none. The world is what it is. 'Bout time you unnerstand that. You best git to moving now. Take this wit you."

"Well it's a stupid world," she said, and took the pouch of drinking water he was offering.

"Yeah, likely is. It ain't the world though, it's the people what's in the world. Stupid. Ain't no law against bein stupid."

She stood and extended a hand. "Good-bye then, Mr. Moice."

He gave her a small knap, rolled and lumpy. "A few vittles for the road," he said, then added, "Good-bye, Miss Loli. Keep to the trees where you can." He took her hand in both of his. "You be careful, missy. What's out there's a whole lotta world, and mostly it contains a whole lotta hurt."

She put the food in her blouse and nodded and he stepped back quick, like one anxious to be rid of something. He disappeared back the way they'd come.

She looked down at Taylor, who appeared a damn sight better than he'd looked a day before. Not well of course, but a damn sight better just the same. She wiped her hand across his mouth, at a bit of droll spilling out the corner. He stirred and his eyes flickered but didn't open.

She looked up the road and saw not a soul. The wind had picked up and was beginning to work the trees hard. The drizzle had been replaced by something more substantial as well. She fingered Moice's pouch, for luck she told herself, and took up one end of the litter and pointed herself toward home and stepped out of the tree line and onto the muddy lane.

She thought, *it is what it is,* and moved out.

The messenger rode up on horseback, the rain and wind to his backside making his clothes all astir. Sitting the horse he had had the look of one tired beyond his years, but when he swung down Purdy saw he was no more than a boy who had aged poorly. She supposed that's what war did to a person, aged him and aged him poorly.

Under the brim of Enoch's preacher hat, she watched the stranger, a Confederate with a uniform that fit him better than most she'd seen, as he moved among the aides and the wounded. He sidled around a pile of thrown-away arms and legs and seemed indifferent to the suffering of the place, as if he'd seen it all before. It occurred to her then that he *had* seen it all before, probably too many times. She wondered what he'd do after the war with all the images he must have in his head.

The messenger trudged through the mud and entered the house around back. He walked right past her at the old water pump and up the steps into the kitchen. He did it without hesitating, as if he knew his way in such a place, and didn't bother even to wipe his feet. She lost him after he went inside, but he wasn't gone more than a minute before he returned and trudged back the way he'd come. He'd left his horse hobbled to a small bush and he untied it and slicked some of the water off the saddle and climbed back up and trotted out without any more ado. He rode not so much like a man in a hurry as one anxious to be quit of a place.

She watched him ride out, not at all sure why she cared. Perhaps envious he could leave. She might leave too given the chance, then knew she wouldn't. She wasn't made that way. This was her home. Enoch's home. Their home. She took the preacher hat off and the rain slicked her hair and wet her face. Oddly lukewarm but good feeling.

The rain, which had been steady but mizzling all the long morning, intensified around suppertime. Tarps were put up and the operations continued with hardly an interruption. The fighting had largely ceased the day before, but the wounded continued to come in droves and the lines grew longer as the hours passed.

So too the number of dead grew and in the July heat and humidity something had to be done. They were buried on the sloped hillside overlooking Old Dutch Road, in Enoch

Gamble's front yard, all but at his doorstep. Rain or shine, the holes were dug and men planted in graves marked only by the fresh turned earth. The most useful implement for miles around was a spade.

The major gave use of his tent over to Purdy and she spent the better part of the day on the cot, sick and unable to bring herself to witness the work of the hospital. She slept restless or not at all, keeping an ear all the while for Hannah or Loli. Coal made himself of some use with the cook, who had taken a liking to the boy for some reason not altogether clear. Purdy didn't argue the matter when she saw the boy moving back and forth between the cook's wagon, the house, and the barn. For him to be useful, even to these unwanted strangers, was perhaps a blessing. *It is what it is.* Enoch's words exactly.

"It is what it is," she said aloud, trying to mimic his tone as well as the words. It gave her pause to remember such things. She wished she had one of his smokes. She lay on the cot and slid his leather hat down over her face and smelled what was left of him.

Whatever remains it is enough. God how she missed that man.

She lay on the cot and the pattering of rain on the canvas was not enough to drown the noise of the soil being turned around her. As the shovels did their bidding they clinked and slid into the earth with little hahs that sounded like the last gasps of the dying. She thought of baby Noah, poor dead Noah, buried over yonder in a too shallow grave after a too short life.

The world around me is more dead than alive. She closed her eyes and for the first time in five days she cried.

Of a sudden the pattering rain sound gave way to a deafening SWOOSH, followed by an intense crackling. The world outside the tent livened up and a raucous noise overtook everything. A sound both strange and familiar at once, it forced its way through the ears and pressed generally upon the brain, like an inflammation of the worst sort.

Purdy was up and out of the tent in the single beat of her heart. She looked one way and then the other, the intense heat near unbearable and forcing her sideways. A skunk, a few squirrels, and a score of other rodents scurried past her feet and she turned in time to see a burning man and then another stagger out of the tinderbox that was Enoch's barn. Fingers of flame raced up the side of the structure in seconds—nothing on God's earth could have gotten out of their way. A tree alongside the burning barn caught and for a moment it looked as if the hillside might go up generally.

Another man, this one of slighter build, moved crabwise out of the inferno as one of the barn's side walls collapsed inward and showered sparks to the sky. He was the last to make it out, for despite the rain the flames were intense and scalding and there was no time to get the wounded clear. Their cries as they cooked were mercifully short but haunting.

"My God in heaven," Purdy said, making the sign of the cross in the air.

She followed the burning men across the yard as they staggered. One went headlong into a tent and it too burned and in the ensuing mayhem another tent and the cook's wagon caught as well. One of the burnt, he of the slighter build, stumbled about with a spastic lurch. It brought a bilious nausea to her and then her lunch came up as she realized what and who she was looking at.

"Coal!" She went to him even as others wrestled him to the muddy ground.

One of the men died immediately, which could only be called a blessing by any sane man's way of reckoning. Another lingered, his clothes burned off so that he lay before them naked and blackened. The skin of his arms and back was blistered at best and charred at worst. He made a ghastly sight and didn't have a prayer of surviving an hour.

It would have been merciful to bury him then and there someone said. The others didn't disagree.

Coal's eyes were open. His face had taken the flames badly and the whites of those eyes looked intense and bright against the blistering, like fried eggs in a charred skillet. His lips had that dead blue hue again and he was moaning something guttural, all the time sounding out of his head, as if he had learned some foreign tongue whilst being incinerated. His hair had burned away and the spot the mule had kicked all those years back pulsed in and out like a poor man's measure of what life he had left in him. The flames had mostly incinerated his shirt and poached the skin of his trunk and bad arm so that they had reddened and blistered worse even than his face. He lay on the wet earth smoldering, wearing nothing more than soiled undies and a pair of old shoes.

She thought to hold him, but as she tried he grimaced and didn't quite blink. His orbits closed down a skosh, sank inward before moving outward again. Unsinking as it were. She stared aghast, bending forward so as to make herself big in his eyes. She took hold of his good hand, the entire arm almost untouched by burns. Coal stared back, but when she moved to and fro his eyes stayed put and when he tried to blink it was mostly just a suggestion of closing and the pupils rolled up and the whites filled those eyes. She had a bad moment when she realized the truth of it.

He no longer had eyelids.

FOURTEEN

The rain, lukewarm in the humid air, fell hard to the ground and rose again as steam. It rolled out and around Loli and the lieutenant and hugged the ground like smoke obscuring a battlefield.

She dragged onward but ever slower and the road muck clotted her shoes and made walking a chore. The rain had soaked her to her very marrow and every time she looked back at Taylor on the litter he seemed not to have moved. She convinced herself she was pulling a dead man but couldn't bring herself to confirm it. Snot clogged her nose and ran over her upper lip and filled her mouth and it was all she could do to get a breath. She'd been crying for a mile or more. Or maybe she had only covered half that distance. A body couldn't tell distance in a steamy rain.

She'd feared she'd miss the willow in the rain, but it was there all the same, as royal and ancient as it had always looked. Twisted, gnarled, misshapen, gigantic in the span of its branches. Those branches at once somber, lowering, and towering. Its scarred trunk was of such a girth three grown men with arms splayed fingertip to fingertip could not fully embrace it. So vast was the shade of its canopy, it was said two people could sit beneath it, each having no knowledge of the other. A magnificent example of God's creation, with nothing common about it.

A person could no more miss it than she might miss the very nose on her face.

She crept under the canopy. Under that edenic covering, the thunder and lightning seemed distant, nonexistent even. The grass here was knee high and dry and was all embracing when she dropped the litter and fell to the ground. She played her hands and fingers in the blades and thought in her exhaustion she might spend all the rest of her days in that very spot. She had herself a long cry and a brief nap. She drank from the pouch Moice had given her, which water tasted gritty and bitter. She ate the victuals, a stringy and tough rodent she could not identify, but it filled her belly as few other things ever had.

In short, she had herself a brief picnic at the base of that willow, though in all of it she dared not check Taylor. There was nothing she could do. Either he was dead or he wasn't. She afforded nothing in-between. She even commanded herself not to listen for the sound of his breathing, indeed could not have said with any authority whether such a sound there was.

Besides, she was almost home. She'd made this part of the journey before, maybe ten or a dozen times over the years. She would come to Tischer Creek, then up over the hill to their barn, which sight would be the most welcome relief to her tired bones. A couple of hours more at most.

She took up the litter and resumed her trek, leaving the willow behind to remember her or not as it had probably been doing with travelers for centuries. Came then thunder and lightning and a dismal, summer rain that wouldn't quit. The rain heated the air or the air heated the rain, she knew not which, and it all served to make for a great misery.

It seemed this was an abandoned place and not a soul was about nor had she seen another person for hours. She was not alone however, as the surrounding forests gave up plenty of sounds to accompany her hike. Calves bawled in the distance and owls hooted from perches high in the trees. Perhaps now the sound of a bear charging, over there the grunts of wild boar. The steady chirp of crickets. She heard something heavy crash in the woods, a tree felled by lightning maybe. Plenty of other noises she couldn't place. She'd heard stories of a far away land called Africa, where the things hiding in the trees could tear a man to pieces.

She didn't want to think of such things. Instead, she thought of Mr. Moice, of her father, and wondered what the relationship between the two could possibly have been. "It is what it is," she found herself saying aloud. She wondered if Mr. Moice had made it back to his place. She wondered if she would ever be able to find his place again and decided she must at least try.

Of a sudden the misty horizon in front of her brightened and the wind brought the report of something burning. A raven cawed and she stopped to look at the disturbance before her. She realized she'd come nearly as far as there was to come. Tischer Creek was a stone's throw in front of her and beyond that her family's place just over the rise.

She sank to the ground in exhaustion and began to cry once again and didn't stop for a long while. When she was all cried out, she closed a nostril against her thumb and repeated the effort on the other side, then wiped her face with her arm and breathed deep of the smoky air.

"We made it Mr. Taylor, by golly we made it."

Ben Taylor did not answer.

Walking had at first relieved some of Hannah's cramps, though as the hours passed her discomfort intensified again. A twisting pain crowded her, what her mother referred to as crotch fever, which she found none to pleasant. A usual part of her monthly and at home she might have taken a bit of Fromen's root.

Wet and sticky down her frontside, she'd improvised with a wad of lint between her legs, enough to soak up the worst of it. But she could feel the clotted ooze between her thighs now. And the small, spoiled odor as well.

She approached now the rear of a building and the solitary form of a man came gradually into view before it. Visible in profile against the light, he stood bent in the rain, with the dark shape of the building looming behind him. Draped scarf-like over his shoulders was a thin band of purple silk with a cross of gold embroidered in the middle and at either end. It hung below his knees with the tips mud-dipped and dirty. It was a stole and since he wore no collar, indeed no other vestments of any sort that might announce him as such, this was the sole suggestion of his priesthood.

That and the reverent way he knelt over the soldier on the ground.

The stone dwelling was an old church. She saw the soldier was one of many laid on the ground in the gloom behind that house of worship, so that the scene before her was like some twisted parody of a minister before his parishioners. The lad on the ground was not moving however, and his chest was not rising. And like the other members of that stilled congregation, he was not covered. Coming closer yet, she observed how his countenance was pale, his face a mask betraying his youth. He'd lost an arm and most of a shoulder; his blouse was suffused with a mixture of once molten flesh, pulverized bone, and clotted blood.

Hannah stopped and held herself as a cramp caught her pelvis yet again. The pain was tolerable, though just. She had now occasion to see the priest had something in his hand, a book of some sort. She imagined more than saw it might be a Bible, thought again of Levi and the rest of her family at the farm on Old Dutch Road, of the way her own father had preached to them often from a large book that was coal dust black and gritted with the same, of the words Holy Bible rubbed into obscurity on its cover.

She looked at the tired priest and could not help but see her own father. She felt his presence heavily at that moment.

She was a few feet from him, bent as he was over the dead soldier, who spanned the distance between them. She watched as he worked with a single-minded devotion, brooking no distractions. By his look and appearance, which was disheveled for one of his calling, it was apparent he'd seen much already, that he'd been at his work for many hours. The lay of dead before him promised many more hours to come.

She bit her lip as her cramping came and went.

The priest was ancient, to look at him. He bent still lower, crouched such that the tips of the stole dragged the mud at his feet. Holding both the book and a small vial in one hand, he carefully unscrewed the cap with the other and dipped a finger into the oil-soaked cotton it contained. Recapping so that no rainwater was allowed to spoil it, he anointed the soldier's forehead and spoke. "*Per istam sanctam unctionem et suam piissimam misericordiam, idulgeat tibi Dominus quidquid per visum deliquisti.*" As he finished, he hesitated a moment for reasons known only to him and God, then added, "Amen."

He rose, took a weary step to his left, and bent to the next corpse.

"Father?"

Only then did the priest appear to realize her presence, and then only by the barest hint of his head moving up. He had dark rings around his eyes, like coal smudges, and his stubbled face wore the trappings of his age and his surroundings. Gloom personified. She was immediately sorry to have disturbed him.

"God bless you, child." The priest nodded in his hardly-at-all manner, wiped the wet from his eyes, and returned to his duties as if never interrupted. She sat in the rain for some time, watching as this man of the cloth performed his sacred anointing on one poor soul after another. As the muted sun moved across the storm-tossed sky, she tried to imagine her husband at the end of that line of dead men—good men, she told herself—but couldn't.

The priest moved down the line doing his necessary work. She stumbled up the line in the opposite direction, searching for Levi. She walked to the other end. She grimaced behind her cramps and knelt at a man turned on his side.

He was the build of her Levi, or at least she thought he was. She hadn't seen her husband in months and she sometimes wondered if she still remembered what he looked like. She had an idea what he looked like, but she was no longer sure if that was the same as knowing what he looked like. Even if her memory was sure, it was likely, more than not even, that Levi had changed.

Her father had gone off to war, then returned two years later. She had seen him through the window glass of his coffin, seen his stilled face, and thought at the time how war had used him up. She was sure the man in that coffin had been her father, her mother had said as much, but he hadn't looked like him. The face in the coffin had been thin and gaunt; Enoch Gamble had been well-muscled, with ginger hair and rose in his cheeks. Of course, the fellow in the coffin had been dead. Maybe it wasn't the war that had thinned him, but death.

Even if she had an idea—a good idea—of what Levi looked like in life, would she recognize him in death? She had not before entertained such thoughts and they gave her a headache.

She reached out and touched the chin of the dead man before her, turned his head up. She stared a long while at this soldier, unable to speak and feeling a twisting in her gut. Her breath came hard and she stilled herself against the sight of his half face, for the other half was gone. She looked at the half that remained, looked at it a long time and from every angle the light would afford. At first she couldn't be sure it wasn't Levi, but in the end she decided it could not be, that she would have a sure knowledge in her soul if it was him. She looked down the line at the priest and said a silent prayer and then bent to the knapsack and pulled it free of the boy. She crossed herself and slunk around the corner of the building and into an old churchyard.

She was not prepared for the sight that greeted her. For as far as the eye could see, the earth had disappeared and a sea of broken men prevailed. Hundreds upon hundreds of twisted and splintered bodies, with every conceivable torment among them—as if the fertile ground of high spring had just passed and Mother Earth had grown these poor souls up for harvest. Here lay the dregs of war—the terrible and unimaginable product of its frenzied machinations. The men here had been subtracted, but only very slowly. They had been set aside—those with injuries to severe to be treated.

Here men lingered and died. This was God's waiting room.

She shuddered and another spasm caught her, which all but doubled her over—blades slicing at her innards. She felt the wad of material at her crotch and grew suddenly hot all over, a pig sweating under the knife. She saw double and the world wavered.

In the midst of this great mockery of the human condition, a sweet sound of salvation carried to her ears, and it was as if her soul had been freed after a lifetime of bondage. A barbarian shown the secret of the wheel for the first time could not have enjoyed a greater epiphany.

Amazing Grace, how sweet the sound,
That saved a wretch like me...
I once was lost but now am found,
Was blind, but now, I see.

She stood and the verse went on before her. She had never heard such a pure voice. Her cramps dissipated. Only after she saw them—three young women standing in the yard of the stone church, in the rain and weather—did she realize "the" voice was actually three. They had an energy, a pure musicality about them. She knew nothing of music, but the three lifted their voices to the heavens as one and it was as if they were singing in the finest hall in all the land.

The finest hall in all the land?

Yes, Hannah thought, that was it exactly.

Was this not, after all, God's country, and not, in the final estimation of all things, a perverted devil land? Could any hall elsewhere be any finer?

These three—angels, for she could think of no other term for them—sang with a reverberant quality that placed their rendition of the hymn first among any tune she had ever heard. It was as if she was hearing it for the very first time, as if every note and word of the hymn was meant for her and her alone.

Yes, I am a wretch, have been a wretch, have lived a wretched life.

Yes, I have been blind, but am blind no more.

Everything she'd experienced, the hell she'd come through in the days just passed, suddenly had purpose. They had shown her the way, had shown her the meaning of suffering. All at once, in the lee of the churchyard, surrounded as she was by the vast and terrible congregation of damaged and inflamed men and soldier boys, herself laid bare with her monthly bleeding, Hannah Gamble Griel's life changed. Find Levi or not, never again would she be able to ignore suffering in the world, no matter the form such suffering might take.

She put her eyes to the sky—*the glorious sky*—and hugged herself, sang "Allelujah, Allelujah," and jumped and danced with a spirit joyous to behold, whereupon she moved among the tormented men, touching them in the fashion of a postulant among lepers.

An observer might have thought she'd lost her mind.

***

The charred remains of Enoch Gamble's barn smoldered in the wet air. An old wagon had sat over on its side in one corner of the place for years. Three of its four wheels were the only thing bigger than a steamer trunk to have come through the inferno—save, of course, the eighteen or so corpses scattered among the ashes.

Back in the house, Brody sat the edge of Coal's bed and leaned over to better examine his wounds. The men had carried him through the house and up the stairs to the widow's bedroom, which they'd cleared out. He lay crosswise of the bed because that was how they'd set him down and nobody was of a mind to move him again. He was covered in bloody humors, soot, and ash, except where touching hands had smeared and peeled the residue—and with it his skin.

Everyone in the room, they were all men save Purdy, gave their attention to Coal. They stood each beside the next, not a one moving except to breathe, which breathing sounded profound in the distressed silence. Purdy herself sat the bed beside Coal. She might have cradled his head in another time, but now she too sat unmoving, hands prayerful before her mouth.

She sobbed, mumbled "my boy" over and over, and "Enoch" several times.

The surgeon bent and his brace clicked. Coal's eyes looked unnaturally huge in their places. They remained still and didn't follow him as he came around the bed. His lips went from dead blue to purple, and back to dead blue again. Brody put a hand flat to Coal's chest and felt the work of his heart, which was pummeling hard and fast and furious, like a steam engine about to blow. The boy's chest moved up and down, all the while making a terrible rasping not unlike a bellows that had rusted mostly closed and wouldn't open again. Only this bellows was underwater, for each time he took a breath in, he was choking, and with each exhalation came a frothy, black spit.

Someone had cut the rest of Coal's clothes away. In places the boy's skin had lost the pink look of flesh, had become too shiny and too white, like something you'd find tacked to a store dummy. Brody pressed it with a finger and it didn't blanch. He pressed it again and when it still didn't blanch he shook his head and caught himself shaking his head and stopped.

Purdy took Coal's unburned hand and held it loosely, as if to hold it any tighter might reduce it to dust. His hand twitched now and again and she couldn't help but think of the seizures he'd used to have. A seizure didn't seem such an affliction just then. He struggled to catch his breath as she watched.

He looks like a drownt man.

"You go on boy," she said, not really knowing what she meant by the words. It wasn't a clear thought. She'd run out of clear thoughts. Every thought she'd ever had in her whole life entire crowded in on her at that very moment. The only truly clear thought she had was that the room smelled—reeked—of burnt eggs.

Everyone else was standing. Most had put kerchiefs or cloths to their noses. Heads were bowed as if in prayer.

Brody stepped away from the bedside, still facing Purdy. "Madam—"

"There ain't nothing?"

"His wounds are mortal."

"What?"

"He is dying."

"You're supposed to be a doctor. Do something. Ain't there nothing?" She would not look at him.

"God himself—"

"Don't speak of God, major. I know God. Ain't no god in this room. This here's man's doing. If you hadn't come here..."

"But we did."

Now she looked at him. A hard stare with piercing eyes. For such a look they'd have burned her at the stake in the time of Old Salem. "Yes, you did, every cur-sed one of you. You came and this the price, paid by a little boy."

"If there was anything to be done, anything at all..."

"Get out. All of you just get out."

They filed through the doorway, leaving her to her grief. Brody was the last and he paused as she called to him.

"Major?"

"Yes, madam?"

"There ain't nothing then? I mean, really nothing?"

"I will send some laudanum to ease his passage. That is all I can do. I am truly sorry."

"How long does my son got? How long's he gonna suffer?"

"He will die before first light, madam."

Sure words, spoken like a prophet.

FIFTEEN

The old stone church turned hospital was a sprawling mess, with no rhyme or reason to its layout, and everywhere she turned, Hannah encountered not but misery. The wounded congregated in great heaps, in endless combinations of twisted limbs, supine bedfellows, ghastly embraces, tortured still images. A mind bending diorama she hoped to forget but was sure forgetting would take a long time coming, if ever.

In the late afternoon, in a clearing that had once been near the center of the church cemetery, she'd come upon the haggard remnants of dozens upon dozens of men sitting or kneeling against the earth. The place had been alive with movement, yet she'd been hard pressed to pick out anything remarkable. The driving rain had lulled and all was mundane: they sipped coffee out of tin cups and chewed at a bit of hard bread or pork; small groups played at cards or checkers and whistled amongst themselves; a small darkie boy with big eyes entertained with his prowess at various animal calls. A pair of soldiers played chess on a board of hand carved soapstone. Those able enough read or wrote letters for their fellow injured. A man loudly quoted Scripture passages, from memory, as he had nothing before him. In one place a man cried, while a few paces away another laughed. It wasn't the activity that caught her eye, but the vast spectacle of it. So many occupied that hallowed space that not a grave marker was visible. She had the odd illusion a man's parts were as dispensable as his clothes. It dawned on her every being there lacked something—a shirt, trousers, an arm, a piece of a leg. The few standing were an exception, but the blood upon them seemed more to prove the rule than counter it.

She went among them, making herself useful. She smiled all the while, and tried to look enthusiastic for each and every man she spoke with. She said to one after another a phrase she picked up from the quoting man: "For everything there is a season and a time for every matter under heaven."

She knew the Lord's Prayer and the Twenty-Third Psalm by rote, but she couldn't recall the rest of Ecclesiastes, except that it talked about love and war and hate and peace and killing and dying. A jumbled mess, only not. And so she said these words, and others besides, to whoever wanted to pray, and they all wanted to when she asked. Many—most—came near to crying.

The tents, she realized as the day advanced, were the worst. She made her way through a score in the space of the afternoon. She discovered the best of the wounded had been in the clearing, that those too corrupted to move had been left in the few available bunks and on the floors of the hastily constructed shelters here. The ventilation was poor and they stank of putrid meat and moldy canvas, of human waste and vomit. There was nothing clean anywhere, but after a while she found that rather than steel herself against it, she got used to it.

The world, and everything in the world, had gone all to rot and decay, but a deep breath and a silent prayer as she entered gave her strength, for in these places all but abandoned by the usual civilities of the human condition, the need for comfort was great.

The soldiers, most were boys and this too became horridly apparent as she moved through the compound, ranged in condition from dead men breathing to those who wished to be dead to those she hoped would die soon for their own sake. These last were at once the most sacred and profane things she had ever had the misfortune to see. A man breathing with half his chest blown open to the air; another who had somehow survived two days absent his entire body below his navel. She came to a tent where a man moaned constantly "Kill me, oh God just kill me." This last she had wanted to pass by, but it wasn't in her power. She went in as if reeled like a fish, as if pushed by the wind, as if there could be no other design but to put her in that place at that moment.

It was wet and humid inside that tent, oppressive. The man, he continued to call out even as she went to him, took no observation of her as she approached. Indeed, it was only at the last, when she was fully upon him and placed a hand to his cheek, that he reached out for her. His manner of so doing was clumsy and desperate, so that she immediately realized he was blind. Once latched, he would not let go and clung to her as a castaway would cling to a log drifting alone at sea. He begged her not to leave.

As darkness fell, she knelt in the mud, held fast in the arms of the blind man. They clasped hands and she began to pray yet again. She prayed longer and harder than she had ever prayed in her life. She prayed for the blind man to see and for him to find salvation. She prayed that Levi was alive and that she'd find him.

But mostly, she prayed for the madness to end.

It was evening when Loli came upon the tumbled down rocks of Tischer Creek. These rocks were huge things, some the size of houses and others less but each and every one substantial. She laid Taylor out on a slab of gray stone and he looked not unlike a dead man. She sprinkled him with water from the creek and toweled his forehead and he was of a sudden resurrected. His eyes worked back and forth under their lids and his breathing deepened then shallowed, then deepened again. He began to gag and she turned him up on his side and he vomited a thin-looking black bile. His skin was hot and wet from the rain or sweat she knew not which. She could do no more for him and so left him propped sideways on his bad arm. At least he was alive.

She waded the stream, which had risen to waist high with the rain. When she looked back the lieutenant had not moved. He lay with his back to her. She ignored the ache in her bones and climbed the rocks and the rise above the near bank toward her homestead. She passed through a fallow cornfield where many of the stalks had been trampled and of a sudden came to a man lying lengthwise upon a stretcher. His head was buoyed by a rucksack and his right leg was but a bandaged stump just above his ankle. It jutted obtrusively from his trouser leg and was blunt and club-like. His remaining foot showed itself naked and black dirty. He looked generally uncomfortable and followed her with slitted, narrow eyes as she came on.

If she'd a mind to stop, she changed it as she drew closer and saw the others behind and around him. A man in long johns and nothing more save his hat leaned against a makeshift crutch and smoked. He drooled from one corner of his mouth, or maybe it was just beads of sweat. To his side was a soldier with both arms stumped below the elbows. What bandages had been put there had long since bled through. Every now and again his drooling neighbor leaned over and took the cigarette from between his own lips and put it to the double amputee's mouth and he would press his lips and take a long toke on it. The ash flared red and his cheeks, narrow and gaunt already, sank inward with the effort.

She came upon a man sitting an old rocking chair beneath a tree. He was wrapped in a quilt and looked ancient, as old as ever there was. His mouth was open wide and he was laughing with oblivious and mad abandon as she passed. Next came one kneeling on the ground beside an oak. An unlit cigar hung from his mouth and he had dropped his pants by way of examining a long wound running the length of his thigh. His manhood hung in the air between his legs and as she came alongside he began to shit. He never looked at her.

She went on past a score or more of them to the top of the rise, where she came upon the ruins, still smoldering despite the rain. It could have been a foreign land for how different the grounds now looked and it took her a moment to place the ashes as what had been their barn.

She hollered for her mother. She was weary from the day's travels though, and what with the rain and other commotion her voice didn't sound like it carried far. She circled the ruined barn, taking it in from different directions, convincing herself of the fact of it.

"God in heaven," Loli muttered, then, in a louder voice, "What happened?"

"Fire," a bushy faced man said, as if the single word summed everything to a logical conclusion.

"Are those—"

"Yeah, they's bodies. Too hot to move just yet they is." He was a Southerner, and as if he could taste the burnt meat in the air he gummed his lips as he spoke. Loli hated him immediately and intensely. She closed her eyes. "How?"

"I ain't knowing fer sure," the bushy man said. "Hell lady, it were a barn. Barns burn. It be a common thing." He said this like it was some sort of ancient knowledge, known the world over except by her.

She opened her eyes. "That ain't right." Stop gumming your goddamn lips she wanted to add but didn't.

"Well they's the bodies what prove it," he said, as if they were the natural culmination of this ancient fact. "Seen a boy come out still breathin' though. Seen it me self. Poor sonofabitch be better off he dead."

"A boy? What sort of boy?" Her spittle turned rancid.

"A boy's all. Go see fer yourself. Took 'im up to the house they did. The major hisself was looking after 'im."

She was on her way before he finished his sentence. The back door was open, or rather there was no longer any door to close. She crossed the kitchen, the floor caked and sticky with the blood of scores and more of men. She made her way through the close confines of the front parlor, where the smell was rancid and intolerable. The taste in the back of her throat made her gag. A fetid sickness groped her guts.

A few soldiers sat the lower steps but beyond them the stairs rose empty to the second floor. She bounded them slower than she might have in past days and they creaked under her weight. At the top were two doors and a hallway. She stuck her head in the first room, hers and Hannah's bedroom in a better time. A gray bearded old fellow and two others occupied her bed. He turned his head as she looked in. He had a large wart or some such growth on the side of his nose and her bed looked puny with him and the others in it. She turned away and gave her attention to the other door.

Her ma's room.

She crossed the hall and then for some reason hesitated. She already knew what she'd find and didn't need to see it. Or maybe she was entirely wrong and who lay beyond the door was no kin to her. She put her hand on the knob but it wouldn't turn. Her hand, not the knob. She couldn't breathe. She stood in the damn hallway driveling spit down her front until the knob turned of its own accord. Loose in her hand, it was being turned from the inside and so the thing was out of her control.

She would know soon enough whether she wanted too or not.

She drew breath and found she had to know. She forced the issue by taking the knob firm in hand and turning and pushing hard against the shut door.

Loli pushed into the room and the man she had seen on the roadside, the one they had called the surgeon and who had given her his few words of advice two days before—*just keep to the roads and away from the fighting. And...get inside soon as you can*—sidled past her.

They made a stilted eye contact—*I know you*—and moved on, each passing the other without a word.

Loli faced her ma across the bed, where lay her brother with a sheet pulled to his chest. A candle burned in the corner and even by its stingy light Coal appeared gaunt and all but incinerated. The particulars were mercifully hidden—she would never have recognized him but for the look in her mother's eyes, which looked not at her but at him with a fierce and agonizing intensity. Loli followed her gaze down to the bed.

If the body there was Coal and he was still alive, it was only by the thinnest. He no longer belonged to this place or even this world. He was but a temporary refugee from the very dwelling place of the dead itself.

"Oh God, oh my dear God." Loli turned away in the next instant and upchucked whatever the thing was she'd eaten earlier.

Purdy looked barely a whit at her youngest daughter, and then only with her side vision. She didn't raise an arm or put out a hand. She stood pale and ghostlike by the candle flame, the color gone all out of her.

"Oh God, oh my dear God," Loli repeated, and God might indeed have been in that room, though at first glance his presence wasn't anywhere evident.

Part III:
Peace. Perfect Peace.

SIXTEEN

The wagons carrying the wounded bumped along the swollen, rutted roads and misery was redefined. The wind blew gale force and great claps of thunder and dazzling flashes announced the rain, which kept up the whole night long without the slightest relief. The water found its way into everything. It seemed as if the heavens had opened, as if the sky had burst and the land had now to give up the terrible burden of flesh and bone spilled upon it.

The Confederate wagon train stretched seventeen miles into the black and stormy night. It was a busted up, unsettling affair composed of unsprung, flat-bottomed boxes—drays and carts of every sort. Anything with wheels for a ten-mile radius had been confiscated, along with all manner of beasts to pull them. These bleating animals were themselves a menace, alternately terrified or confused, limping in their own right. Most had not a mind to move except by the crack of the whip, and it was a sorry sight to see these exhausted creatures pulling against the suck of the mud. More than a score fell dead in their tracks, others were shot dead for their reticence. All these had to be dragged to the side of the road to make way for the rest.

The roads became great clogged arteries of humanity at its worst.

"Where in God's name you been the last two days, girl?"

Loli couldn't think. She tried, but it was like rubbing two sticks together in the rain: no sparks. She might have been standing beside her brother's bed for five minutes, five hours, or five days. It made no sense.

Two days? I been gone two days?

She wasn't sure if she meant *only* two days or two *entire* days. Time had suddenly constricted with the whole world spinning down to that one moment. She of a sudden felt deathly cold, a body mouldering under the earth. Was she dead? Was this Hell?

She began to shiver and couldn't stop. She lifted her gaze from her brother to her mother. She looked old beyond her years, like she'd aged ten years since Loli had last seen her.

Where in God's name you been the last two days, girl?

She had no idea. Her mind was not so much a clean slate as it was a dumping ground. Too full, she couldn't cull anything from it: *Hannah in her nightshirt holding Noah; Mr. Moice taking off Taylor's arm; dawg and his thin ribs; Purdy on the ground after being slapped; Ben Taylor dead or not so dead on the litter behind her; don't ye make me come after ye; alone with a big negro; the lanky soldier at the aid station who'd sought to confuse her; Mr. Moice pulling them through the swamp; the turned earth beside baby Sam's small, open grave.* And none of this with any meaning, any emotion. A jumbled mess. Even the last thought, *Ben Taylor propped alongside Tischer Creek,* meant nothing and might have happened a month ago or ten minutes ago.

Where in God's name you been the last two days, girl?

She had absolutely no idea, knew only the here and now and even that much was dubious.

Ma's bedroom, Coal on the bed—near burnt to ashes. Nighttime outside, not quite full dark. She knew this last because she could see it through the window. She knew all of this—and nothing more—only because she could see it. She looked at her mother.

"What happened?"

Purdy's forehead pulsed beneath her tawny skin. Had her skin always been tawny? Had she always had such deep lines over her eyes?

"He burned," came the plaintive answer.

He burned. Simple, direct. *She wants to cry*—then the crazy thought her mother would never cry again.

"Look at him. My boy don't got no eyelids."

Loli didn't need to look, had seen that much already. His lidless stare wasn't the sort of thing a person could miss. "I'm sorry, ma." She'd stopped shivering.

"Your brother's going to join your pa."

"I'm sorry."

"You shoulda been here girl," Purdy said.

It is my fault, then.

"You shoulda been here seeing to him. He listens to you."

"Please, ma."

A silence loud enough to hurt the ears. Neither spoke. Purdy looked ever like a woman on the verge of tears but they never came. Every time Loli looked at her, she seemed to have aged further. Sometimes she was looking at Loli and sometimes she was looking at Coal. Either way, her eyes burned with an intensity hot as anything that might have been in that barn. It hurt Loli to see her mother so, to have her mother look at her so.

"I'm sorry, ma."

Purdy worked her lips like she might spit. "Look at your brother."

"I seen him."

"No you haven't. You get down close and you really look at him."

Loli felt her breathing ratchet up and her waist tightened, like she'd cinched her belt a notch. "I done said I'm sorry."

"He ain't got no eyelids." Purdy's eyes were working hard looking at him, then her. "My boy—he ain't got no eyelids."

Loli's breath hitched as she nodded her head and turned away from the both of them. She moved to the door, opened it, and stepped into the hall.

"I ain't blaming you girl," Purdy said as the door was closing. "It'll be torture enough you blaming yourself."

Moments later Loli was outside, beneath an eerily clouded night sky. The rain ran on and off and before her the ruins of the barn smoldered. The air reeked of burnt manure. Men, the injured and those assisting them, lay on the grounds amid the ruins, mostly sleeping but she was aware of a background thrum of noise, talking and moaning, the sound of spades digging in the night despite the rain, the heavy clatter of the rain itself. Other noises besides. Somewhere behind her a horse neighed.

Strawberry Festivals. Coal had made himself sick gorging on berries of one sort or another at last year's Strawberry Festival. She had told him no, to stop eating, but he hadn't listened and had spent the night upchucking all the berries he'd eaten. It had been her responsibility to watch over him that day and she had failed him then too.

Where had Coal been when disaster had come? No way to know, not now. Certainly in the barn, else how could he have been burned. She stepped into the rubble, which steamed in the rain and felt warm even through her shoes. She began to move around, not certain at first what she was looking for but looking anyway. She turned over planks and burned out boards, upended the remnants of a plow. With her feet she scraped through the soot and ash. She found nothing very interesting.

After a few minutes, a piece of polished metal caught her eye. She ignored it, had no use for such a thing, but it galvanized her into knowing what she was looking for and she went at it with renewed energy. The rain came harder now, became a deluge. She went down on hands and knees to keep her place, the rain washing away the ashes and pushing her this way and that. It carried the taste of char into her mouth and blinded her besides. She stayed with the hunt though, used her hands where her eyes proved useless. She searched for hours, until her hands raw'd and her knees bled and she spat black mud with nearly every breath.

She only noticed when the sun cracked the morning sky because the rain lessened at just that moment. The bushy-headed soldier from the night before appeared at her side and offered his canteen. She coughed, spat black, took a swig, and spat black again before finally drinking.

"What come of the bodies?" she asked.

"Bodies? They's gone missy. Back into the earth. Ashes to ashes you know. That's what bodies do."

"So you buried them?"

"In the night, afore the rain. They wasn't something to be looked at in the day."

"They might of had loved ones."

The bushy-headed man looked out over the washed rubble. "If so, they wasn't in no condition to meet 'em. They'll look all the better after some time in the ground."

"I need to find something," she said.

"We all is looking for something, missy."

"Something in the rubble, something important."

"What that be?"

She told him.

"Well, could be a tall order. Could be it got washed away."

"Where in the rubble they find him?"

"Lemme see now. Weren't in no rubble." He turned and pointed. "There."

"I don't follow."

"He come running out the barn and fell just there."

"You sure?"

"I ain't slow and don't stutter none."

She saw by his eyes the confidence he felt in what he said. "Okay. You show me?"

And there it was. Round and polished, like all the rain the night just passed had been for nothing so much as cleaning this one stone. And it was exactly the size of Coal's palm. Coal's rock. His ticket home. She had to get it to him before it was too late.

Lieutenant Ben Taylor finally roused to some semblance of awareness long after nightfall. He opened his eyes and had a bad moment before he realized the night was black dark. Black dark and wet as wet can be. The rain was coming down in sheets and for this he was thankful, at least at first.

His tongue, which was swollen big and protruded out of his mouth, appreciated the wet until it began to fill his mouth and he couldn't swallow. He gagged and spat before managing to roll himself over onto his stomach. It was a near miracle he didn't puke. If he had, he would've died, drowned in his own spew. As it was, he began to cry and felt stupid in the darkness, helpless as a baby. He'd even shat himself.

He was a long time lying there, a long time gathering himself. He cried out in the dark but there was nobody to hear. Claps of thunder echoed off the rocks and lightning streaked the night. He tried getting to his feet but wasn't strong enough to hold himself upright. He sat propped against the rock where Loli had left him. One foot dangled over the edge. Initially it had hung over the water, in the free air. Now that same water lapped at his heel. Before long it would cover his foot entirely and then it would start to come over the side of the rock where he sat and not too long after that it would cover him.

He had an idea he'd drown when that happened.

He panicked, like a horse he'd seen shut up in a burning barn. He'd been just a boy, but he remembered. His father had tried to corral the animal, but it had retreated deeper into the barn, deeper into the danger. What followed he'd mostly heard and not seen, but hearing was enough. The heavy clang of its hooves against the wooden sidewalls, the hurricane whoosh of the flames fanning to an inferno. The horse made then a sound like he'd never known one could make—a terrible baying, a sound more fit to a deep-mouthed hound than a horse. It was a devil sound. The unendurable and awesome sound of death itself.

The creek water crashed past him and he tried with everything he had to stand, but succeeded only in falling back and tumbling into the water, right into the danger. The cold shock of it nearly undid him. A large, hulking shape came at him in the dark, a flash of lightning at the last minute revealing a massive tree trunk turning with the raging creek. It flowed by him, but he was stricken all the same. He was certain of just two things: his name was Ben Taylor and he was about to die. The water swirled in the depression and he could hear nothing save the roar of death rushing at him—the terrible sound of that long ago horse filled his ears and he thought: *I don't want to die.*

The cold water rushed around him, swirled over him, dumped him this way and that. He clawed at the rocks with his hands—only just that moment realizing he had but one. It felt like he had two, but every time he tried to reach with his right arm his hand grabbed only air.

He shredded the fingertips of his left hand trying to hold on against the granite. He fell back and now the water pressed him hard against a cranny. It was all he could do to keep his head in the air. He tried to swing his right arm—his phantom arm—around the rock and nearly got pulled back into the torrent. He used his legs and left arm to brace him in the base of a crack.

I'm gonna die here.

He forced himself to be calm, to look around. He was floating in a depression about ten feet across. Beside him, a long arm's length away—*Where's my right arm? My goddamn right arm?*—the rocks parted to a 'V' shaped ravine. And just past that, the water disappeared in a boil to cascade downstream. The depression trapped him, but he didn't need to climb out of the depression, only to drag himself up the ravine. Of course, if he fell into the boil—well, he wouldn't be a one-armed, fevered cripple much beyond a few more minutes, would he?

He pushed the thought from his mind and inch by tortured inch—he had to consciously remind himself he didn't have a right arm, could only use his left—he dragged himself the several feet around the bowl of the depression to the ravine. This was the easy part, he discovered, as he began to push up between the rocks. In the depression he hadn't had to fight gravity. Now however, he was moving uphill and it took all his might to push off with first one foot and then the other. Uphill was the way out, the only way to distance himself from the rushing, rising water.

But it was rising too fast and he wasn't strong enough. Every time he looked up, he came near to drowning, such was the downpour out of the sky, which was all the worse for the darkness. He couldn't see the rain, only feel its moment, its weight. Worst of all though—far worse—was the devil noise of the rising creek. It filled his ears the way the water filled the depression: ever rising, ever tumultuous. In his mind, the dead horse lived and died all over again and the awesome sound became his entire known world, the center of his universe.

He forgot himself and fell back when he reached up with his phantom arm. "Goddammit!" he shouted, but of course his voice was lost in the rush of the cascading water.

He struggled on for some indeterminate period, eternity close by all the while. The water leeched the warmth from his body and the strength from his muscles. And as it topped his head and breathing became a memory, he had one last conscious thought: *I am drowned.*

In his death throes his mind wandered. He had the wild idea he was being wrenched upward, manhandled. He took a breath—a wet, soggy, gaggy breath, but a breath nonetheless. He opened his eyes and a beast of a man towered over him. Big hands, muscular, calloused. Those hands grabbed hold of him in the hollows of his armpits—*I still have both armpits*—and twisted him up and away in a single motion.

Time skipped and he was out of the water, lying sideways in the mud, half his face numb. Before him, standing on not quite two feet for one was but a stump, stood a giant. Gulping to catch his air, Taylor imagined his sanity had completely unraveled.

So this is how it is to die.

Except the image of the huge nigger man standing beside him wouldn't go away and seemed to argue otherwise.

Purdy Gamble slept not a wink all that long night. Outside the storm howled and the rain fell like the reenactment of Noah's flood. She sat up at the bedside of her only son and watched as he struggled for every breath, as if there wasn't enough air in the whole world entire for that one little boy. When he grimaced she grimaced and when he looked once or twice as if he might be smiling she smiled too. She rubbed her finger over his lips, which were blue and no pink at all, and she thought maybe he kissed her finger.

She wanted to towel him off, but every time she tried he tensed. The best she could do was hold his better hand in hers and to occasionally run her cheek along the back of his palm. She tried not to cry but mostly she failed at this. After awhile, a drip of water seeped through the ceiling and she watched it puddle on the floor beside her, watched each drop make a little ripple of circles and then how the circles would disappear before the next drop. She thought maybe that's how they were, God's people, just drops in a puddle making little ripples. She tried to see a trace of the circles after they'd gone and before the next drop, but saw nothing. Yet the puddle grew.

Maybe that was something too.

She trembled and stepped away from the bed, found the chamber pot in the corner and took down her under things and used the pail. Afterward, she went to the window and opened it and stood before it taking in great lungfuls of air. The rain washed her and matted her hair. When she turned back to the room, a person couldn't say if she'd been largely crying or it was just the weather writ large on her face.

She stood in the middle of her bedroom, a room she had shared with Enoch for twenty odd years, until he had taken the long walk down to Old Dutch Road two years before. They had talked of it the night before, how it was something he had to do. She had known it was, but knowing it and living with it were two different things entire. Now he was dead, buried out back beside their firstborn, the nameless baby whose legs she'd broken getting him out. What had happened with the baby hadn't seemed a just thing at the time, nor Enoch's going, and especially not him returning in a box.

Now this.

Whatever remains, it will be enough.

Coal stirred on the bed and she saw how before long there'd be another hole in the ground out back under the willow. She thought back to the night she and Enoch had talked, how he had said he'd never be able to live with himself if the war came to them and he hadn't done a thing to prevent it, how the effort needed good people for that very reason, how living on this good land meant defending it, even dying for it.

He hadn't been talking about little boys, of course.

She went to the dresser and pressed her wet hands against the top drawer, hesitating. She looked back at the bed and for a moment the pain of it all nearly brought her to her knees. She steadied herself against the dresser and opened the top drawer, stared down at the contents. She mouthed a few words, then spelled them out, "h-o-l-y-b-i-b-l-e."

She ran her hands over the book, the words 'Holy Bible' all but erased by the touch of her fingers just so over many years. For only the second time in her life, she wished she could read.

But in the end it wasn't the Bible she lifted from the drawer. In the end, she appeared to find more warmth and solace in the second item. She wrapped her hand around the grip. The steel blue pistol felt both heavy and cold in her hands, but not foreign. She had learned to shoot as a girl and Enoch had renewed her acquaintance with the weapon the day before he'd left.

"You gotta be able to defend yourself," he'd said, "I ain't gonna be here and things might get rough."

She held the weapon high in one hand, rubbing the barrel with the other. Enoch had insisted upon loading it the day he'd placed it in the drawer.

"The time comes, you don't want to be fooling with having to charge it."

She brought the cool steel to her forehead, the gun pointed skyward, and prayed. "God, grant me strength…" she stopped, found she couldn't finish.

Strength for what?

To kill my own son?

The words went unspoken and with the pistol in one hand and the book in the other, she stepped back to the bed and kissed the unburnt skin on Coal's arm. She pulled a chair close and sat down and began to pray anew, this time with the Bible at her forehead. She fingered the pistol and prayed again and kissed the book a dozen times in the night.

The candle flame flickered and the room flickered with it and she saw the tiredness in Coal's eyes. They looked ridiculously alert though, ridiculous because his eyelids had been burned away and he couldn't close his eyes. Every time he tried, which was with every breath at first and less often as the night wore on, his eyes rolled upward until only the whites stared out, as if seeing the back of his eyeballs had been the goal in the first place. She wanted nothing so desperately as to reach over and close those eyes, to rest them. A dozen times she reached for them, gripping the pistol hard each time, but his eyes never closed and she could never bring the gun up where he might see it. She had an idea resting those eyes would be a good thing, but she couldn't bring herself to do the resting.

"It'll all be good in the morning, Coal," she said over and over.

But it wasn't of course. In the morning he still clung to life like a person who actually had one. He still stared out from lidless hollows and Purdy stared back, wondering if he could see her. If so, he never acknowledged her.

She was still holding the Bible in one hand and the pistol in the other when he passed out of this world an hour after sun up.

Whatever remains, it will be enough she had once thought. But it wasn't. Not even close.

SEVENTEEN

The fiddle player tightened his bow in the lee of the wagon. Slightly built, elderly, he ignored the rain and picked at the strings and turned the pegs and tuned the fiddle and played a few notes by way of warm up. When he was satisfied with the sound, he laid the bow on his lap and cracked his knuckles and stretched his neck. Taking up the bow once more, he began a long, lamenting melody.

He played as if he'd waited all his life for this one moment and the vibrato was a tremulous, eerie thing that seemed to hug the countryside. Solitary in its musings, it reminded of home. Wandering in its stirrings, it rang of ma and pa, of Billy Bob and Mary Jo, of gals back home, of wives and children kneeling nightly and praying beside quilted spreads stuffed with feathery down. It awoke those parts of a person poisoned by a war nobody wanted, a conflict everyone hated.

Hannah listened to the music as she sat alongside the cot of the blind man. He was a cachectic, distant lad with ash gray skin, scruffy whiskers, and concussed eyes. He sweated much and from time to time passed a little fart through his dressings, for he had taken a knife in his belly as well. The flies alighted on him frequently. He had some hours before finally given up on his death chant and now he slept, however fitfully. He had said nothing for some time, but it was clear the musings of the fiddle player aroused something in him. He fluttered his eyes, which then came open with a melancholy glaze. The whole of him began to move generally then, like a man needing to get at something beneath him. "Bayonet!" he screamed, and now he arched his back and flailed about like a man possessed of an evil spirit.

Hannah, who had been only half dozing herself, came fully awake.

The soldier was now every inch of him alive, his eyes big and wandering. He seemed to be looking for something. Those same eyes, blind and blank and bleak just a moment before, now became the herald of passion. Hannah bent over him and those eyes fixed upon her and she saw a whole theater of emotion come through them. As if he was watching great actors on a stage and reacting to and repeating much of what they said and did. And in the effort his mouth moved and his lips trembled and words poured out in a great confused morass: "I can't do this. Oh my, can't do this no way." The blind man put a hand up, waved it back and forth in a beckoning gesture. "Levi?"

Hannah startled. Had he just said 'Levi?' Had the blind man just said 'Levi'? Had the man she'd spent the entire evening with just said her husband's name?

She hadn't heard it right—couldn't have heard it right.

"I don't wanna die, Levi," the man said, his voice quivering. His arm fell on the bed, made a thud the way a dead arm dropped by a mortician might.

"What'd you say?"

He bucked up of a sudden. "Levi, we gonna die sure today."

"Levi? Levi? Levi who?" She grabbed at him, shook his shoulders. "Levi Griel?!"

"A coward? Me?" He quivered again, minding not the woman, but the man he saw somewhere deep in his mind's eye.

She thought, *he's crazed, fevered, and blind. Dying. He doesn't know what he's saying.* Or maybe he wasn't saying anything at all. Maybe she was imagining the whole thing. Maybe she was the crazed one.

He grabbed at her now, at the front of her dress. He seemed to be looking for a fight. "Tell me this," and she saw how his blind, contused eyes had narrowed, how a look of fear had come over him. "Tell me this, Levi, when it's all over, how they gonna tell a dead coward from a dead hero, eh? How they gonna do that?"

He fell back, ash gray and exhausted, his gaze once again in the here and now, once again showing only a hollow stare. The eyes of a blind and dying soldier. He said, "I'm killed," in a tiny, matter of fact voice, like he'd been thinking on it a long time and had finally decided there was no working around it and nothing more to say on the issue. He didn't look at her though.

His eyes rolled back and forth and a light breeze came through the open flap of the tent. There was an up tempo in the fiddler's music, followed by a series of deep-strung notes and tranquil tones drawn long across the bow. The soldier's eyes, blind but not paralyzed, rolled in the direction of the fiddle playing. "What sort of day is it?"

"It's sunny," Hannah lied.

"Always wanted to die on a sunny day. I wish I could feel the sun on my face. What's your name?"

She told him.

"My girl's name's Julie." His last words in this world.

His eyes rolled back and forth a few more times, at first in time to the fiddle, then less so. She wanted to ask him so many questions, but this was not the time and there would never be another.

When his eyes had stopped and he was done and at rest, only then did he seem to look at her. She closed his eyes and stepped out into the air. The warm rain pelted her face and she tasted the spoil it carried. She stifled a gag and moved across to the nearby clearing where the fiddler was still at work by a large fire. She wondered if he knew the effect his music had. A small crowd was gathered and a petty sutler had set up a grill and offered boiled peanuts for pennies. She watched a negro boy give over an Indian-head for a bag and skip off.

It was the most normal thing she'd seen in days and she very nearly smiled.

Moice came out of the trees to a dawn shrouded in a glaucous mist. But even before he came out of the trees he knew something was wrong. His nose told him, for the stench of an army camp is unforgettable, and surpassed in superlative degree only by the stench of an army encamped at hospital.

He had approached the farm, as was his usual doing, from its rear. This, of course, meant he had to cross Tischer Creek, and it was at the creek he came across the all but drowned Lieutenant Taylor. He'd recognized that stump immediately, for it wasn't everyday he had occasion to cut an arm off. He had fished the man out of the water in the blink of an eye, thinking peripherally how he hadn't cut the rebel's arm off just to watch him drown in a summer downpour.

Moice had waited the storm out kneeling beside the half-drowned man, their surroundings both ethereal and unearthly in the mist. He had seen much in his near three score years, and he took in the sights around them with nary a word. Several tents hung slack in the weather, their canvas siding flapping back and forth. A pair of worn trousers hung from a scorched branch above a fire pit. Papers beat about here and there, tossed in the wind. Half-smoked cigars and the butts of cigarettes littered the ground. Broken tables, pots, pans, upended chairs, a weathered couch that looked somehow coffin-like. A dumping field with a thousand thousand odds and ends; a hodgepodge of stuff once useful, now rubbish. And among it all, stained and clotted with the ichor of men—both the profane living and the sacred dead—the bandages.

The field was abandoned—lifeless as far as he could tell— yet every item on it said otherwise. A man could collect all the bandages hereabouts and be so weighted as to never move again. And the bandages were not the whole of it. Here and there, showing bright against the summer grass and brighter still in the wet mud, crimson clumps of blood and other vital incidentals argued the point. Proof of life it was, proof of man's inhumanity to his fellow.

As if Moice needed any such further proof. The blood in his veins ran cold and he felt lightheaded. He knew what would come next and even so, as his heart began to thump and his breathing quickened, he felt as a helpless child. He looked about for a hide, felt too exposed in the open, but had no time. The world around him began to turn topsy-turvy and he managed only a short move back into the trees. He came to rest heavily against an old oak. Trembling now, he found himself looking at the stump of his foot, which reminder did him no good.

And then would come, and then did come, the worst of it.

What came was no ordinary fear. A hideous, creeping pall enveloped him, like night replacing day, and just as slowly. No part of him was left untouched, most especially his mind—which seemed now not to think but to churn. And he had not thoughts, but a kind of terrible churned brain-work, the sort of muck one might find shoveling out a hog pen. He began to blather, the words coming very fast and in no discernible order. He could have been speaking in tongues. Only the names of his dead wife and son told otherwise.

Was he soliloquizing with the dead? Or were the dead speaking through him?

And then something more. Another name, like a white hot poker branding his black skin. And when the charnel smoke wafted away, what was burned there was a single word hard against the back of his eyeballs, where he couldn't get away from it. Korley.

Korley Misipi.

For an instant, he thought maybe that was a place, but that wasn't right. Mississippi was a place. But Korley, Misipi—that was a time.

Before Korley Misipi, he'd had a wife.

Before Korley Misipi, a son.

Before Korley Misipi, he'd been happy.

Before Korley Misipi—and it was always Korley Misipi, like the two words belonged to one another—he'd had a life.

After, his son was dead and his wife dying, and he'd never known another happy day in all the long span of time since. What he had done was exist—no better—and if it was within the power of a man to will himself to die, Moice would have been a thousand times dead.

It is October, 1842, a late and rainy afternoon. Within the sordid limits of a flea-infested backwater hovel off a no-account tributary of the Mississippi River, a bell tower looms three stories over a town square. The tower is part of a church which has crouched on this land for three generations and so like the land, is weatherbeaten and old. It is sturdily built however, despite how it leans. That leaning can be seen for miles, because the land it occupies is the highest spot in the county and a gathering place for the masses. On a clear day from the top of the tower, a person can see beyond the Mississippi River, across the breadth of Arkansas, and well into Oklahoma. On a still clearer day, the Okies can be counted if not heard.

Or so it is said.

The business of the day near done and the light is just beginning to fade, good for perhaps another hour, two at the most. Despite this, the ruckus is just beginning. A white girl, the princess daughter of a local dry goods merchant, has apparently been violated, maybe this day, maybe the day before—or maybe not at all. This is all about as clear as mud, which under the leaning bell tower in that picked over town square is clear enough.

The nature of the violation, as told by her merchant father, has changed with the advancing sun. In the late morning, he tells anyone who will listen how a nigger slave boy saw his daughter swimming in the local swimming hole. That she often swims naked, that all the girls of the town swim naked in Copper Creek, is common knowledge. But by the time lunch is being served, and this may or may not have been encouraged by a few shots of whiskey, it is the nigger who is swimming naked and the girl—the sweet and innocent and *white* princess—is now just washing her hair on the banks of the stream. Later still, as the tables are being cleared, with more people listening and more drink being had, the nigger brute is forcing himself on and, presumably, in her.

To anyone who will listen, and this turns out to be almost everyone in this sorry little acre, population somewhere north of a hundred, that godless boy—a savage buck of a man in the making—has taken the merchant's daughter and ruined her. No less than a crime against nature it is.

"She might even now," the offended father is saying, "have the burden of a nigger devil growing inside her. What'd you do if'n it was your little girl?"

"The world ain't safe what with that heathen in it!"

"Cut off his pecker! That'll show 'im. That'll show 'em all!"

"Kill the nigger!"

As it happens, whoever has witnessed whatever has occurred cannot with any certainty identify the boy involved. But this hardly matters. It is generally known that a certain negro of about the requisite age, a boy of thirteen by the name of Davidius—the son of slaves known simply as Moice and Sufee—had been stacking goods for the merchant in the week just past. And so, with no more information than that, the crowd settles upon his guilt and determines a sentence and all the while neither the boy Davidius nor the father Moice know any of these goings on.

The boy is taken in the late afternoon, clubbed in the head with an axe handle while chopping wood in a light drizzle. Moice, who is informed through Sufee's screams, comes too late to save his boy from the crowd. He goes immediately to his mistress, an illiterate middle-aged woman of limited means. Her only belongings are a tiny house and the three slaves, all left to her by her husband at his death from smallpox a year earlier. She is not intelligent, at least not in matters of business, least of all in matters doing with slaves. She is not of a mind to keep so troublesome a boy around.

"But he ain't never been no trouble, mistress," Moice says.

"You dare raise your voice to me, boy?" the mistress says. "You best to learn who yer betters is. Get out my sight."

"Please, mistress." Moice has never before or since pleaded with anyone.

"I told you get out my sight. I'll think on it. Let you know come morning."

"He gon' be dead come morning, mistress."

"One more word and I'll have them back here after you!"

Moice leaves his mistress' tiny house and gathers Sufee. They take not but the very clothes on their backs and together they follow the crowd, but at a substantial distance and through a screen of trees, all the while frantic and afraid and all but out of their minds with grief.

The rain falls in sheets and still the crowd presses ever on toward the leaning bell tower. They number the entire town and then some, ever multiplying. There are dogs as well, bitches and dogs filling out the low places in the crowd, yipping and yapping as they sense their masters' heightened blood. These dregs march up the hill pushing and pulling the bloodied child, who is at once both worthless and the exact center of all their attentions. A cold rain comes now at their faces, now at their backs. They carry torches to light the dusk and the flames bend every which way with the wind, distorting their faces in the fevered light. They carry as well clubs and whips of wire. The dogs bare their teeth in sorted sneers of perverted excitement.

Reaching the crest of the hill, their numbers swell still more—it is an event now, a real happening, and nobody wants to miss a real happening—until they bulge like a living, breathing devil and trample the sign at the edge of the town square. It breaks apart and a jackleg preacher, aiming to get out of the mud and slop, stands on the largest piece of the hand-lettered sign. 'korley' it reads, the 'k' no bigger than the other letters, the word still legible in the black muck of the yard. The preacher scrapes his boots against the protruding edge of the sign, scraping the mud off the soles. He smiles lewdly at the people around him, or maybe at the festivities—it isn't clear. He watches the merchant spit in the boy's face, then slap him over and over. The preacher clears his throat and brings the word of God to the moment:

"Come now people and give the nigger savage his due. Move up, move forward, don't crowd now, more's the chance. Don't hesitate as he certainly wouldn't in your stead. Send him on to Hades but first let him know we'll brook no such heathenous behavior from this black beast or any of his kind. Look on him and see not a young lad, but a serpent from Hell. Revile him, spit on him, use the lash and all the better the club. Protect your loved ones though, and care to avoid his eyes now, for those is devil eyes, and to look upon them is to be branded—if not by the foul fiend himself, then by He known the world over by the several names of Lucifer, Mephistopheles, Beelzebub, Satan, Moloch, Belial..."

The crowd becomes a mob and responds to the preacher's words as the heart responds to exercise. It quickens and squeezes all the harder, until with the next pulse it must surely burst. They strip the boy till he is naked and every time he moans or moves even to breathe, as if in doing so he is about to rise up and kill them all, he is slapped, prodded, smacked, or whipped. Sometimes all of these. The thunder and lightning increases, and the jackleg preacher intones how all of this is the will of God, even as a dog rips open the boy's sack and pulls one of his balls out between its canines.

On the edge of this horde is a young man, barely twenty, on his first trip to the Deep South. He hails from Southern Pennsylvania and has come to this dark place on business, has bought and sold much cotton for his father back home. He is unlucky enough to be caught up in the maelstrom, though he has no mind or stomach for any of it.

He leans against a low wooden building, a decrepit structure that looks as diseased as anything in this shit hole town. That is how he has come to think of Korley, Mississippi in just the past few hours. A few minutes before he had been caught up in the crowd, pushed along in this fecal stream, until he lost his footing and was kicked in the face—maybe more than once he thinks but can't be sure. He's lost a tooth and can feel the warmth of blood trickling across one cheek. He'll have a right shiner in the morning.

He is thinking that he has to get to his buckboard, has to get out of this place. He looks on at the scene before him with a horror he will never again equal in this life—not even on the fields of battle he will encounter a score of years later. His mouth tastes sour, tastes of the spew he threw up as the boy passed him in the surging crowd. Only passed is not the right word for it. Dragged. The boy was dragged past him by a half dozen men. Twisted faces all of them.

He had looked into the boy's eyes too. He hadn't seen much, they were swelled the size of plums and he thought the boy was already gone or at least too gone to look back. He hadn't been dead though, not yet. His legs had been jelly, moving all wonky and the like, but not the dead weight of the already departed, the already murdered. And there were his hands of course. They weren't yet gone. Bound behind his back by a cinched tight piece of rawhide bound around his wrists, those hands had yet been fisting—tight then loose, tight then loose—over and over. Several of the fingers were crooked too.

It is then the dog rips apart the naked boy's scrotum and Enoch Gamble vomits.

He can't save the boy. Doesn't even consider it. What he wants is to save himself. He has no interest in pursuing this thing to its climax. He can't get past the crowd on the road though. The only movement is up the hill, as if the laws of physics have suddenly reversed and gravity pulls up and not down. *A man dragged to his own execution would go easier than I...*

The idea dies in his throat as he realizes what he is thinking.

Gamble will spend years trying to tune out the fetid claptrap of this jackleg preacher and the image of this boy being thrown off the bell tower. At odd times and in odd places, he will hear again the clap of thunder and the awful scream as the boy falls through the air, then the awesome and terrible and sudden silence of the rope pulling taunt and his neck stretching beyond this world and into the next. The ratcheting of the neck coming apart is the worst thing he will ever hear, worse even than the cries of his fellows lying wounded on one battlefield after another so many years later. It is only by the grace of God the head doesn't come off altogether, and in the years to come Enoch will thank his Maker repeatedly for this favor.

Moice and Sufee flee for their lives even before their boy hangs. They aren't cowards, but they aren't fools either. The mob has tasted blood and, like a many-headed monster, there is no telling how much it will take to satiate their appetite. One or three—the more's the fun.

For three days the pair moves only by night and then only by the deepest woods. On the fourth, a dark and dreary and moonless one, they are found by three men. These men have hunted them down, or so they say, but they have brought no dogs and in every such case Moice has ever heard it is the dogs that find runners out. More likely, they have just been lucky. It matters little, as they have less sympathy than a rabid hound would have had. To keep him from ever running again, the trio chops off half of Moice's foot with an axe. Then, as he lies fevered and half out of his head, they rape Sufee in the early hours after midnight. This last, they say, is their reward for having to chase them down in the first place.

It is in the middle of this carnage that the young Enoch Gamble comes upon them. He sees them, they do not see him. He sees what they have done and what they are doing. He draws a pistol from his belongings, says a silent prayer for forgiveness to his Maker, and without any warning, shoots in the head the man raping the negro woman.

Enoch is surprisingly calm and methodical as he turns the two-barreled weapon on a second man and shoots him dead too. The third man pulls his own gun and fires at Enoch, but his lead goes wide, ricochets off a rock or otherwise, and strikes Sufee in the belly, high on the left side. Moice grabs the axe—his blood still wet on its blade—and sinks it sideways into the man's chest, hacking through the arm in one swing. The man stands a long while—long enough to fade ghost white as his life blood pours out from the innards of his gone arm and sliced-open chest. The axe juts from his side and as he falls dead, Moice pulls it out and it becomes his from that night on, along with the forepart of his foot, which looks not unlike a ham-hock what with the bone and gristle visible along the cut edge.

It takes three more weeks, but Enoch, Moice, and the dying Sufee make it north.

And now, all these years later, Moice lay at the base of an old oak, looking like a man hollowed from the inside out. His eyes darted to and fro and his lips quivered incessantly.

"Korley, Misipi. Korley, Misipi. Korley, Misipi…" He chewed his lower lip till it damn near came off. A trickle of blood flowed down his chin. His fists balled in the dirt. Slowly, very slowly, his fists opened and he began to right himself.

A stone's throw away, the rebel lieutenant lay supine in the grass.

Neither man, it seemed, had much sense about him.

EIGHTEEN

Purdy finally left her bedroom, moving through her house only reluctantly. The place was dead to her now, like her son—whose body lay yet on the bed she had so long shared with Enoch. The dreary light of morning filtered through the dirty windows, those not yet cracked and broken anyway, and cast gray shadows about the walls and across the floors. It was as if another house entire had grown up in the night. It creaked and groaned around her in ways she had not ever to this moment known. She felt a pang of loss—perhaps the only thing she could feel that morning—and her menfolk died all over again in her heart. They were everywhere she looked.

And nowhere. She slipped in the blood on the kitchen floorboards and, looking down, saw 'EG' carved in rough hewn, square block letters. She stared a long time at those letters, the only ones—aside from the words 'holy bible'—she'd ever learned to read on sight. She'd seen the initials hundreds of times over the years. As she fingered the book in the pocket of her dress, she wondered that she had no idea why the initials were there. She supposed that once or twice she'd thought to ask Enoch about them, but it had seemed a small thing. Now she'd never know and that bothered, like a pebble underfoot she'd never be able shake out.

She found the major in the front room, bent to a soldier who'd lost three of his limbs, including both legs at mid-thigh. The poor bastard was laid out in a space half as large as he would have needed just days before, next to an old sideboard that had housed her dishes. Enoch had fashioned it for their tenth anniversary, honed it from the yellow pine growing thick in the nearby countryside. A hollow, empty thing now, the shelves barren and her dishes nowhere to be found. Like something out of the casketmaker's trade now. One of the lower doors sat askew off a busted hinge, the other gone altogether. The floorboards before it looked no better, soaked dark as they were with body fluids of one sort of another. She ignored the wasted fellow. She was weary and numb to such things now and her sum total of thought on the poor man was that he would die and it wouldn't change a damn thing.

"I had me a pair of dogs once," the poor bastard was saying in a halting, slow rasp broken by his need to breathe. "They got themselves in a fight one day and the bigger one he knocked the other's eye out. That damn mutt took to jumping and his eye was hanging on the side of his head bobbing up and down. He kept beating at it with a paw, making a noise I ain't never heared a dog make since."

"Son, you have given much for your country these past few days, do not give up now." Brody took the soldier's hand in his own.

A few paces behind the pair, Purdy stared at the back of Brody's head. The room around her was quiet with the labored breathing of men trying hard either to live or die, hard to say which in most cases.

The steel in her hand felt heavy, but bringing her arm up still seemed harder than it should have been.

The poor bastard of a soldier grimaced and she saw that, saw how he kept talking through the pain.

"That mutt was crazy and I had to shoot him, doc. Putting that eye back in was beyond me. I might of been able to do it, but he never woulda been the same again. No sir, never woulda been, not after that. Something like that, it changes, wounds the spirit. Kills it even."

"Corporal." The major's voice.

Precise, always so damn precise, Purdy thought.

"I'm like that dog, doc. I ain't never gonna be no good again, not after all this. Let me die now." His eyes grew big, voice stronger than it had right to be. "Shoot me, man, for God's sake shoot me." The soldier pulled himself up by Brody's hand, up close alongside Brody's ear. "Or give me a Springfield and I'll do 'er myself."

He lay back and Brody stared at him, as if the words had stricken the power of speech from him. Purdy stood behind him, the major not aware of her presence.

"Gawd," Brody drew the word out a long while, as if it had two distinct parts, "will forgive you those words, son. He will forgive all of us."

He pulled away from the soldier's outstretched hand and ran his own hand through his hair before putting his cap on. He leaned over the soldier again, said loud enough for all to hear: "We all have a job to do, son. Yours is to get better, get better and maybe fight another day."

The sound of the pistol going off was an explosion in the quiet room.

The force of it knocked Purdy back a pace but she didn't fall. Brody swung around and stepped away in one and the same motion, his cap moving in the opposite direction like it had leapt off his head. The soldier who had a moment before begged to be shot gurgled once or twice through a new opening in his neck. His hand went to his throat and bright blood flowed briskly over his fingers. He had enough presence to look up to Purdy and that was it. The blood stopped pumping and his hand came away from his throat, falling with a thud.

Brody stood frozen for a long instant. It seemed to Purdy the only part of him not frozen was his mouth, which slowly opened. Then he turned and looked at the soldier, making no effort to staunch the blood, which very shortly staunched itself in any event. He looked back at her then, mouthing *What have you done?* His lips moved but she didn't hear the words, didn't hear anything. As if the report had deafened her. Her arms felt heavy a thousand times over.

Brody slowly stepped aside the soldier. For an instant her eyes met his and she saw for the first time the lack of sleep in him. He pulled at his suspenders and the brace on his leg clicked and she was reminded how he was a cripple. His movements were those of a winded runner, or a not quite whipped dog. Not quite, because he still had determination about him. His leg, crippled though it was, did not slow him down.

"Your people, they've left." she said. Flat, maybe a question, maybe not.

"Mostly." He stared at her, a look of what—incredulity?—on his face.

"You didn't go." Another maybe question.

"So it would seem."

His own face was sallow and thin, as if the war had worn on it. He had the eyes of the long suffering and enfeebled, eyes that had sunk inward. He took a deep breath. "Couldn't leave these men."

"You'll be caught," she said matter-of-factly. Her arm, the one with the gun, swung at her side.

"So it goes." He took a step toward her and somewhere in the far distance, his brace clicked.

"You don't care?"

"I do not have such luxuries, not in this time, not here." Another step and the brace clicked again. "I care only about what happens to these men. They have families. Wives and children. People who love them. They deserve the best of me, all I can give."

"Families and loved ones. This I know." Purdy gave her attention to the window over the surgeon's shoulder, her eyes alighting on the willow tree in the yard, to the loved ones entombed at its roots. She said flatly, "I'm burying my son today."

"God bless you, Mrs. Gamble," the surgeon said.

Then he struck her upside the head with the heel of his hand.

There was no minister for he was dead, shot through the chest on the steps of his own house of worship. In his stead no one stood, for all were too tired, too haggard, too lost in both mind and body to step forward. All anyone wanted was get it over with, for this would not be the last burial this day.

"I guess I understand why you did it," Brody said. "But it was wrong."

"No more wrong than your coming here in the first place," Purdy said. She was seated on a chair in the backyard, close by to the willow. Her hands were tied in front of her. "No more wrong than anything else what happens in war."

"We are not animals, madam."

"My face would be the exception then?" It was swollen and bruised from cheek to ear where Brody had clocked her.

"Another man might have killed you and he'd have been in the right."

"That might have been a blessing."

"Well, they might maybe still string you up."

"It don't matter no more. Nothing matters no more."

"I am truly sorry for that, because if it's true, all of this has been for naught," Brody said.

She looked away, nodded.

"Including your own husband's death."

"I told you once to go to hell, major. I guess what I really meant was, see you in hell."

"Couldn't you untie her just for the funeral?" Loli asked.

"I offered," Brody said.

"Ma?"

"It don't matter, girl. Coal ain't gonna know no difference."

Coal was laid to rest beside his father under the willow, his death shroud a Confederate army blanket. He lay in the grass beside the open grave and his mother pulled the blanket back from his face with her tied hands—a final look at the young, blue lips of the newly departed. This was how she would remember him, blue-lipped and gone to his Maker prematurely. She stared hard at his face, all the while his lidless eyes staring back at her, wide and accusatory, like maybe she should have taken better care of him. The soft rain washed into those eyes and she wiped it away and it collected again.

His sister, her face smudged with mud and the ash of the barn, opened the blanket yet further, found his hand. The good hand, for the palsied would not do. She was wordless as she curled his stiff fingers around the polished stone and bent to kiss his cheek, like an angel breathing life anew. When she rose, a touch of the blackface was left on Coal's cheek, where it would stay until the vagaries of time and mortality conspired to erase it.

In the rush of last night's long train of wounded, a score of injured had been left behind. For a few there was no room, others too wounded, still others not wounded enough. One of the able-bodied, as able-bodied as came in that season of carnage, stood across the grave from the others, slicker wet with peat and mud, hard breathing, shovel at order arms like a sentry. Coal was no kin to him, but burying is a solemn act in any land, so he stood by and breathed hard and felt the ache in his muscles and perhaps hoped the rain would lighten the digging yet to come.

It was left not to a pious man but to one of science to say some words over the boy. Major Peter Brody had not seen four hours' sleep in four days and so what he said was short. He looked at the boy's mother, at her hands, at the length of rope holding them. He looked at the small mound that was the nameless baby, at the larger that was this woman's husband and this boy's father, at the sister who he supposed had now to inherit this ruined land.

The willow tree worried with the breeze and the rain and the sound of its leaves rustling over and around all of them was a whisper in the wind. Somewhere in the hills a mongrel dog barked loud enough to make itself heard here. A barn owl screeched. The major looked finally to the boy, who lay beside the earthen pit dug for him. He clasped his hands, either in prayer or in thinking.

Brody, wearing the same soiled gray jacket he wore the first time he set foot on this land, spread his arms wide and said something like "precious in the sight of the Lord is the death of his saints," a passage he recalled from his reading of Psalms. "I am told," he went on, raising his hands higher still and looking the very part of a preacher, "that God does not play favorites and takes us all to his side sooner or later. But I believe he must have favorites, and that he puts them here only to strengthen us. And that once strengthened, he calls them home again. At his side the blind receive their sight and the lame walk. The deaf hear and the dead are raised up and the dumb have the gospel preached to them and their understanding. God rest his soul, the boy will be made whole again."

He spoke these words not so as just anyone could hear, but especially so as Loli and Purdy could. Beyond this, he did not pay particular attention. He was beyond exhaustion and had delivered this graveside sermon nearly in his sleep, and it was sleep that fought hard to claim him now. He took a moment for himself, wiped the rain from his face. He was so tired, yet there was much work yet remaining. He came around the grave, knelt beside the dead boy, and pulled the shroud over his eyes.

"He is in God's hands now."

It was then he noticed the shape of a large man, still a ways out, lurching forward through the grass. In his arms he cradled a second man. *Something odd with the negro,* Brody thought.

He was reminded of his own lame, lopsided step.

NINETEEN

Loli caught the surgeon's look and followed his gaze out beyond the tents. She had time only to think *God forgive me I forgot him* and was up in an instant, moving toward the negro and the man he cradled. She waved and hollered, "Mr. Moice! Mr. Moice!" forgetting the place and the solemnity of the moment.

She was at his side a moment later. The big man continued to move along, the unconscious rebel looking small in his arms.

"Miss Loli." Moice nodded at her and panted by way of breathing. Blood still seeped from the puncture wound where he had bit his lip.

"They killed—eh, my brother he died. He got himself burnt up. I didn't think after that. Is he okay? He gonna make it?" Her words ran together.

"He alive, missy. Lost his wits is all. Likely as not the fever will get 'em though. You gots a doctor herebouts?"

She turned. "Ma!"

Purdy was standing now. Enoch's preacher hat, which had been in her hand all through the short graveside service, was on her head again. "Who's that, child?" she said, then answered the question herself. "Moice, that you?"

"You know Mr. Moice, ma?"

"Who's that you carrying, Moice?" Purdy said.

"He is a rebel officer," Brody said.

"It's Ben Taylor, ma. The man what helped us with Hannah." Loli had run ahead and was close enough now to her mother that she didn't need to shout anymore. "He's the one what helped with Noah. He's hurt real bad, on account his arm got blowed off." She nodded at Moice, looked at the surgeon.

Brody, the fatigue and pall of sleep lifting from his person, took command. He directed Moice to place the officer inside the house, on the kitchen table. If it seemed a travesty to refer to it as a kitchen, nobody said as much. It was plain to all the place would never function as a kitchen again.

Moice ascended the three steps to the kitchen and put the man on the table as ordered. He stood looking down on the soldier, maybe wondering if he'd done the right thing in removing his arm, and was interrupted by the surgeon. "Get your black ass out of my way so I can work boy."

Loli took Moice's hand and pulled him out of the room and into the yard. There were perhaps twenty people present in that yard, most all rebels and most all too sick to have been moved out in the train of the night before. A few men were more able-appearing and these stood beside the small body which in turn lay beside an open grave under a willow tree. They were staring at the negro.

Loli explained to Moice: "That's my brother, name of Coal. Got himself burnt up when the barn caught fire." She turned her attention on the bystanders: "What you people staring at? This here's my kind friend, Mr. Moice." Back to Moice again: "I wasn't here when it happened but I was here when he died. I wish I had been here cause maybe then it might not've happened. You have to come meet my ma."

Moice hesitated, stopping in his tracks like a stubborn mule. "That ain't no good idea, Miss Loli."

"Why not?"

"I told you this ain't none my affair."

"Then why are you here, silly? Besides, I think maybe she knows you."

"Yeah."

Purdy decided the issue by coming over from beneath the willow tree. She stood in the slow, mizzling rain, her eyes going to and fro over him as if seeing him for the first time. When she spoke, it was out of the corner of her mouth while she continued to eye Moice. "Loli child, what's this man done to you?"

"Done to me?"

"Yeah, don't be afraid. What's he done to you?"

"Mr. Moice ain't done nothing, ma."

Purdy addressed herself to Moice. "What'd you do to my child?"

"I showed her back here's all."

"He found me and Mr. Taylor in the swamp, ma. Took us back to his place—"

"He did what?"

"He saved our lives. My life anyway. If'n Mr. Taylor lives, then he saved his too."

"Perhaps you better start at the beginning, child. And let me sit down, I'm feeling just a little, eh, unwell. Enoch, honey, I hope you're listening." She took the preacher hat off and held it in her hands before her face, as if smelling it. She smiled at Loli, a distressed sort of turning up of one side of the mouth. It didn't seem meant to indicate pleasure.

Loli told the story, starting with having met the surgeon once before, at the aid station, and about how she had come across Lieutenant Taylor in the woods. She told too about the soldiers who'd chased her into the swamp, about how Moice had rescued her and Taylor. She had an idea Moice had killed them but left that part out. She left out the amputation too, indicating Taylor had lost his arm before she had come across him. She told how Moice had given them a roof for two nights, and how he'd doctored the rebel till he was well enough to move. When she was done,

Moice was the picture of a saint and Purdy could only stare at the two of them a long while.

She finally said: "I don't think there's no way you could make up such a story as that one, child. And if even half of it's true—and I didn't teach you no lying ways so I suppose it must be—then I guess I owe Moice here a thank you. First though, praise be to Jesus for steering Moice to you." She turned to Moice. "Thank you."

"I'm obliged to ya," Moice said. "Mr. Enoch, he always said how you was quality folk, ma'am.

Purdy said, "I never understood the hold the two of you had on each other, how you'd disappear together for days at a time. It was the one thing he never would talk about. What was it?"

"It ain't the sort of a thing what bears talking. We was friends is all. He done something for me once and I've spent a lifetime trying to repay him. When I seen Loli being chased, something just went off in me. I couldn't allow it. Even if it kilt me."

"Moice, my husband is buried right here under this willow. You know that, you done the burying after all. And beside him is my first born baby. You put him there too I recall. And beside the two of them is our grandson Noah. And now, beside all of them, is my last born son, Coal was his name. I wish you would stand by us now as we put Coal in the ground."

"I can do that."

"Just stand by us is all. You don't gotta do nothing."

"Yes, ma'am."

And so the three of them—Purdy, Loli, and Moice—stood by the grave and watched as Brody's men lowered Coal into the ground, then closed the earth over him.

"He at peace now," Moice said, and something in his voice made Purdy glance at him, a sharp, daggered look. "Perfect peace."

TWENTY

Brody had seen a lot of arms blown off in his near two years behind an army scalpel, but this had to be the cleanest blast wound he'd ever encountered. The beds of both the flexor and extensor muscles were recognizable where they had been cut through above the elbow. The stump was smooth, it could have been knife cut, but it was burnt as well. He thought on that a moment.

The proper word, he realized as he stared at the lieutenant's stump wound, was cauterized.

"And a cauterized wound is a surgical wound," he said *sotto voce*, thinking how the work wasn't half bad. By 'wasn't half bad' he meant it wouldn't have to be done again. The stump would require some debridement, probably several debridements, but there was a fair chance it would heal, if the man lived. There was always that, of course. If he lived.

He poked with an dissector, checking for laudable pus. He found none, but it was probably too early for it.

The lieutenant moved then, turned his head and opened his eyes. He looked right at the surgeon. "Caint feel my hand," he said.

"I am not surprised," Brody said. "It is a fairly bad wound."

"My hand?"

"Gone, but you still have your life to lose. We must concentrate our efforts on saving it."

"Oh God, my arm. Did you take it off?"

"Never mind. It is done and there is no going back. Lieutenant, you have given much. Nearly a full measure and more. Our task now is to get you back to health so you may resume your place in this army. I suspect the time is not far off when experienced combat officers such as yourself will be in very short supply."

Taylor might or might not have heard this. He grimaced somewhere in the middle of the words and drifted away. Brody waited a moment to see if he would come around again, then dressed the stump in a wad of cotton lint and wrapped it in plaster.

Hannah waded through the tall grass across the field. It was not quite dark yet and the sound of men and shovels at work was heavy in the air. When she finally found them, she discovered three negroes wearing Union uniforms. They'd stopped digging for the night and were laying out bedrolls and had started a small fire.

She announced herself as she came into their camp. They stopped what they were doing and looked at her dumbfounded, clearly uncomfortable with her presence. Yes, they told her, they were from graves registration. They had been tasked, only just this day, with burying the men on this end of the field as quickly as possible.

"Seen any red-headed soldiers hereabouts?"

"Ain't sure," one of them answered. He was the senior here, a corporal he said.

"Could we look?" Hannah asked.

"I suppose we could check in the morning."

"Could we look now?"

"Gonna be dark pretty fast, Miss."

"It's important."

"The dead ain't going nowhere overnight," a second man said.

"My husband might be out there."

"Our condolences, Missus."

"Alive."

The second man said: "Ain't seen nothing move on this field all afternoon. Well, I did see me a hog out there somewhere, rootin' round." He snickered.

Hannah ignored him.

"Missus, if'n he's out here, he's dead," the corporal said. "Ain't nothing alive out here 'cept us."

"And the hogs," the second man said.

"Shut up, Rosley," the corporal said.

"I'm just sayin' how it is."

"Supposin' you keep how it is to yerself. Shut up or I'll shut you up."

"You and whose army?" Rosley said.

"Listen you two," Hannah said, "I'm only asking, while there's still some light remaining, that you point me in the right direction."

The corporal said: "They up dat away." He pointed up the hill, where the bodies were scattered randomly for a mile or so directly in front of them.

"You going up that way you gonna need something to cover your nose. It's powerful bad lady," the third of the soldiers said.

"Much obliged." She turned to leave.

"You're going up there tonight?" the corporal said.

"I am. If my husband's up there, he's hurt bad. Maybe he's dead, but I don't feel it if'n he is. Either way, I aim to find him tonight."

"That ain't gonna be no pretty sight. Some of them bodies is swolled real bad, lady," Rosley said.

"He ain't swolled if he's alive, now is he?" she said.

The corporal sighed. "My man's right, but I suppose you ain't gonna hear it, is you?"

No answer.

"All right then. You white people is nothing you ain't stubborn. And you always doing things the hard way. Rosley, you and Kelly, get that old mule over here and hitch the cart. We might's well help the lady."

They looked for an hour, until it grew too dark to look anymore. At that, she thanked them and walked off into the night.

Ben Taylor shivered on the ground. Loli gave him a sip from the medicine Brody had given her and covered him with one of the few blankets available, a handcrafted patchwork quilt that had no business in the mud.

"No, I'm fine, really. Give it to one of these poor souls what's in more need than me."

But she insisted he have it. "You're shivering. You going to catch your death wind."

"I'm okay. Look," he pointed to his stump of arm, where the plaster bandage was wet and red. "I'm more whole than most any man here."

She wrapped the gift around him anyway, doting like a mother, or perhaps a lover. Later, she and Purdy returned and found the blanket given over to another.

"They're all deserving," Taylor said.

They all three watched as one of the fellows was taken by the orderlies, disappearing into the wet curtain coming down all around them. The renewed rain swallowed everything.

"That's not how I see it. And besides I don't care. That's off my own bed. I brought it for you. Don't be proud. Or foolish,".

"What about you?" Taylor said.

"I'm warm enough, and I'll sleep dry tonight," she lied.

"Why you helping me?"

"Because you helped my sister, Hannah. And because you need helping. And, well, just because."

Taylor said, "Hannah? Oh yeah, the baby. Sad thing that. How's your sister doing?"

"Tolerable I hope. She ain't been around in a few days."

"I'm grateful. Really, I am. But I can't take the blanket."

The quilt lay over a young boy beside him. His face was powder blackened and his teeth chattered like it was winter in July. All the while he talked a fool's talk. Loli reached for the blanket but Purdy stopped her.

"Perhaps it's best, child." In another minute though, the sergeant on the other side of the boy snatched the covering.

"Give it back," Taylor said.

"What's it to you?"

"The boy caint speak up. I'm speaking for him."

"Mister, I caint hardly stop shivering no way. I'm wet and cold all through. He's dead already and y'all know that. Got no call to cover the dead on a night like this."

"Put the blanket back over him or I'll kick you in your jewels," Taylor said.

"You ain't got the strength," the sergeant said.

"I do," Loli said. "And you best believe I'll do it."

"You go ahead, missy. I like to die anyhow and maybe that'll brr—bring, bring it on. I caint, caint stand one more minute of this." The sergeant's voice quivered.

Purdy felt the man's need. The boy couldn't be long for the world, not this world anyway. In the black dark, she saw the sergeant had lost both his legs at mid-thigh. She decided he had earned his right. "Problem here is we just ain't got enough quilts." She nodded at Loli and they dropped the argument after that.

They came for Taylor not much later. A captain leaned over him and pronounced him fit for travel. They were loading up a few more wounded, getting together a smaller train of casualties than the previous night.

"We should make the river by daybreak," the captain said, the implication being they'd be safe on the other side.

He moved on and was followed by a pair of stretcher bearers. Purdy had seen them earlier as they roved about the grounds. The two started to lift the lieutenant to a standing position, but Loli and Purdy stepped in and supported his weight. They crossed the yard to a buckboard. There were three men already seated in the bed of the wagon.

Moice came forward to help lift Taylor into the wagon.

"There now, rest on that hay pile," Loli said.

The "pile" was a few bits of straw that did more to dirty the wagon's floor than cushion it. Taylor groaned as he settled into place.

"Go with God, Mr. Taylor," Moice said, then stepped back into the shadows.

Taylor, who had no idea what the man had done for him, caught only a vague glimpse of the negro. "That's a might big nigger fella."

The horse neighed and the wagon lurched forward a piece, throwing Taylor over onto one of his companions.

The man said, "Oh God. Could you just kill me now? If you has a decent bone in you, just kill me now."

In the merciful dark Loli couldn't see the owner of that pathetic whine, but the dank smell of dung mixed with sour vomit filled in enough of the details.

She slipped a canteen of water in alongside Taylor and pulled him close to her. She was careful with what remained of his arm. "This is just for you. No arguments this time. Ma says you got a ways to go before you'll be home. I wish I could go with you. Maybe you could come back and see us some day?"

"I might just maybe do that. After this war."

She began to cry and covered her mouth and left her good-bye unspoken. She stepped away from the wagon.

Purdy said, "Seems you've made an impact on both my daughters."

"I'm appreciative."

"It's I who should be appreciating you." She took off the coat she was wearing. "This belonged to my husband. He was about your size." She put it around him, then laid him gently against the side of the buckboard. "Enoch would have liked you, I think."

"The war?" Taylor asked. He was drowsy and all-in with fatigue, but he hadn't lost his insight.

"That's right. He won't never be coming back." Purdy felt compelled to return his gaze. His hair slicked back in the rain, and around his eyes the glint of water droplets conspired and she saw something of the young man the war had beaten out of him, the innocent he must once have been. "And so it must be with each of us in our time. We don't none of us know what tomorrow gonna bring, Mr. Taylor. It's as the Good Book says. Our life is but a vapor that appeareth for a little time, and then vanisheth away." She looked out yonder and back again. "Good-bye, Mr. Taylor. And Godspeed."

TWENTY-ONE

Only a handful of injured remained at the Gamble farm. These were the men whom Brody had determined would surely die if moved, would probably die anyway. Yet he couldn't bring himself to abandon them. And now, with darkness settled all around them, he waited. The Yanks could not be far off and he would be captured, probably before the night was out. Certainly before another day had passed.

The rain had finally stopped and the injured were laid out in the grass behind the house. The house itself stood as if alone in the world, a big, quiet, diseased hulk. Even in the dark, especially in the dark, it looked aged.

"Thank you for the use of your tent, major."

"It is the least I—"

"Thank you all the same," Purdy said. She had come up behind and alongside the major and he had turned to meet her. "Loli thanks you too. May I sit?"

"It is your homestead."

"It is my husband's place, and my place."

"What was his name?"

"Mr. Enoch Gamble."

"I will remember that name," Brody said.

"He is buried right here." She pointed yonder, to the willow tree twenty yards distant, to the patch of dirt—now mud—under it. "He lies beside my two sons."

"Two?"

She told him of the breech baby.

"I had no idea. You are a remarkable woman, Mrs. Gamble."

There was an awkward pause. She turned away for a moment, wiping her eyes. When she turned back she said, "What will become of you?"

"A yankee prison camp, I suppose."

"You can't do no good for your men in such a place."

"Perhaps I shall be paroled. Perhaps there will be an end to this damn war someday."

"You don't believe that?"

"That I shall be paroled, possibly. That the war will end any time soon, no. These two factions—sides—have dug in and we will all do hard time before it is over. You and yours, Mrs. Gamble, are, unfortunately, not the exception but the rule. This is war and life is cheap."

She started to say something but her thoughts were interrupted by hoofbeats. More than one horse by the sound of it. She stood. "Come with me, major."

"What?"

"Do you want to spend the rest of this war in goddamn prison? Come with me."

The sound of the horses coming up the trail from Old Dutch Road intensified. The major rose and they walked across the yard to the back of the house, where they ascended the several steps to the kitchen. The major's brace clicked and he limped as he went. Even so, they moved quickly and once inside the major took her hand and together they made their way to the front room and then the stairs. They ignored the stench, which was of decay.

"The way I see it, you have a choice."

"I am no coward, madam. And I will not beg for my life. Or my freedom."

"Of course you ain't. Never said you were. But you can't do those outside any good now and going to prison, well, who does that help?"

"I have a duty."

At the top of the stairs she guided them to her bedroom, where Coal had died not twenty-four hours before. It was black dark but their eyes adjusted quickly. Horses neighed outside and they could hear men moving about in the darkness.

"To your men, I know. But I've seen your work, doctor, and your bigger duty is to the men whose lives you haven't yet saved but will. Put these on. They belonged to my husband."

With that, and brooking no more resistance, she hurried back outside.

"Who's caring for these men?" a Union officer called out.

"I am," Purdy said as she came down the steps at the back of her house.

"These are rebel soldiers," the captain said.

"So they are," Brody said from the back doorway.

The officer turned to face the new voice. The man at the door wore trousers and a flannel shirt. On his feet were work boots of a sort that suggested he had just come in from outside. On his head was a wide brimmed, black preacher hat.

"My apologies to you, sir, I did not realize a man was at home. Your name?"

"This here's my husband, Mr. Enoch Gamble. He owns the land you are standing on, captain. Owns it all."

"We've won a great victory these past few days, and the rebels are in retreat," the captain said.

"And you are claiming their wounded?" Brody said.

"We are," the captain said.

"And how will they be treated?"

"They'll get the care they need and those that survive will rot in prison."

"They'll be treated humanely?" Purdy asked.

"We are Christians. Not barbarians."

"Then take them," Brody said. "I'd just as soon be rid of 'em."

"Any others about? Wounded or otherwise? Those who treated them perhaps? We suspect a rebel hospital was set up somewhere in this sector."

Purdy was thankful for the cover of darkness. She looked at Brody. "No others, they've fled. Moved out this early morning in the rain. Check the house if you like."

Brody came down the steps, the clicking of his brace obvious as he moved. "Yes, check the house."

"You've lost a leg, sir?"

"Just lamed is all. First Bull Run."

The captain eyeballed him. "No one in the house, then?"

"No."

He turned to his men. "Collect up these rebels and be easy about it."

Once the captain and his men had left, Purdy and the major stood in the darkness. "His clothes fit you better than I thought they would."

"They feel a mite conspicuous to me."

"Well, they needn't be," Purdy said, followed again by that awkward silence, which was broken only by the appearance of Moice.

"Miss Loli is still sleeping," Moice said.

"Thank you for watching out for her, Mr. Moice," Purdy said. She looked at Brody again. "You can't stay here."

"Yes, those men will be back. Just point me in the right direction."

"Moice," Purdy said, "I wonder if you'd be up for a little adventure."

"An adventure, ma'am?"

"You think you can get Dr. Brody to the rebels?"

"He a friend of yours?"

"Yes, I believe he is."

"Well then, if'n he's a friend of yours he'd be a friend of Mr. Enoch. And I'd be obliged to show the way for any friend of Mr. Enoch. Not happy maybe, but obliged."

Dr. Peter Brody took a few minutes to retrieve his medical bag and a change of clothes which included his uniform. "I suppose if I'm caught I could be shot as a spy," he said.

"You won't be caught. Mr. Moice knows these parts better than anyone. In fact, I'd trust my own life, or that of my daughter, with him."

"Godspeed, Mrs. Enoch Gamble," Brody said.

"And to you, doctor."

Purdy walked the violated acres of her family farm. The occupiers had taken everything she'd held dear. Her home was in shambles, barely fit for dogs. The land was a torched boneyard. Even her husband's grave looked to have been desecrated. Not violated, she allowed, but desecrated all the same. And Hannah was missing, maybe gone forever. Coal *was* gone forever. She still had Loli and thank God for that.

There comes a time in a person's life when everything they've worked for—everything that's important to them—suddenly takes focus. For Purdy Gamble, that time came in the wee hours past midnight standing on the Old Dutch Road, as she looked up at her homestead from a bend in that road. Moice and Brody had left and she'd gone for a walk. But time had gotten away from her and now, in the veiled darkness, she saw the remains of her home for the first time. She couldn't make out the details, but the shadows were distressing enough. The farm was as dark as she had ever seen it. No gray, just black dark. Sable sky and the inky earth below. She felt a chill in the misting air; too cold for a July night.

As she got closer, the homestead became even stranger; not a place she knew. That thin-ribbed mutt of a dog didn't come out to greet her. No laughter, nor even of people present. Closer yet and the silence enveloped her too. The night was still in a way she'd never imagined a night could be still, as if somehow the hundreds of sounds that made the darkness familiar had morphed into something unholy.

Somewhere, the wind wrestled a door and the banging of it again and again made her think of the hammering she'd endured in Falmouth, where the casketmakers had been busy. The closer she got to her front door, the louder the slamming became and in the end, the run up that lonely piece of trail from Old Dutch Road to her front stoop was the hardest quarter-mile of her life. The yard's open air smothered her. And, like the walls of a coffin, that banging closed in on her in the silence. An image of Loli pale and dead blue came across the blackness and was too real not to be true.

Loli? Where was Loli?

Her feet began to run of their own accord and took her into the yard. She stumbled in the dirt. A stretcher lay in the weeds. Clothes scattered here and there. A broken wagon wheel. Piece of a man's smoking pipe. Pages from a notebook. Everywhere the loathsome buzz of flies. The trees were like exhumed things, how they had lost their leaves, how their branches withered against the sky skeletal, their tips like finger bones.

In this clockless place, her mind skipped a moment—the way a rock skips the surface of a pond, touching only here and there—and when it touched down firm again she was at her front door with no idea how she'd got there.

"Loli?" Her voice cut the dark like a torch. And though it was agony to speak, it was worse agony not to get an answer. The silence was unbearable.

She pushed open the door—the jamb was still splintered from before and how long ago that now seemed—and there was the scrape of metal on wood. She bent and picked up a busted latch. Rimmed in blood it was.

Even in shadow, the outlines of the front room were wrong. She found an inch of candle and struck a lucifer to it. The stone fireplace loomed huge and dark in one corner, a monstrosity and no comfort at all. Broken furniture. Black streaks along the walls. Dark puddles here and there. Stale smell of urine and animal musk. And the flies. Oh God, the flies.

Falmouth. It all came rushing back.

She went room to room. More of the same. Filth and crud everywhere. Bandages, broken blade of a hack saw, bloody blankets. A urinal that hadn't been emptied and a bucket of shit. Only the busted out windows allowed a tolerable smell. Tolerable but no better. Her head pounded. The bandage makers had missed the drapes hanging in her bedroom, part of them anyway. They floated tattered and torn in the breeze, half-dissected for their cloth. One hand to a wall she steadied herself and grabbed the billowing material with the other. She sobbed, and in her crying slipped to the floor. The devil's own day was at hand.

Her mind skipped again—a painful, blinding flash of light this was—and of a sudden it occurred to her that she'd left Loli sleeping in the major's tent, not in the ruined house. She rose and in another moment crossed the yard and found the tent. Loli was as Moice had said, asleep on the cot. She lay down with her, up close and spooning, her breasts flat against Loli's back. The girl stirred but didn't speak.

In that instant, Purdy's headache vanished and she felt more nearly alive than had seemed humanly possible only a moment before.

TWENTY-TWO

Purdy didn't want to see her ruined house in the light of day again. She found it difficult enough to go into the place in the dark, when she could barely see the carnage. Everywhere she went memories lurked, like wounded wolves waiting to pounce. By day it would be too much to endure.

Neither she nor Loli coveted much from the place, but the few things they did want they took. Loli had given her favorite quilt to Taylor. She took the only other thing that had any meaning to her, a store bought hairbrush her father had given her on her birthday the summer before he went to war. It had come with a small looking glass but she'd dropped that and cracked it not a month later. Nonetheless, she grabbed the looking glass too.

The only thing Purdy really wanted was the tintype she'd had taken with Enoch a few days before he died. She also had the wide-brimmed preacher hat of course. She entered the blighted house and climbed the stairs to what had been hers and Enoch's bedroom. The tattered drape lay on the floor where she had pulled it down. She found the Bible exactly where she had left it. She picked it up, then one of Enoch's favorite shirts and tried to smell him in it, but it was no good and she tossed it away.

On the way out it occurred to her she should take something for Hannah. In Hannah's room, she eyed the cradle Enoch had made so many years before, the only furniture in one piece after the hell of the previous days. She considered a moment, but there was no way she'd be able to carry it. She looked past it to Hannah's dresser, largely empty. Under it was a small square of delicate white linen.

We should have buried Noah in it, she thought. His death seemed a year in the past now and she shook the notion off. She took the cloth and ran.

Out in the yard, torch in hand, she couldn't bear the thought of the cradle gone to ashes. She and Loli went back inside and made the arduous climb to the second floor. They wrestled the large cradle down the stairs and out into the yard and set it under the willow tree, under the same tree where they'd buried so much of their lives in recent months.

Purdy took the torch in hand. She'd had a regular life once, but that was forever gone now and this place had become wretched and deplorable. A curse upon the land. As long as she lived, she would think of her life as divided into two great arcs. The dividing line, the terrible awesome moment when everything had turned, was not a crystallized point in time. Rather, it was a blurred hell of destruction, a misery of weeks. On the one side, she'd been Enoch's wife and the mother of his children, a role she'd relished; on the other, she was Purdy Gamble, wife of a ghost, mother of shadows, the matriarch of ruins.

Purdy stood before the back steps. She'd stood those steps maybe ten times a day for twenty-odd years. She wondered what that came to in round numbers. She walked up them one last time, feeling them sag into the mud with her weight, and peered into what had once been her kitchen. She had only to toss the flame and it would all be history.

She knelt and skittered the torch across the floor. It stopped against the far wall and for a moment the issue seemed in question. But then the wall caught and the flames ran up the vertical and across the ceiling.

She turned away and stepped back, suddenly spying the corner of floor where Enoch had unaccountably carved his initials. She stood transfixed. She had only time enough to regret not pulling up that piece of floor before Loli pulled her out and the fire roared.

In a few minutes the house Enoch Gamble had built with his own two hands looked like nothing so much as a large funeral pyre burning in the night.

The pair stepped further into the back yard, away from the house. There they stood a long time, hugging each other close, the warmth of the fire upon them. After awhile, Purdy turned away,

Standing before her was a young woman. She was dressed in the oversized shirt and pants of a soldier, and her face looked yellow in the pyred light, but Purdy recognized her on the instant.

She put out her arms and Hannah came forward and the three of them embraced under the willow. The family Bible lay abed the cradle beside them.

Loli picked it up and thumbed it, finding the tintype and turning the image for all to see in the firelight. Her parents sat ramrod straight and looked like strangers to each other. Loli had tears, but no word passed among the three of them.

Purdy looked at her daughters, thought *not a time for talking.* Later it might be, but not just then. She took off Enoch's hat and wiped her forehead with the back of her hand and brought the hat before her face, where she held it prayerfully. It still smelled faintly of him.

Or maybe she just imagined it so.

THE END

ACKNOWLEDGMENTS

Writing a book is a long, lonely road. Not a slog, mind you. I never find writing a slog. But, for me at least, it's an intensely solitary experience. I'm not much of a people person when you come right down to it. Oh, I try to be. I'd love to have scores of friends I can call at all hours of the day and night, to golf with or invite over for a movie night. Another couple to go out to dinner with would be handy. And somebody to trade tools with or play catch with on a Saturday afternoon would be fun.

Problem is, my life doesn't run that way. I've never been able to make friends easily, and, if I'm being truthful, I'd just as soon not be bothered with making dates to play ball or shoot hoops. And what happens if you just don't feel like going out to dinner on that previously scheduled night? I like my alone time. Maybe I'm selfish, or maybe it's all on account of how much time I have to spend doing other people's bidding at my day job, being a neurosurgeon. Sixty hours plus a week, used to be eighty or more. When I'm off, I want to spend my time my way.

Usually that means either watching baseball, curling up by the fire with a good book, or writing. Sometimes a variation of all three. The writing is daily though. Over the years, I've realized I need to write the way others need to breathe. It's sustenance.

But no man is an island, and no writer is truly alone. Even if it's just coming up for source material, or to eat and drink, you just can't do it alone. Besides, that'd be boring.

Thanks to my wife, Jean, for putting up with this attitude all these years. She's there when I need her and mostly even when I don't. And god bless her for knowing there ain't much difference between those two.

Thanks to my kids too, Edison III, England, and Ehvyn. They've had to listen to more than their share of stories, which I could see in their eyes was pretty painful at times, especially when I cajoled one or two of their friends to tag along. I hope they noticed their friends kept coming though, and I hope the stories have gotten better over the years.

My mother is, perhaps, my ideal reader. She's never been able to wait for the next thing to come off my pen and for that, thanks. She's been nothing but encouraging over the years.

David Poyer deserves a round of applause for his patience and assistance over the years, as does Lenore Hart. I've learned more from their edits than I ever learned elsewhere. I appreciate their faith and persistence with me over the years. I've no doubt it was a slog for them at times. Thanks, folks.

Tim Farrington helped me when I was at my lowest. Thanks, Tim.

Over the years the nurses and techs at my hospitals have listened patiently as I read the occasional passage or bounced ideas off of them. Linda Vogel in particular deserves special mention for her time and encouragement.

There are, undoubtedly, many others I could name, but I'll stop here. I haven't left anyone out on purpose. All who have been along for the adventure know who they are. You are, each and every one, close to my heart.

Now let me go and write.

ABOUT THE AUTHOR

The Matriarch of Ruins follows *Not One Among Them Whole* in Edison McDaniels's ambitious and acclaimed Gettysburg Trilogy. His writing is informed by medicine and the supernatural. His work received honorable mention in the seventeenth edition of *The Year's Best Fantasy and Horror*, and has been published in *Paradox Magazine, The Summerset Review, The Armchair Aesthete, On The Premises Magazine*, and others.

McDaniels, a graduate of Stanford University, is board certified in adult and pediatric neurosurgery, with over 7,000 operations to his credit.

Visit Edison McDaniels at www.surgeonwriter.com, where you can read his blog, Neurosurgery 101 — about life and some of its harder or more interesting moments.

Northampton House Press

Northampton House LLC publishes carefully selected fiction, lifestyle nonfiction, memoir, and poetry. Our logo represents the muse Polyhymnia. Watch the Northampton House list at www.northampton-house.com, or Like us on Facebook – "Northampton House Press" – to discover more innovative works from brilliant new writers.

www.ingramcontent.com/pod-product-compliance
Lightning Source LLC
Chambersburg PA
CBHW022030240626
47154CB00007B/2338